1369

Jack Flash

Blank Frank
Is the Messenger
Of Your Doom and Your Destruction

Yes, He Is the One Who Will Set You Up As Nothing
And He Is One Who Will Look At You Sideways
His Particular Skill Is Leaving Bombs in People's Driveways.

Blank Frank
Has a Memory That's As Cold As An Iceberg
The Only Time He Speaks Is in Incomprehensible Proverbs

Blank Frank
Is the Siren, He's the Air-raid, He's the Crater
He's On the Menu, On the Table, He's the Knife and He's the
Waiter.
 *Eno *

        . . . I knock three times on the door of nine-oh-
nine. 909. Just like the song.

"Hello? . . **Citadel** warden."

No answer. I slip my hand across the sensor and open it using the **PS**ynaps upgrade with an implanted Nano chip in my wrist. More specifically, in the fascia over adductor pollicis muscle. A concept based on pre-existing **R**adio **F**requency **ID**entification chip technology.

Only **PS**ynaps **PS**ecure offers this feature. Many test subjects retain carpal tunnel symptoms from lateral transdermal implants inserted directly in the wrist. Too many small bones. Bones and ligaments tend to reject implants, generally speaking. Hence the relocation to the meatiest part of the hand.

Delicately placed in the dermal layers, just above the muscle but far enough from the bone. The less invasive the better . . . but the itching never truly goes away.

Few test subjects have developed tumors at the site of implantation. Some experience a permanent numbness in the hands, though I have had no such complications.

The creaking door reveals nothing inside. Darkness. I hear breathing in the corner. The lights come up after sensing my presence. Part of the **A**uto-**PS**ynaptic **C**ognizance feature via **PS**ynaps.

Her smallish body is slumped in the corner next to the bed, a needle lodged deep inside her vein. I smell the warm blood flowing from the puncture wound at the crux and down onto her forearm. Were it dry already, I might be too late. A large cut on her forehead, maybe from the fall. It will require at least 13 stitches.

Her body looks positioned . . . posed. Staged. Unnatural. Like some prop or dummy, not flesh and blood.

I take a moment . . . to remark on the peculiarity of the emergency notification I received minutes before arriving at her door. Someone wanted me here. Exactly here and now. A smoking candle wick in the living room overwhelms my olfactory. I check the bathroom.

Empty.

Well . . . not exactly empty. At least two grams of dope lay on the marble counter near the sink. Between some used needles and a bloody 900 g.s.m. double loop Egyptian cotton towel.

I quickly dab my finger into one of the packets and taste a fine Afgani flavor in my mouth. So I pick them up, quickly putting them in my pocket.

I notice that a few light bulbs are missing above the sink vanity. Broken pieces on the white marble were clearly used for smoking ice. The chemical stench of it still hangs heavy in the small room.

Next to the broken glass, lay foil packets which appear to contain more of the acrid drug. I despise speed. Only in the face of unplanned physical withdrawal, would I ever consider it. **Midnight runner** is no friend of mine, and I leave that shit where it lays.

At the **Citadel**, should it be your preference, pure oxygen will be piped into your living quarters through the air conditioning.   Should your palate require enlightenment, certain mood altering substances may be vaporized and mixed with your air supply . . . record players in every room, if requested. The finest suites host jukeboxes, so you dont have to be up and down every thirty minutes or so. Changing albums or flipping sides.

Our jukeboxes are the product of our own fabrication, as they are no longer manufactured. The internal components of many machines are harvested. Used for spare parts and general maintenance. One may find a plethora of equipment within the Engineer's workshop with which to construct the smallest or largest of answers.

The appearance of the washroom informs me that she is a solitary tenant. No evidence of a male. Or another female.   Of any other person at all. Except for the fact that one of these broken lightbulb shards is still warm. And the wick . . . still smoking from a recent yet unsuccessful snuffing. Could be nothing.

They do not pay me to investigate, only to solve problems after the fact.   I am a copacetic coordination consultant . . . . and it does not get any better than this.

Holstering my weapon, I return to the girl. Who is actually rather pretty for a junkie type whore. I remove my homemade balaclava before I slap her good and hard.   Hoping to wake her from the terminal two-step she currently dances with mister d. Her short black hair sways from the effort, making her dull blue eyes roll deep inside of her hollow, bleeding skull. Still no response . . . .

Now that she seems incurable . . . I radio for a bus via PSynaps, of course. They can take over from here. Paramedics being a whole other kind of animal: sponsored junkies and loathsome opportunists.

Now I wait.

Counter-clockwise . . . anti-clockwise . . . the antithesis of forward progress . . . of time . . . of future . . . of productivity . . . . An entity which goes on and on . . . and beyond . . . with or without us . . . never even knowing our names . . . or caring to learn them for that matter. I have learned to accept this.

I have discovered that some tend to find this an uncomfortable fact; as the discovery of insignificance often is. A person seems to enter life in search of a purpose. More simply put, a name to call their own. An identity. A public face. Well . . . I have many public faces. Perhaps you have even seen me yourself.

I am not exactly preferential to the concept of nomenclature. Nor am I an appreciator of kudos. Were credit given where credit is due . . . credit would likely label me a killer. I cannot afford to be labeled such a thing. So, I must forever alter my appearance, to mutate . . . adapt.

It is quite true. I am now and for many years have been . . . an executioner of evil. That being said, I must enjoy an entirely anonymous lifestyle . . . it is the only way to survive. I have personally been many things throughout my time as an equalizer.

I have been called many things, and possessed many names . . . and titles. Worked many trades . . . as a waiter . . . or a cleaner . . . a bag man . . . an auteur . . . a lieutenant . . . a shaman . . . a patriot . . . a crater . . . a healer . . . an exterminator . . . an iceberg . . . a music man . . . a hunter . . . a driver . . . a mole . . . a siren . . . an air-raid . . . a killer . . . a spook . . . a rogue . . . and . . . as of late . . . an unidentified army of one.

If it puts you at ease, that is, should you find it more comfortable . . . having a name to call me . . . then you may refer to me as Francis. Frankk, if you please.

My congenital name is no longer of value or necessity . . . and the less you know about me . . . the safer it will keep you . . . in the end. The end . . . more near to us now than ever before.

Time gives us one option . . . one direction. One speed. A rat race through an electrified maze riddled with felonies. A race that carries a life sentence in the crouch of every alcove. We have been taught to accept this. We are given only one choice.

What if we want a different choice? If we want to go against the grain? Like salmon, to spawn against the common accepted flow. To defy gravity. To defy time . . . defy the impending tick ... tick ... tick ....

What if we want a new ending? Or a new beginning . . . what if we want to change the past from

10

the present ? Or the future, for that matter? If we were no longer slaves to a fourth dimension, then the possibilities are limitless.

Many survivors have found salvation as workers in the hillside compounds, stretching from Hollywood to Santa Barbara. Consuming the Santa Monica and San Gabriel Mountain ranges. Extending up parts of the Sierra Nevada.

Other survivors reside as sheep in the remnants of the midwest. Far enough inland from the destruction on the coasts, and protected on the north end by Quebec. Which now, claims the majority of, what was once referred to as Canada.

The world of private security blew wide open when the entire planet suddenly decided to explode into madness and slowly devour itself. The military certainly wasnt going to spend time saving you.

As a private security contractor, I typically found myself on VIP detail. Charged with the escort and protection of principle clients. Or the delivery of cargo to them throughout their time inside the green zone. Convoy commission. That was then . . . .

Now, I am merely a glorified babysitter. No one in their right mind would willingly accept a job like mine. I had little choice in the matter. For me, this is merely a job of necessity. The fact is . . . no one is truly safe any more.

Meanwhile . . . I insistently attempt to wake sleeping beauty from her self imposed purgatory. When her mouth falls open, I see that her throat, more than anything else, resembles the inside of a locker room shower drain.

Unsuccessful in my attempt, I quickly toss the room. I discover a couple of rolled up euros near the nightstand, and again over beside the urine soaked scarlet tufted settee.

Seems I missed quite a gathering. Not my type of crowd, anyway. Not that I was invited . . . but I'm making up for lost time.

I check the whore's purse, but all it contains is a loose grip of dirty needles. I prefer clean ones. These I find next to a crumpled t-shirt, rife with cigarette burns and what I can only imagine to be seminal fluid.

The shirt has a large syringe in the shape of a space rocket that proclaims: **American Heroin!**.... **Give it a shot! Blast off!** I silently agree.

Additionally, and to my great delight, I find a small baggie in of a side pocket. Containing what I can only imagine is blow. Or more smack. No time to check, in the pocket it goes . . . fill the hole. Search complete, time to call for support.

"Unit 8, gonna need another set of eyes up here, looking pretty grim,"

I speak to myself. Though I am not truly insane. Insane people will talk to themselves, it is true. Not the case here.

A receiver/transmitter located in the upper left molar allows dialogue transmittance once the program has been engaged. **PS**ynaps. Quite useful but most of all . . . it feels completely natural.

I wait for 8 before moving her body. It is far better to have a witness with these things anyhow . . . like the needle removal, and whatever else need be done.

While turning on the cold water in the translucent shower, I see a few short green hairs around the drain . . . non-pubic. Possibly non-human.

This girl is shaved below deck but not recently. Maybe three days growth. Her hair is bobbed and black.

No surplus of rubbers anywhere, so I assume she's no escort. Or maybe she is . . . just doesnt give a fuck. Lazy bitch.

"8 . . . what is your twenty?"

I holler into my molar receiver as I gesticulate in front of the brain-damaged-dope-whore.

"In the box, en route to you," he chirps back.

I drop my hands back to my side. Get her awake soon, or it will be comatose vegetable time for our little homecoming queen of the damned.

I consider doing a shot while I wait because I am feeling edgy. Bad idea. I havent prepared a rig in advance, so it could get dicey with both 8 and the paramedics each on their little fucking ways. I decline and resolve to wait a bit longer.

I slouch onto the floor, next to the white YumanMod Victoria bed.   Sliding my back down black Vintage Flock wallpaper.   Coming to rest beneath a print of Jonathan Yeo's *Analyze This*.   A Baroque framed vintage stag rag collage of Freud.

I havent had the time to fix my mood today. Due to that fact that I woke with a start, summoned by anonymous exigency.   Instead, I remove a glass pipe from a small leather case and pack it with white death . . . **kryptonite**. I take a long . . . slow . . . slow . . . pull . . . .

. . . until I see stars and my hearing goes all thin and tinny, I inhale so deeply. Quickly, I pull her mouth to mine and breathe into her. Exhaling with great force . . . and my head is like a wind chime . . . resounding like some filthy fire bell riding a bottle rocket and a Roman candle on Chinese New Year. Ring . . . a . . . ding . . . ding . . . ding ding ding. . . . . . .

Almost there . . . one more long, slow drag off the pipe . . . and I exhale another thick cloud of smoke into the crisp air of the room.   A pesky musca domestica, the size of a human pinky, becomes caught within the plume. It zags . . . loops, hovers a moment, and hits the floor with a thud.

Problem solved. I begin to converse with the girl. However . . . she declines my advances . . . .

Which is okay because I can hear him walking down the hall. Heavy, uneven steps. Finally, the pudgy four eyed monster that is Unit 8 clumsily stumbles over the threshold.

The help has been slipping in recent years. This Dodo is the result of many recent pay cuts within the **Citadel's** spending plan. He looks at the ground behind him as though it were responsible for tripping him.

"Bout fucking time," I growl while getting to my feet.

My heart and head rushing at once. My vision going a little purple and grey. My body wanting nothing more that to lay on the floor but I fight the urge . . . and . . . thus far . . . I am winning.

"I got here as fast as I cou- " he begins.

"Shut the fuck up," I cut him off. "Get her feet, and move her to the shower."

He does this while looking insulted. We slide her to the edge of the bed. As we stand her up, a black onyx dildo slides out of her, landing on the carpet. I watch closely to be certain it doesnt touch my foot.

This type of mini cock is all the rage with women survivors. It generates energy from a rechargeable core powered by static electricity via skin contact as well as an internal spiral mainspring. Loosely based on automatic watch technology.

Offering hours of pleasure, provided that the operator has sufficient internal friction and motion. It zooms around the shag carpet in little circles at full speed, until it running out of juice.

8 is weirded out, steadily moving toward panic with every passing second. A diverse, yet exotic mixture of lube and sex has filled the room. This, compounded with the residue of the burnt candle wick and smoked cocaine, creates a nauseating effect.

"Smells . . . strange in here," he remarks.

"I guess she was into some off-color shit," I dismiss.

We move her to the shower where I whip the needle out of her arm. Tossing it into the corner where the others have collected.

The cold water has no effect on our sleeper. I look at the ceiling and notice that it somehow looks different from the other rooms.

Upon closer inspection, I see where the junkie-fuck . . . or fucks, shot bloody streams of water at the white ceiling with used syringes. Some kind of calling card.

Lowlife motherfuckers always need to clean their rigs, post shot. This way, the hypodermic can be used again in the future. (Needles are difficult to come by and extremely expensive.)

Instead of aiming at the sink or the toilet like any other self-respecting recreational relapser . . . these junkies opted for a Jackson Pollack type assault on the interior decor. Very cute. A few more slaps to her face but nothing that would leave a serious mark.

"Come on you lazy bitch, dont die here," I say.

Too many questions to answer . . . were she to expire. Too many names are at stake these days. I cant sit back and let this dirty bitch become a believer tonight.

It would be a detriment to our outstanding reputation. Far more damaging than a cunt like this is worth. The **Citadel** is known as a place where one may evade whatever it is they are attempting to escape . . . . I will have a lot to answer for . . . so . . . .

A few more wet slaps . . . . And one more for good luck and clarity. Then some shaking. Nothing. I slap myself. Nothing. I slap 8. Hard. To be sure he is paying close attention.

He promptly begins to well up. I roll my eyes and we move her back to the bed. Or more like I move her. 8 is one useless fuck.

I instruct him to remove the sex shit from the bed. The dildos, lube, and leather restraints. Still greasy and riddled with bite marks. All recently used, I suspect. The idiot isnt even wearing gloves.

No, no. He just waves at the pile of deviant idols . . . as if he were chromosomally deficient, and swatting at some housefly as it attempts to land on his birthday cake. With the many health risks occupying the world today, I do not take chances.

I toss her dead weight onto what I hope, for her sake and my own, is not her final resting place. Her breathing is shallow and sporadic. As she lay there motionless and spread wide . . . I suddenly recognize her. This particular party girl is rather well known. Her name is Reevus Longue. The hair is different now, but everything else looks the same.

This girl has been checked and rechecked prior to her admittance into the **Citadel**. Her friends run deep in this community. So, we allow her inside despite her capitalistic cannibalism. Certainly, it is one of these friends who anonymously contacted me with the "urgent message" at oh-dark thirty this morning.

This kinky bitch, she cant be older than twenty. I bet she likes it all. I imagine her say,

"Anything goes, but be sure to fill the gimmick first."

Probably been in the sex trade for a solid ten years already. Pedophilia has become a national predominancy.

This is what happens when the demand for something is so high, yet the supply is virtually nonexistent. Little girls are rare. The youth are endangered, but young girls are the most coveted living creature of all. Children are now specialized down to the very helix and only produced under strict government supervision.

In the hillside compounds, they are farming babies of their own, without consent. They do most things without consent up in the hills. The governing body tolerates this because it shares in the vast dividends reaped from the film industry. Along with any associated entertainment, and its subsequent media.

As I stand up, now wet from the shower, I notice some of her blood on the sleeve of my Hugo suit. Bullshit. Cunt. May never get that one out. It's not exactly easy to find a size 38 any more, the size is too common.

Supply has dwindled down to a murmur, and prices have grown exorbitant, to say the least. If there were a custom tailor in town, I'd gladly go that route. But there are none to be found, and believe me, I have searched high and low.

All have been utilized in the hills for the purpose of costume design. Occasionally I am lucky enough to procure a suit of true quality, from a costume dealer working outside of the compound.

I have been charged with the maintenance of my own Irish pennants. Along with any tears that may come my way, as a result of my occupation. Stains are a whole other problem because dry cleaning is no longer an option.

I hear the rapid footsteps of paramedics coming down the hall. These scumbags are sponsored addicts in possession of minor medical comprehension. They work for the **Citadel**. Their job, to safely rush victims to the current medical professional on retainer. She will become their problem now.

"You handle 'em, I dont have the stomach for it today" I instruct 8. "And if the bitch croaks, do not let them hang out in the room like last time. And dont leave the fuckers alone with her. Not here. If they want to do it that way . . . that fucking badly . . . then make 'em take her to the bus."

I snatch a little FM radio off the nightstand. One complaint about PSynaps, there is practically no music to be found. You can manage to locate a few ambient Nature loops. And plenty of film and media. Some movies offer soundtracks, though they are never released to the public. Music has been utterly ostracized. Fear I suppose. Music has been outlawed in general. Too emotional. Too painful for mass consumption. Too inspirational.

If you want to see a live music performance, you have to turn over a few rocks, or delve deep into gutters. It's not as easy as going to a secure movie theater to view a new film release. But there are always live music shows to witness. A guy I know can locate things like this. He is able to procure most things. Except, of course, a new razor to shave with or a fresh toothbrush.

Also, ice cubes, salt, coffee, and chocolate are pretty much a thing of the past. He does manage to get me my cigarettes, which are becoming exceedingly difficult to acquire. I smoke Chesterfelds because they are made in America and more available.

My favorite actor smoked them. He fell victim to Rapid Deceleration Syndrome. Driving a Porsche on a desolate stretch of road where highway 41 meets the 46. Then known as the 466.

The paramedics these days have their own little bag of tricks hidden up their little sleeves. They offer adrenaline, epinephrin, saline and anything else you could want or need. She's in store for a fine time. They may even pump her stomach with a charcoal milkshake, just to be on the safe side. Good times.

This girl is essential to someone. Why else would the anonymous tip have come through? Someone who knows how to manipulate the PSynaps feed in order to prevent a trace and wants her alive for some reason. Is it scandal prevention? The press is currently such an authority in the world. Even the death of this wretched wench, would create a stir. No matter. Now that she is in such capable hands, I make my grand exodus.

The time has come for me to enjoy my own bag of tricks. I calmly brush past two medics as they rush in . . . first, the one with bad skin, and then, the one with the greasy moustache. The stench of cannabis haunts their auras. Bloodshot eyes on both of them. Walking swiftly but not too quickly, I approach the elevator. For all they know, I could be a killer.

I have been one. Many times in the past . . . but not today. It always amazes me that wearing a suit seems to legitimize you in nearly any given situation. Like you belong there, wherever you may be. Unless, of course, you happen to be a politician. Were this the case . . . I would hang you by your silk tie, set you on fire, and use your skull for an ashtray.

I punch in the code for full access, selecting the thirteenth floor. The building has yet to be fully upgraded. Only doors to the rooms are **ʃS**ynaps regulated. Apparently, there is an issue with funding. In the meantime, I still have to remember the code.

Disappear Here

Of course, I know . . . I do . . . I know that a building doesnt have a thirteenth floor. It is **unlucky**. Not one entrepreneur in the entire history of corporate enterprise would willingly invite rotten luck into any business venture.

I suppose this is why there are exactly thirteen steps leading up to the gallows pole. **Judas Iscariot**, the thirteenth disciple to join the festivities during the last supper . . . .

At age thirteen, a Wiccan or Pagan will commence in the study of witchcraft. Coincidentally . . . thirteen is the number of members in a coven. Also, and possibly unrelated, the very age at which a Jew becomes a man or woman.

Unlucky or not, a thirteenth floor is terribly uncommon. No remaining building actually has an elevator button for the thirteenth floor. None but for those housed at the **Citadel**. Our rooftop is one of a kind.

A jet leaves a vapor trail overhead . . . lacing the clouds with chromium oxide for rain. The consistent rain is the only thing that keeps us holding on to life.   Eighty percent of collected rainwater is filtered and fit for human consumption.

Some horticulturalists sell vegetables grown in the remaining twenty percent.   Which is considered impotable, but acceptable if the p.h. is adjusted prior to utilization.   Reverse osmosis is the most effective form of filtration.   Any self-sustaining survivor requires their own vegetable garden and a green thumb.

This roof was once the pool level . . . though there is no need for any of that nowadays. Considering the fact that the sun burns so hot, it can kill you within two hours of direct exposure. Sunblock is highly recommended during your stay.

Back in its golden age, there were hundreds of alcohol-poisoned-coke-addicted-adrenaline-junk-stars.   All squeezing in tight tight tight from edge to edge, doing their damnedest not to plummet onto the street below.   Pure **debauchery**.

Once, a promotional event included a live human free fall from space.   Culminating with the space monkey's soft landing onto this very pool deck. Mojitos were sold by the passel.   Which was ideal because the entire stunt must have cost a bomb.

These terrific hedonists, would cling desperately to one another, in the collective attempt to achieve an eternal high whilst sinking to the ultimate low.   Somehow managing to self-preserve amidst imminent blackouts . . . day after day after day. Penultimate versus determinate.   Showing up, time and again, always with well tailored silk Hawaiian print shirts and low SPF tanning oil.

Come to spend whatever money they had, or could render. To rub up against one another in the sweet sunshine. The ground was as needle ridden then, as today. A few feet of sand have accumulated over the years, but still I wouldnt walk barefoot. They always have a way of surfacing, despite being buried so deep.

Patrons of this bar in the heavens could spout irrevocable, corybantic abominations like,

"Last week I dropped a hundred thousand in cash on a vasectomy reversal . . . for my standard poodle . . . . My girlfriend thinks that he's . . . we call him Samson . . . my dog . . . is so hot. So sexy!! Soooocoooo . . . she got this brilliant idea to . . . like . . . let him cum inside of her. You know, Samson . . . . For many obvious reasons, one being . . . like . . . the beautiful puppies they could have together . . . . "

Back then, the days here were typically spent watching coked up debutantes attempt to consume drastically over priced cocktails. Emphasis on cock. While ingesting sterno-heated buffet bar food that would taste shitty even without all of that cocaine in their systems.

Feeding from filthy plates left full, due to the ingestion of blow. Wasted. As the world starves around them. Wasted. Strong alcohol consumed out of dirty plastic tumblers. Putrid calories for licentious mouth-breathers.   Selfish one way motherfucking food converters.

Things were fully operational maybe fifteen years ago, not that anyone knows exactly, when the sun was always shining bright, and the was ocean still calm. So calm that you could lay beside your girl and get tan. No solar flares capable of scorching the skin off your body.

No fear of aggressive stingrays, truculent sharks, hordes of jellyfish, or giant tube worms. Nor the portentous slack-jawed cuttle fish. No acid rain, or fire breathing leviathans.   No plastic shells to collect from thick saltwater, supersaturated with High Density PolyEthylene.

On a beautiful, clear afternoon, a mild sunburn would be the worst of your fate. It could be fatal just to paddle out nowadays . . . fatal to venture outdoors at all.

Kill City has always been a funny town. Full of diverse people who all thought the same way. Stuck in their little microcosms, avoiding interpersonal interaction. Which is why there have always more dogs in this town than anywhere else in the world. People here prefer pets over humans for companions.

Again, the reason there are more cars now abandoned in L.A. than anywhere else in the world. No one wanted to share rides, or utilize public transportation. Now most cannot even afford the Metro. It only comes twice a week. Running downtown, then to Venice, and up through Santa

Monica and Malibu.   Then back southeast to Hollywood.

The way it is now . . . it seems like all I know is struggle. So far as I can recall, my entire adult life has been squalid, hard-worn, and cut-throat. Survivalist. Bizarre.

The current average life expectancy is roughly fifty-nine years of age. I only know of a handful who have made it so far, or beyond.

I'm around forty-five by my estimation, but I look about thirty-eight. Even that can put people on edge. At this age, I'm still the oldest person I know. Nobody celebrates birthdays. No one even mentions them.

I do not know my exact age. Once you live alone for so many years, eventually you forget how to celebrate your birthday. Then you forget the exact date. And before long, when there is no one to remember for you, even the exact year of your birth will become entirely obscured.

Moments from your childhood will begin to escape you as well. Only the most vivid imprints seem to survive. Allowing you to recall, upon rare occasion, a beautiful or dangerous memory from time to precious time. Even if only in the form of a nightmare.

What remaining parental units there are, hastily hand down American and world history to their children, in vain. Without a true knowledge of past events. Without fact verification, or the necessary research required for the discovery of all things no longer taught in schools. Reducing modern education to a century long game of telephone . . . and we lost our souls long before knowing of their existence.

I havent seen a child in years. The youth will copulate but refuse to procreate. Finding the responsibility far too severe. The new panda bear. Too hedonistic to contribute in any way at all.

Recently, the youngest humans I have seen are those in their late teens. Early twenties. The government is farming babies anyway. Killers. Purebred. Elite. Like me. Children that often kill the host during their birth.

Not to say that I wasnt natural born. My father was reared within the agency network. Which meant that I would be, too. Observing me from birth, to youth, to puberty.

On on the edge of seventeen, in my sixteenth year of life, I recall being approached by a woman. A nun. One who held the devil's hand as she slept. She gained my trust to bring me in willingly.

Everyone now carries a weapon. Usually hard artillery. I wear two to four guns depending on the day. Because it's never dull here and that's a fact. I carry a few blades as well, including a full tang titanium damascus that I affectionately refer to as my deadly feather.

Also a straight razor in the left boot and an Italian stiletto in my right. A neck knife worn against the skin. I am prone to hiding ice picks or nine inch nails up my sleeves. I even utilize small explosives. Sometimes, an M67 fragmentation grenade is just what the doctor ordered.

If a man or a dog attacks you, it is within your right to issue death. If it shits on the sidewalk . . . death. These are preventative measures, designed to prolong our existence on this lonely, dying planet. Sunset Boulevard is now lined by a rivulet of sewage which has collected over the last decade, but it would be far worse without the law.

Part of the general groundwater defilement was caused by wild dogs, feral kitties, and wayward humans. Those who were regularly defecating and pissing into the wind. So much so, as to destroy the sanctity of the water table. The unsecured landfills, drilling and nuclear power had a devastating effect on it, as well.

It was a funny day when our daily elected talking puppet ordered a general decree on water wasters, polluters, or any known associates thereof. License to a righteous kill is only valid when accompanied with proof of guilt. Offenses are typically verified through captured evidence, in which case, submissions are gathered via the PSynaps retinal upload feature.

I still pick off sick pups with potshots from time to time. For sport or eco-purification, take your pick. If you can control your canine, then you've got nothing to worry about . . . but if you cant, well . . . it's a hard journey for those resistant to change.

Especially in this day and age. Expect no pity from me.

Southern California's climate was, at one time, particularly exceptional. Sunny days and chilly nights. Which kept the insect and rattlesnake populations under control. Mosquitos could not survive. Houseflies and gnats were kept at a minimum. Now the climate is warmer and wetter. Resembling more Louisiana than Los Angeles. More La. than L.A. Thanks to this change, the insects have tripled in size, and mosquitos now thrive and grow as large as hummingbirds.

I have learned not to worry about these things any more. There are no hospitals to cure what ails us. No teachers or intellectuals to answer my questions. No adults to make the youth responsible.

Sometimes I remember, with great difficulty, what it was like in my adolescence. How life was easier then. Fatter. Superfluous. How we always wanted even more than we were given. Now we're happy with whatever we can steal.

I can get it all, anything you need. For the most part, anyway. Large caliber cartridges are difficult to come by, however. No one makes the molds large enough any more. With resources in severe decline, smaller caliber weapons have become the tool of preference.

Accuracy is king. I do okay with my .22 and I do better with my .38. Explosives are available, though not in major supply. I still have a few loose connections within the agency that I call upon from time to time. Which is the only reliable place to secure ordinance any more.

I use my punch code paired with a little key I carry. This enables me to run the elevator car independently. No key, no roof access. The cables of the car groan from the tension of forced work. Our elevators, now twenty years old, and not a repair specialist alive, should we ever need one.

We have one Engineer, a pedantic Guatemalan, who fixes whatever may break around here. As the elevator car whines upward I enjoy the view. No stops or starts. No tenants. Just a mainline to the top.

A Chet Baker song drops from above as I rise, and through the glass I view the expanse of the city beneath me. The notes meander and roll around my head prior to falling on my ears. The slow, somber melody transports me deep inside my troubled mind. I tend to prefer songs from an artist that are recorded during the peak of an addiction. Usually a heroin habit. Heroin is a drug that seems to lend itself to the music . . . whatever the genre. However, Sly Stone was one freebase junkie who, somehow, managed to make extraordinary music.

The devout always boo and hiss, quick to judge drug addled musicians. What the devout do not comprehend is that, without mood enhancers, the music would be as banal as their own lives. What musician wants to write a song about suburbia and the supermarket? Who wants to listen to a song about such things?

Yet, inevitably there comes a point in time for every musician when the drugs will win and the music will die. But for that fleeting moment of productivity . . . those few years . . . or even months . . . even if it is only for one album . . . there is simply nothing better.

As I look out, I see remaining shreds of buildings. Their I-beam carcasses left for dead and never reclaimed. Erected by greed. Dismantled by Nature. The owners already done-in or dying.

I do not notice what is playing on the screen behind me. Yet the light coming from it illuminates the cubes as it flashes against the glass walls.

From here in this little box . . . from inside this tall, thin elevator shaft . . . inside of a building . . . perched atop a substantial and well known hill . . . I survey all that has been left behind. Shit always seems to roll downhill. Does it not? Even these days. Provided that the earth does not simply decide to open wide and swallow the entire damned hill.

The fuckers we get here at the **Citadel** tend to come off as self entitled . . . at first. Trotting into reception as if they own the place. Behaving as if we really need their blood money. What they dont know is that we have a waiting list a kilometer long.

When I jam my Mosquito between their quivering lips, perhaps even chipping a veneer or two, and I ask if they might prefer life on the outside, they always tend to soften a bit. With the sun swiftly setting in the distance, I assure them it can all be arranged. I ask them,

"How would you like it out there on your own?! A stranger in this strange land . . ."

This is no bluff. The stakes are just too damn high. There is life out beyond the fringe, outside of the **Citadel's** bosom.

It has gotten so bad out there, with roving gangs claiming most of the city after dark. Dwelling in what is left of the unclaimed dry areas. Basing the majority of their operations out of so-called "state maintained" parks like Griffith and Runyon. Wattles farm has also been claimed by the state due to its fertile soil.

However, the state does not actually maintain anything any more. Like asking a trust fund baby to mow the lawn for anything less than a new Maserati. Though, even that might not do anymore, because now little baby wants a new Ferrari instead.

Vagrants, who now occupy the parks, have set up various shanty towns. Consisting of tents by the hundreds and even more bonfires. They converge on the city streets to hunt for meat once the sun has set and you are alone, lost in retreat.

Sometimes they attack the monorail during a daytime delivery but only when absolutely desperate. It has gotten severe enough outside that these silver-spooned-cocksuckers would rather fuck with me inside the **Citadel**, than be out there. Unprotected, and trading wits with a rabid collection of cannibalistic misanthropes.

When bleary eyes begin to well up, they kind of grimace and shake their little heads. Then, for a fleeting moment, they look almost cute. Innocent. Must be the same expression mommy and daddy have borne witness to all these years. The look that gets results. The one that gets them what they want. Paid. They know exactly what they do. And I know it, too. However, it is no concern of mine should a tenant live or die. I get mine either way. I am merely an animal trainer.

Once an initiation has taken place, things always tend to roll more smoothly. I have found that you've only got to break that horse one time. Take the piss right out of them, the very first chance you get. It truly doesnt matter. Whether you are dealing with a certifiable freak of nurture or some unholy kingpin from the Saint Petersburg bratva. Simply remove their pride from the equation.

A little one-on-one quality time with yours truly, and they become teddy bears in two shakes of a lamb's tail. Because nobody gets inside without my approval. That is the agreement. A thorough health screening is required by the **Citadel's** medical board prior to admittance.

Following the completion of a physical inspection, I will offer the applicant a general psychological examination. Upon satisfaction, admittance within the perimeter will be granted. Nothing more. If you wish to remain safe inside, financial accounts must be kept up to date and house rules must be respected.

I finger the three baggies in my right coat pocket as my heart begins to race faster and faster. Come on thirteen. I cannot get there fast enough.

After new tenants have been briefed with regard to our policies, they are taken to the decontamination hall on the first floor. Here, they are re-screened for airborne contaminants.

Once cleared, they are cleaned with wire brushes, pressurized water, and other potent purgatives. After which they are tagged and released into their respective living quarters. Joking about the tags, no need. **PSynaps** offers a **PerSonal** tracking feature which is a requirement for any potential lessee.

At the **Citadel**, we get the scummiest . . . and wealthiest shitbags from all over the globe. Some come to Edge city for business and some for vacation. Why? I could not say. Some are simply on the run, like me. My work here is part of my cover. Most of our international visitors are the latter. Agency celebrities. Criminals.

America, though not as operational as their homeland, has become the only option for them. Because they have already burned that rickety hometown bridge to the smoking ground. If the old world got their hands on any of our tenants, it would be a one way ticket to terrorville. This place is where survivors come to vanish.

One thing is sure, it's no prettier or easier at the top of this particular shitheap. Here, life is only a show and tell act. Appearances may seem more valuable than actual clout. But that is merely facade. Sniff out the bullshit, win a prize. The prize not really being a prize at all. The prize is no surprises. Beware . . . things here can go dead wrong, and very fast. Worse than wrong.

Constant as the wind, death omnisciently looms here. I often find myself amid a crisis. One composed entirely of someone's involuntarily indiscriminate neurotic bombast. That is the way it will be from now on, and there is nothing anyone can do about it.

Finally, for fucking finally . . . the roof . . . and I can relax. No cameras. No people. Restricted access only. Due to jumpers. So many want to suicide whilst ejecting from this capitalistic altar.

A perfect view. Three-hundred and sixty degrees . . . . A panoramic view from the top of my world. Or what is left of it. Rather, what has been left for us to make use of . . . .

The remnants. I remember when only the poor rode the bus. Now, the truly poor must walk because the monorail is far too expensive. And if you try to walk around this town, you wont live to tell the tale.

A mushroom cloud appears in the northern distance, off the coastline. Now a regular occurrence. With any luck, the wind will bring us minimal fallout. Our water supply comes from the southern sector of the state. So we should be in the clear.

Any local rainwater collected over the next few days must be tested for radiation. The military death squad is now crippled with fear, hence the radioactive cloud. Some grand display of power. Three hundred miles away, in Death Valley, they've even built another Groom Lake.

The decline of petrol brought travel to a grinding halt, but even more importantly, it made shipping nearly impossible. This factor made the self-sustaining lifestyle an absolute necessity for most. Gasoline is only burned in extreme emergencies, and only if you can manage to find it.

Only the privileged, the prosperous, and the silver spooned have access to the monorail system. Which is the only reliable mode of transportation any more. It's the safest way to mobilize yourself, but tickets can cost you a pound of flesh. The monorail is elevated for cannie avoidance. Run on electricity farmed from the sun and wind.

Just like the **Citadel**, which is lined with solar panels on the east, south and west facing sides. A wind turbine is secured to our roof atop a two hundred foot tower. Turbines line the entire ridge of the hillside compound. You can even hear them from the roof sometimes, if the wind blows just right.

Looking around from this harrowing vantage point, I prepare myself to blast right off this white monolith. I only want to get as high as fuck, and rant and rave like some ornery dog damned unfortunate. Just scream at the sky as the tears roll down my face . . . as the clouds just drift on by . . . passing

overhead . . . paying me absolutely no mind at all . . . .
Putting me in my place.

Mother Nature is one serious cunt to contend with. Wind speed averages from eighty to just thirty kilometers per minute on a good day. I duck into an unused storage closet. One that I tend to frequent in the interest of self medication.

It's also where I stash my rifle. A vintage CheyTac Intervention M-200. Lucky for me, the building's previous owner left a cache of vintage weapons inside of a basement level storage room.

You are thinking . . . *"this guy must be some kind of Lee Harvey fanatic, right?"* Allow me to assure you, I am not. Amateur that he is. Oswald used a Remington.

Yet, any rifle is handy when stray cannies come wandering, desperate for food. If I happen to be on the roof, rifle in hand, I can take care of the problem before they reach the front gate. I can put a . 408 in them from a kilo out in high wind, even farther with a laser rangefinder and a spotter. Night vision is also extremely effective. One good thing about cannies, they're not infectious. Like, say, vampires, werewolves, or zombies. If they were . . . this would be over already.

I open the rusty door of the storage room, which squeaks as it swings agape. Dingy and black inside, with the faint residue of burnt cocaine that never really goes away. **Kryptonite.** Guilty as charged. A few rats scatter for their lives.

I once kept a kitty in here, to control the problem. One day I returned and found only bones. Still plenty of rats. The true power of majority rule.

I load my pipe with some rocked poison, hitting it until my bell rings. It's time to try out that smack, better be careful or end up like the bitch downstairs. Less is more. I believe I heard that somewhere before.

Now, I love heroin . . . this I cannot deny. I adore it. I also must confess that it truly seems to change me. And not for the better. Deconstructing me to leave only the shell of a man. A hollow soul. A husk. And an utterly useless one at that. Nodding off in the corner, drooling on my shirt . . . and . . . dozing . . . off . . . in the middle . . . of . . . a sent . . . e n   .   .   .   c   .   .   . e . . . .

. . . . The only remedy I have found, thus far, is to cut the heroin with a little cocaine. Blanca. Marching powder. Just a sprinkle, of course. Too much and your heart will be doing flip-flops until it passes out . . . forever. Ask Belushi

The secret to survival is in the proportioning of things. Fifty percent heroin + fifty percent cocaine = death. Yet ninety-five percent horse + five percent blanca = high yet functional. If you do not want to add cocaine to your shot, you can always smoke it instead.

Simply chalk it up to being an occupational hazard, nothing more. I need to relax. I do it to survive. Survival is good. Everybody needs to survive, dont they? I know I do. Having to deal with these damn assholes all day . . . every day.

Not to mention the many injuries sustained and endured through nearly thirty years of hard service. Sore joints have nothing on my scars. My fingers chewed to the bone by many a resistant creature. My ears slashed more times than I care to remember, my nose cut from my face a time or two. Which is the best thing about a new face . . . the fresh start

But first . . . I've got to taste that last baggie I found. The one from her purse. See if it's more smack or rat poison or what . . . . Nope, it's coke. We're in business. All systems go. Soon I'll be as high as a kite on white dynamite.

I dump a moderate amount of smack down my glass syringe . . . follow that with a touch of blanca . . . tap tap. Now I carefully replace the stopper, turning the rig needlepoint up so I can push out the air. Once I clear the air, I reach into my pocket for my flask. You can always use spit if you're in a jam. Though I prefer not to shoot saliva.

I draw about .5 cc of self-made wheat vodka through the needle into the reservoir and shake vigorously. Remove the deadly excess air and find a vein, which is not a difficult task because I'm all lean tissue. We all are any more . . . and . . . I've . . . got . . . it.

A smooth jab with a small, sharp needle leaves almost zero evidence of inappropriate behavior. I need to procure some new points, mine have been used to death.

Even when I calmly slide the dull needle deep into the scar tissue covering the vein . . . I am not certain . . . but I swear . . . I can actually hear the skin pop. Still . . . I . . . am . . . the . . . happiest.

I register, then applying slow yet steady pressure on the stopper, I merge the drug with my blood. A pearl unicorn jams its diamond horn deep into my gaunt forearm, releasing the drug. Releasing me.

Tasting the dope in my mouth, at the back of my throat. I go black for a minute. It's fucking, o h . . . s o o o . . . s o o o o o o o . . . goooooooooooooooooooooooooooooooooooooooood. Fucking . . . . freaky good . . . .

Darkness . . . .

However late it is, I know that it's never late enough. No clock necessary. The lights in the hallways here are always dim. Regardless of how bright and hot it is outside. Electricity is maximum expensive any more.

Even personal hygiene has become a challenge. When I do floss, which is rare, I am sure to rinse my teeth with purified water. Once opened from the flossing, impurities in standard tap water could enter my bloodstream through the capillaries in my gums. The contaminants within it could easily end my life.

I am attempting to breathe. Like an orgasm. Shit. Got to puke- . . . it's too pure.

Once I get that out of me, I feel perfect. Pop in some gum and light a Chesterfeld. Funny how life is like a cigarette . . . the start is as good as it ever gets. After that first drag, the tobacco becomes saturated with tar. Each consecutive drag grows more and more polluted.

I couldnt handle this dope if I was a freshman, way too fucking pure. They would find my bones . . . face down in this dirty little closet . . . my flesh consumed by rats. A proper coffin for a lowlife like me.

Only myself to blame for this current debacle . . . I put myself here. Enough of that now. It's time to float over each floor in an awesome deluge. Shaking this vapid superstructure down to its core.

Before I can get out of the closet, my PSynaps streams in to enlighten me of a new tenant's arrival. A warm sensation overwhelms me and I am positive . . . it's not the drugs. My nervous system has been hard wired with soft fiber optics. Many other survivors, too. We link to a source known as PSynaps and nothing more. The human mainframe . . .

Sea Grave

    . . . I recall upon occasion . . . that I was a smiling son in the advent of my youth . . . content to be loved by most . . . but not all . . . . though . . . in the end . . . it was the wickedness of the world that would harm me the most . . . . Madness would become a way of life for me. For you. We found happiness in slavery.

    This particular day was one I would never forget. Regret perhaps, but forget . . . no. I remember the beach. How silken silicon glistened in the beams of sunlight . . . . The breakers were perfect.

    Six high . . . and so was I. Getting wet, catching set after set after set . . . continuously pushing my arms to absolute failure within the deep green wash.

    When I was too weak to continue, I caught a wave in, to touch the sand again. I found myself walking along the beach in the direction of my home . . . . Alone.

    Before exiting the sand, near the pavement I noticed a small box. Black in color, with a handle on it. Deeply worn and telling of hard times . . . of worry. Of chaos.

    As I continued on . . . beyond it . . . . I felt something . . . . A force . . . . A thing that I can only describe as electricity . . . an attraction . . . emanating from its scarred surface.

I will not tell you that it called out my name, because I know that would discredit me.   It may have, I am not certain.   Who could be sure?   I have never been prone to exaggeration.

So, I walked on . . . beyond the crossroads. Not far from the beach, still far enough from home. I was determined to get back before the sun sank below the horizon.

Because bad things . . . horrible things happen here after the sun sleeps. The evening fog rolls in, with the marine layer; encompassing everything from the coast to the Inland Empire. The shadows will close in, drowning you deep inside.

As desperate as I was to get home that day, I soon realized that I could not continue. It was either a severe curiosity . . . or perhaps . . . I was unconsciously drawn to it.

Approaching Santa Monica Blvd., I gave into impulse and made a u-turn.   I had no choice in the matter.   I was going back. I gripped my board tighter, to muster the courage to continue.

My bones led my body and the rest of me followed. My organs were rejecting the idea like a coat of electric eels, set on stun. My heart thrashing with desire and adrenaline. And hope. I increased the pace to outrun the sun.

Upon my arrival back at the beach, I found nothing. The box was no longer there.   Rather than burn precious minutes foraging, I forced myself to retreat once again.

On my way back home, now twice, catching the very last rays remaining in the day. Quickening my pace, as the sun would soon close its weary eyes again. Turning its back on this decrepit section of the west.

Until tomorrow comes around. If it ever does. The sun's final golden bolts reaching toward me from far beyond the forgotten sea. Its beauty now lost on me . . . for I am far, far later than I should ever be.

I double-timed it, as the salt water quickly turned from liquid to solid, forming a light white powder over my body. My eyebrows gray from chalky residue. My wetsuit clinging desperately to my inner thighs, chaffing with unending fervor.

Suddenly, from the fetid, brown shadows a man approached me. Preparing myself for the introduction, I noticed his labored breathing as he came from behind. I turned around to face him (casual greetings once being an ancient obligation). What I saw, I never would have expected.

Dark foam choked his burning, wide mouth and a blind rage filled his sunken, black eyes. Thousands of tiny, moving insects covered his dirty sweater and hung from his greasy beard. Moving in all directions, in concert. My feet, picked up without thought, and carried me away.

The sun, so quickly setting. Momentarily, I was possessed by that bewitching sunset. One that I will forever retrospect. Black clouds overlapped the blinding sun.

The stranger was quite fast. Faster than I. Reaching my top speed, still he managed to gain on me. His hands, dirty with broken fingernails, clutching desperately at the air just behind my back.

As he was nearing my left side, I half-turned, smashing his face with my epoxy pintail. Which sent him reeling. Coincidentally snapping the board in half.

What a waste . . . considering I spent the entire day using it to carve rights like a plump spiral-cut ham. My wetsuit still chaffing my inner thighs and sack. On the bright side, losing the board allowed me to run faster. Turning the corner, I saw the crossroads in the distance. I ran as fast a my legs would carry.

Not much farther to the house. 1369 Sixth Street. Once it was my home. Now, it is only host to the fishes. Back then it was very much a comfort to me. I could hear him behind me, panting heavily . . . . A wet, stymied wheeeeze. An unmistakeable, unequivocal death rattle.

Whhhheeeeeeeeeeeeeeeeeeeeeeeeeeeeeeeeeeezzzzzzzzzzzzzzzeeeeeeeeee....

It seemed as if he was gaining on me, once again. How could it be?! How can this revolting-cock-sucking-transient - one solely reliant on a diet of Guinness and milk- get the jump on me?

I had speed then and always have. My upgrades are always the best available. As with home security . . . it pays to utilize the best technology. Better safe than sorry.

All of this was before I learned about true darkness. About the things doling out the speed in the blackest of times. Things no one ever seems to mention. Things created by the great void. The void created by Nature, once it was utterly corrupted by us. Our race was ultimately the impetus of our own destruction.

Got to stay ahead, if I can just maintain a little distance. Years of endurance training have failed me. And I knew, I fucking knew I should have brought protection with me. But, hey, live and learn you dumb fuck. Regret will not help you survive. Wheeeeeezzzzee. I hear him just behind my shoulder.

Taking a right at Electric Avenue . . . . Almost home. Just ahead I saw my street. I swore I would never leave the house again without a Mosquito. My bungalow was up ahead in the distance. As I closed in, I saw that something was waiting for me on my doorstep.

A chill shot through my core while my stomach dropped into my knees. I strained my eyes to make out the details. It was a little black box with a handle on it. The same?

I ran past it, unlocking the door and running into the house, slamming then locking the door behind me. The ravenous cunt following me attempted to break through the door.

A steel enforced jam with bolts from top to bottom, extending into the foundation. Wailing out of hungry frustration. Waking my neighbors with heavy thuds, as he pounded like a big bad wolf.

No such luck tonight. I never wonder about home security. I only use the best available, as all survivors should. Even twenty years ago, I had the best security. It used to be about alarm systems and bars on the windows. But here and now . . it's everyone for themselves. No one to come and save you. You must always be prepared. At home, I am always prepared. Armory, munitions, a year supply of MREs. Meal

Ready to Eat. *So . . . on that night long ago, that particular hungry heart had to eat his lunch all by himself. While I was pining over my lost surfboard.*

As I turned around, I felt a presence behind me. An overwhelming chill and pressure encompassed my body, while the stench of guilt filled the room. My heart began to beat faster. My breathing continued to elevate. I looked down, and there at my feet, halcyon, crystalline and ultra-sheen . . . sat the little black box . . . . Scars and all . . . staring back at me.

Stormy Weather

Now are ye undeceived.
Evil is the nature of mankind.
Evil must be your only happiness.
Welcome again, my children,
To the communion of your race.
*HAWTHORNE

"Some eyesores in the driveway . . . couple of bulldozers with 'em, too," my interior transmitter advises.

Dog damned paparazzi shitfucks. Fame is always deadly in my line of work. Anonymity is key. Though, it can go both ways, because even the little x factors are paying dearly for that lead role or a cover shot nowadays. Now that things have gone so terribly wrong, these pappo-fuckers are knifing each other, or worse. For a shot at virtual immortality.

Paparazzi's now have their own bodyguards. Well paid for hassling our clientele, about that big shot. That meal ticket. Turning the talent into something more resembling Sasquatch than anything else. Pictures are worth so much more now, due to their scarcity.

Prompting every famous "it" boy and girl to remain indoors. Living in fortified compounds scattered here and there, throughout the wasteland. Many reside with the fortified walls of the hillside compound, also.

Grocery delivery operations are raking it in as a result. However, the monorail has always held a monopoly on all delivery within the wasteland. Heavily taxing any comestible operation for its use of the rail system during deliveries.

Stalkers and pappos are so bold these days. Taking every opportunity to commit illegal trespass. Private security companies make a killing, as well.

If someone is going to brave a wild pack of paparazzo, it is never going to be the talent. Never. Not even close. Every time, it's the homely assistant or the insecure yet slutty stylist who gets charged with the task. Give the public a few days without a shot of their favorite so and so, and they begin foaming at their filthy fucking mouths for anything. Anything at all . . . .

Now a demand is created for the assistant or stylist's photo. Multitudes of midwestern jackoffs still purchase worthless fanzine subscriptions to virtual rags like Creeple and PUS Magazine. They reign supreme, so publication continues in unyielding fashion.   These stylists/assistants come nobodies/ wannabes . . . are now household names by default. And most of them seem to love it . . . at first

See them around town living it up, shopping and smiling with shit eating grins in the bright limelight. Inevitably, the stalker-fucks begin picking them off one at a time . . . .

And guess what? They even have the live murder footage of said nobody. In the event that the recording is not already comitted to a live news feed, it is promptly sold to the highest bidder. The proud new owner will then broadcast across the world . . . via PSynaps. Members are charged a nominal fee for each viewing.

Acting on the defensive, many desperate handlers and talent managers began sending these homely runners on their 1369 missions with their own bodyguards. But why send a stylist and a bodyguard? Why not just send the bodyguard? Less to risk.

So the bodyguard becomes the temporary solution to the fanatical daily bread. And again, the temporary celebrity status of a random bodyguard is quickly followed by their murder. Usually broadcast on live national television.

Always committed by some star-crazed fanatic on a free-range suicide mission. So the talent and their handlers began wearing masks.

Masks are so useful, even to someone in my line of work. Balaclava, ski, monster, surgical, you name it. If it's a mask, we can use it. Prosthetic noses . . . the whole bit . . . . Welcome to my world.

Unfortunately for these eyesores, this type of behavior will no longer be tolerated at the **Citadel**. No one taints my reputation without retaliation. Time for a little crowd control.

I walk to the closet, opening it, then picking up a handful of dirty needles . . . none with caps, of course. The fucking floor is covered with them . . . . I walk over to the edge of the roof and survey the situation from above.

I see all the little eyesores . . . hounding some new x factor. Shouting just about anything to elicit a reaction from her. I wait until she is safely inside and I flick my half-smoked Chester down onto the collection of party crashers.

After which, I release my handful of dripping, besoiled points. They plummet toward the pavement, sailing swiftly and with ease. Coming to rest upon the stinking throng of riff-raff papar-nazis, as they hoard the open driveway below.

Now, I certainly understand that this may seem a bit unsportsmanlike. But, please, you must remember, the needles belong to me. My blood is clean. This particular occupation requires regular health exams on account of the various and sundry plagues now sweeping the nation and beyond.

There are countless fatal viruses that this planet has become a host to; as a result, the entire world to now suffers from aerophobia. Not to mention trypanophobia.

Not even a bout of ringworm will be tolerated. Every employee or guest is required to offer current and legitimate proof of health. Absence of malice, so to speak. Dropping dirty rigs on them is only a scare tactic. I am merely making a point.

One that is making me laugh my ass off. I hear the reaction from below and it is absolutely glorious. A false alarm, but little do they know. Until they receive their test results in two weeks. Maybe longer. Glorious, all the same.

I follow this up with a nice long piss, that I anonymously take from the roof's edge. They will think twice about muscling in on our operation here. A steep price will be paid for transgressions done to us. Better walk the floors. Make absolutely certain none of those parasites made it past our perimeter.

Fuckers will dress up like anyone to gain access, and convincingly, too. You name it: cops . . . priests . . . paramedics . . . the elderly . . . security agents . . . well known dead people . . . even celebrities . . . the list goes on.

Currently, there are eight individuals living at the **Citadel** who could net a million euros or more for one compromising shot. These people pay me very well to sort out any piece of shit choosing to engage in such unpleasantries. I return to the closet and do one for the road. Then setting up a fresh one all ready to go, hidden in my jacket pocket . . . right next to my heart.

Human Frights

On the seventh floor, I hear fucking . . . one man and one woman. The only type I enjoy personally. Even girl on girl sex, rare as it may be, tends to become tiresome before long. I need a little more cash for my supply shipment arriving tonight, and I am attempting to round up the last of it.

If I come up short, then I will lose my seniority, which means I wouldnt have first pick of the truck. My shipment would be **rat fucked**. I actually do hate to interrupt these two, but I need my munitions.

Aside from that, Davis Honorable is at large, and a notorious tenant here, because his own daughter has filed molestation charges against him in Paris. He exists on borrowed time, bought with the red tape that beleaguers any extradition process.

I slip on my mask, pass my hand over the sensor, and **PS**ynaps does the rest. They are on the couch, but do not see me yet because he is just banging away. A fuckstain regular at the **Citadel**. Merely the son of a wealthy man, which is the absolute worst. Born into wealth and incapable of appreciating it.

This **Jody** comes to us courtesy of France, as I stated. Heir to an existing wine dynasty. Countless international criminals find their way here. Many of them are thieves, child molesters, rapists, and murderers. I've seen plenty. Forced to track and apprehend a pattern killer right here in this building years ago. The authorities, or what's left of them, would not touch it . . . that is another situation altogether.

I sneak behind them, then into the bathroom to check it for drugs. Or information. I cop a bottle of xanadu and another one full of zorcos, painkillers containing minimal acetaminophen. Making it a decent little score today. I am so extremely fucking pleased with myself. But I really need cash, not drugs. Zorcos tend to make me a bit of a kleptomaniac.

Which means I usually avoid them. But in the spirit of things, I pop a few in my mouth, crushing them with my teeth. They hit you harder and faster this way. I wash my mouth with a pull off my flask. Then some water from the faucet.

Rainwater is first collected, then osmotically treated to lower the acidity of the pH. It still tastes a bit metallic, like copper, due to the old pipes, but it cleanses the palate all the same. The time has come to make contact. So, I walk up on them, mid-thrust and say,

"They sent me about the noise. I knocked. Didnt get a response. Now . . . I dont mind if you fuck. Really, . . . I dont. Fucking is great, I absolutely agree. Truly, I do. We all love to fuck. But consider that international sweetheart, Daphne Abernathy, is staying next door. As she attempts to acquire her beauty rest, all she can hear is you (I point at the girl) screaming **"Oh ... dog! Oh ... dog! Fuck me harder!"** Poor Daffs has enough trouble relaxing as it is .... Now ... how do you figure we can make all of this right? Hmmmmmmmmm?! .... I think five should cover it."

As I wait, I begin to fear that there is a language barrier which could ruin my fantastic diatribe. Leaving only myself and the blue eyed cum sponge on the couch to witness its magnificence. But then, at last, the hairy frog croaks something like,

"Allez p'tit salaud, t'es l'suivant!"

"Why dont you dance with me? I'm not no Limberger," I taunt.

He runs at me with rage in his eyes, and blood still filling his erection. He comes at my neck, both of his hands outstretched. I calmly step aside and grip his skinny left wrist, I deflect his weight past and behind me. Whipping his face into the wall as I jerk his momentum back toward me once again. Popping him like a ratty towel used to soak up sweat, semen, and blood from the locker room of some past life. Snap.

Bleeding and broke-nosed, he ferociously fires back at me. Fists clenched and white knuckled. I pull back and release a single jab to the throat which puts him on his knees. I then toss him some discarded jeans I find crumpled on the floor. He digs hurriedly into his wallet, eagerly removing some bills. Happily stuffing them into my hand.

"Avale ca," he says.

I inspect the wad in my hand. Stupid motherfucker thought I meant five euro. I get a crazy look in my eyes and I'm pretty much going snake when I smash the fucker in the face. Then biting him on the cheek. Like an abrupt slap from your mother when you went a little too far.

I patiently wait . . . .

"Hey . . . fuck! Connard! You've got ten seconds to reach in that wallet and empty its entire contents into my hand. I swear if you even try to jerk me off!"

I wait.

Then saying, "Are you . . . fucking *trying* to get pistol whipped?! . . . Mission accomplie."

I crush the left side of his head with my steely right fist. Blood trickles as his eyes roll back . . . he falls limp on the floor. The girl begins to scream, so I give her a look that shuts her sticky, quivering mouth.

To his credit, the Frenchman gets up with speed. Once I allow him to regain his composure, he clenches his fists, preparing for another go . . . but his whimpering betrays him. Telling me that he's had enough. For today, at least.

"Give me what you have," I instruct.

He reluctantly completes the task. Handing me a wad of bills with a shaky hand.

"Good boy. You two have a nice one, okay?" I quip, then continuing. "Keep that cunt's mouth shut the next time you're stretching her out. Use a fucking pillow. Do not make me come back. If you play it cool, Monsieur Honorable, your wife may never know about this. If you dont, she'll get a visit from me . . . and I'll have a taste of my own for the sake of vengeance."

Amateur that he is . . . the fool brings his wife and his mistress to the same location for little getaways. I notice little details like this and pretty soon everybody wants to be my friend. Leverage. Because we all have to eat somehow.

I can buy a lot of supplies with eleven-hundred and twenty-eight euros. The fuck has a family plantation back home, run entirely on indentured servitude. Duplicitous philanderer that he is . . . he gets what he deserves . . . so dont go getting all apathetic on me.

My shot is wearing off and it's time to make my grand exodus. A few more intimidating looks of disapproval from me, just to be sure he's scared.

"Your name is Davis, right?! Well Davie boy, just so we're absolutely crys-tal-line. (I tighten the dog collar around his neck, bringing his bloody face to mine.) I can easily contact her. We keep her information on file. She's only one transmission away, . . . remember that. You be extra careful with yourself!"

When I am sure that the gravity of my statement has sunken deep into his spoiled mind, I retreat for the roof once again. Tethered by my habit. I am using over a gram a day now, and gaining momentum quickly. It is also the only place to get a clear radio transmission. **1370 K N I L . AM** pirate radio. The building's twelve inch concrete exterior is coated with a solar film. It might as well be made of lead.

No time to wait, going to prepare a shot on the way up. A little powder, some vodka, shake vigorously, clear the air, and enjoy the ride. I throw my jacket in the corner of the car and roll up a sleeve.

The door opens just as I find vein, register, and press the plunger. I look maniacally at a shocked woman who stands there, waiting to enter the car. I ask her for some spare change using a terrible cockney dialect. She stands there, frozen. The door closes as I laugh my fucking head off.

Madness.

Luckily, I am still wearing my balaclava. She will simply report a vagrant in the elevator. Happens from time to time. Though we cant figure out how they get inside. Must be the sewer lines. I continue on my way upward. Because you've got to get up to get down . . .

. . . now, I am standing on top of the **Citadel**. Perched in the hills. Enjoying the view almost as much as my high. This particular building happens to be one of the remaining few still boasting a dry lobby. Mainly due to the hillside location. The elements have caused the tide to rise exponentially. Making the actual sea level a modest eighty meters higher now.

The newest rage is a pirate themed lobby. It has become the answer for all of the unfortunates stuck in Santa Monica, Venice, or any neighborhoods west of the fallen 405.

At the **Citadel,** we are far enough inland to stay dry. For a limited time. While supplies last. Forty meters of land elevation separate us from them. At the current rate, I give it about two years before we get wet here. Could be sooner.

We sit on the edge of the hills but not quite in the hills, if you can imagine. We exist on the outskirts. Electric fences fortified by a concrete walls delineate the perimeter of the hillside compound. In that compound exist zombies of another kind altogether.

Our dry lobby wont last forever. Others, in proximity to our vicinity, cant even rent the first floor any more. In the event of a squall, the unwelcome waves will enter their property. Here, we guarantee a safe and dry experience. That's the whole point. Comfort from the elements . . . and your own demons.

On the coast, the situation is more pronounced. Water reaches the second floor from an average swell. And when she really swells . . . look out. Waves can crash over the top of a building twenty stories high. The hillside compound is not interested in our property due to the proximity of an encroaching coastline. If they wanted to . . . it would be theirs for the taking.

Lighting my Chesterfeld, I notice two streetwalkers approach two men in suits and offer their services. One man, taller, wearing a black trench coat. The other, is a wider man, who wears a fedora with a feather. Both wear masks to conceal their identity. Some idle chit chat ensues . . . while, I assume, the details and conditions of the elicitation were negotiated. The men escort the girls down the street toward the abandoned Peterson building.

I notice a black Mercedes parked on the opposite side of the street. No license plate. Cars are so fucking rare now . . . they always stick out like a sore cock. The driver looks as intently upon the interaction as I do.

At first I think it's some **JAFO**, **J**ust **A**nother **F**ucking **O**bserver, but then I reconsider. Probably the chaperone . . . just supervising his investment. A profitable one considering the car. I notify 8 via **PS**ynaps. Instructing him to,

"Follow the two masked men and their . . . friends . . . observe and remain invisible."

I must closely monitor all activity on my street. Then I spot a dusty PT Cruiser heading west down Sunset toward La Cienega. Not the original model . . . it was a reproduction, one with all of the piss taken out of it. So, I pick up a loose brick and hurl it down at the car, smashing the hood. The fey thing goes careening out of control, colliding with the nearest light post.

A post past which, I found myself walking one previous day. As I was walking by, I looked down at my feet, only to find this statement etched into the concrete, *"say you love satan."*

The Cruiser's retrofit hydrogen fuel cell under the hood goes off like a bomb.   Smoke and broken glass fill the air.   Chagrin holds my face hostage.   The silly man-bitch driver exits the car screaming and throwing its purse around for dramatic effect. Clucking like the castrated rooster it is.   To my delight, this makes the chaperone extremely uncomfortable.

This is what you get for driving a pestiferous car down my street.   Miatas beware, VW Bugs beware.   Fiats, too.   Especially if you are guilty of driving a lady's car while in possession of a cock . . . no matter how small, tucked, or queer it is . . . you'll want to stick to Santa Monica Blvd.

"We've received a report of a dangerous individual in the elevator," the lobby desk informs me via **PS**ynaps.

"I will check into it," I say, talking to myself, then disregarding the call.

A quick bump of blanca and I am back in the box.   She's on my mind.   Always creeping in there. Her perfect lips, eyes . . . .

My **PS**ynaps whines again, it's 8 saying, *"They went inside of the Peterson building. Do you copy?"*

"5X5 . . .Copy that," I reply, and the beat goes on. Ding.   Exit stage right.   Grace give me speed tonight.

As I slowly roam the halls of each floor. I make my way down to the lobby, while I pitch a pencil into the air and catch it repeatedly. Well maintained, sharp reflexes help one survive in this modern setting.

Ironically, on the fourth floor, I fail to catch the pencil. It bounces with its broken eraser down on the dingy, once red, now browning carpet. Making a dull thud. The light is so dim that I must peer intently to locate the white stick hiding within the shadows of my four walled world. I fish around on the floor as my hand glances a familiar object.

A human tooth. A molar to be exact. I hold it up to the blinking and sputtering light bulb overhead, as my other hand (seemingly unaware of its counterpart) continues to search for the lost pencil. Locating instead, a nauseating surprise . . . .

Surely, this is the origin of the stench currently occupying the hallway. A tongue. Clearly human and coated with pulsating larvae. Housekeeping services have slipped to an all time low, they dont even clean the hallways anymore. I sling the grimy film from my fingers with instinctive recoil. They dont pay me to investigate. Devoting my full attention to the effort, I snatch the pencil up from the floor with ease. Using it to skewer the dead meat reeking in the shadows.

Walking to the incinerator. Careful not to lose my pencil, as they are difficult to obtain. I fling the flesh down into the dark, dank hole. Which leads down . . . down . . . ever so gently down . . . deep . . . far underground . . . into the belly of our complaints department.

Little
Indian

The moment I saw her . . . I knew her instantly from a previous encounter. By then it was too late. The plane had already left the ground, and things were already in motion. Allow me to explain . . . .

Perhaps it was in Dubai that I first saw her. I was on a mission regarding a prince, or, rather, his first in command. The prince was truly not a threat. But his first man, Mofaz Uzai, was a concern to the agency.

I arrived on a Tuesday evening and by Wednesday afternoon, was making my getaway. Practically a smash and grab. Believe it or not . . . I still used plenty of finesse in completing the task. Arriving the night before to do a little gambling.

I recall a girl in Dubai, a 21 dealer in a private casino, who, somehow, didn't quite fit. It was not as obvious as wrong clothes or hair. More that, she simply did not belong with these animals. She could not blend in with them. She was too pure to be associated with the dregs found here.

Once I had befriended a maid, an enjoyable by-product in my line of work, I had open access to his suite. The maid I chose was the belle of the ball, to be sure. Only the *prettiest biddy would do. Dark flowing hair, falling onto my chest over and over as I stroked . . . stroke . . . stroke . . . .*

Her slightly wide-set eyes, were almond in shape, mahogany in color. Her full, dark lips crushing my mouth. Tongue smooth, wet, soft, pressing on me and mine. Her downy flesh consuming my cock again and again and again. After roughly half an hour, we both reached mutual intensification, deep in a warm embrace. Then, saying our farewells, we parted ways.

I tossed the used French letter into the bowl and enjoyed a nice, long piss that sent chills up my spine. The color in the bowl revealed that I was a bit dehydrated. After washing my dick and dick beaters, I returned to the bedroom of my pomp suite overlooking the harbor.

Pulling the maid's key card from where it was stashed between the mattress and the box springs. Just off the nightshift, she was going home for the day . . . and wouldnt be looking for it until tomorrow morning.

Mofaz . . . the unlucky flotsam . . . . He never saw me coming.

I inhaled a liter of filtered water. Between the flying and the fucking, I was extremely parched. Quickly dressing myself, then packing my lone carry-on; leaving it by the door. I headed up the stairs one floor, to the eleventh. Letting myself into room eleven eleven. Upon entering, I heard the shower running.

Aside from his negative influence on the American oil trade, Uzai also profited from human trafficking and a child pornography ring. Selling stolen sucklings to the highest bidders. Some as young a four years old. Reminiscent of a

66

man named Cavie Lester. It was the kind of assignment I lived for, dog bless America.

Turning on the sound machine next to the bed, I raised the volume. The sound of rain and overwhelmed the room. I scampered into the bathroom, observing him for a moment as he cleaned the crack of his ass . . . .

I holstered my silenced Mosquito. Engaging a straight razor I found on the counter. Wouldnt want to rust my fine stiletto on this fuck.

I quietly opened the shower door. He noticed the cool air rushing inside, forcing him to turn around. I took a moment to look him directly in the eyes. To verify it was definitely him . . . . It was.

I proceeded to take an immoderate chunk of flesh out of his neck. I never saw a razor cut so deeply. Right through to the bone, dulling the blade. Leaving a nick in the cutting edge.

The trick is to hold the razor upside down as you strike. Grasp it in your hand so that the blade hangs out of the pinky side of your fist. This way, you generate much more force than the traditional overhand method.

I bled him out, right there in the shower. Once he stopped twitching, I eased out of there and back down to my room. I entered and went to the bathroom, removing any visible trace evidence of bodily fluid.

After washing my hands and forearms, I removed my shirt, rolling it into a ball, with the razor inside. I tossed it next to my suitcase. Along with a single semi-bloody hand towel. I opened the case, and in a dexterous manner, removed

a black Hugo button-up.   Throwing it on, followed by my
overcoat. Tossing the messy bits inside my case, I blew out of
that casino.

Hailing a taxi, I took it down the street to the
Madinat theater, next to the Palm Jumeira. At the time, it
was next to a police academy . . . .

A fact that remained elusive to me until it was too
late. No matter, I paid the driver and exited the Japanese
sedan. I purchased a matinee ticket and entered the theater.

Inside, I located a trash can in the men's room.
There disposing of my Mosquito, bloody shirt and hand towel.
I did not stay for the show.

From there I hailed another cab, taking it to a bar at
the Sevens Stadium. One I am not familiar with and cannot
recall the name of . . . but it came highly recommended by the
first driver. I downed three reposados in two minutes and used
the toilet before heading to the airport in a third cab. Once I
arrived there, I paid that cabbie, tipping him well but not too
well. To be memorable is always undesirable in my line of
work.

My level of security clearance was so high, especially
then. Even for international travel. It neared the stratum of
respect upon which diplomatic immunity rests. Walking right
through the pilot's entrance holding my carry-on without a
hitch. Weaving through the maze of back corridors that line
the perimeter of the terminals, I was suddenly struck with an
uneasy feeling.

My tequila was wearing off, and fast . . . I ducked
into an upscale lounge, using an employee entrance.
Assuming the cover of a lost tourist, I sidled up to the bar.

Ordering two platinum level tequila shots. Then I decided not to order a 150 year aged Gran Marnier. Opting for the standard version instead. I finished them within five minutes. The bill was about 105.00 euro, roughly 7,400 Rupee. I tipped thirty percent. Good but not too good. Never be too memorable. Ever.

I checked my watch, eleven to three. The sun, high in the sky, and so should I be. Egressing back out of the employee portal, while the red-eyed bartender was supposedly urinating in the restroom.

Taking the snaking hallways that ran behind all of the scenes. I followed it to a lobby, one that held many patient travelers. I gingerly approached the attendant's desk and kindly retrieved my boarding pass for the flight.

After which, I located a vacant seat, positioning my back to the window overlooking the tarmac. So I faced the room. Calmly waiting for the plane to fuel, I ate half of a yellow xanadu bar and one psoma. Government issued.

We began to board the plane. I always hated to fly. I was just a regular guy with a coach seat on a routine, regular flight via aeroplane. Nothing to worry about, the hardest bit was behind me. I just sat back and enjoyed the ride back to headquarters in the motherland. Then I was up, standing in line, ready to board.

While we waited, I purchased some kind of wrap from an adolescent that contained fried egg, lamb, and chutney. It reminded me of the egg banjos I had in the service. Except that this particular one was delicious by comparison.

Smelling so divine. I recall hoping that it wouldnt make me sorry I gave it the opportunity. I really needed something in my stomach to keep those pills company anyway. I tore into the handheld edible. Before I knew it, I was licking my paws. Eyeing the room in search of one more, but the child was gone.

Alas, it was finally time to go, I handed the cute stewardess my boarding pass with a smile. She waved me forward. Finding my seat next to the window, I checked the runway for abnormal behavior. Nothing so far. I stowed my small overnighter at my feet and clasped my seatbelt. Almost out . . . on my way . . . just breathe . . . .

The pills were kicking in, and before I knew it, the plane was pulling away from the terminal. Lining up on the runway for the grand exodus. Another twenty minutes, and we were gassing it all the way to the heavens. I could finally relax . . .

Once in the air, I quickly used a lavatory to remove the prosthetics from my face. Detaching the nose, eyebrows, and facial hair of my cover. Cleaning any adhesive residue from my skin. Walking to my seat, as the G force was bearing on me. Directing me as the pills kick in, and the bird flies higher.

And up, up, away . . . only one problem . . . as I return to my seat . . .

. . . I recognize the flight attendant . . . .

. . . . From the casino . . . .

.   .   .   . My eyelids are far too heavy . . . .
. . . .

Nancy Drew's Bone Awl

8 better have it right. Slipping on my frayed balaclava, I creep through the doorway of the Peterscn building. A block down from the **Citadel**. The track by Bone Awl I heard walking up is blaring, so I close the door behind me. *Live on Jupiter* erupts from a makeshift stereo in the corner of the sprawling cluttered first floor of the building. What used to be reception.

I peer around another corner and see the two gentlemen carnally engaging the women. Saliva for lubrication, girls on hands and knees, the two men mounting them from behind. I notice that the two gentlemen are sprinkling something on their members while sodomizing these damsels in duress. A white powder, most likely cocaine.

I recall a friend I have in the compound One who happens to be a voiceover artist. One who also happens to love coke. I would ask him how it is that he keeps his voice and nose so clear, knowing that he loves doing that shit every single night. The guy hates needles . . . so I know he's not shooting it. So how? How does one remain railed out of his mind all night long if I never see him snorting any?!

The answer . . . he shoves it up his ass! Think on that. Right up there . . . like a gold tooth in a prison camp.

And get this, he swears that it gets him higher, because the blanca is absorbed directly into the bloodstream without first going through the liver. Like mainlining but without the rigs to carry around and no marks on your arms.

I confessed to him that I would never be able to shake his shit smelling hand again. Forget about sharing finger foods with that sicko. Yikes. I did, however, thank him for the valuable tip. I felt like he understood where I was coming from, but who can ever be sure in a situation like that?

Returning to our casanovas . . . they are, perhaps, imparting this very same . . . precious knowledge to our ladies of the night. I feel that I should let them finish. Though I know how hard that can be, especially on too much blow.   I will respectfully allow them a few minutes and check the bathroom.

Fumbling around in the dark, I inspect the contents of a discarded black trenchcoat.   Italian wool. Cashmere. I find some more xanadu . . . yawn.

Is everybody eating this shit?   Doesnt anyone take oxxytrope any more?

Searching every pocket . . . I carefully feel around inside. A smart man would put his gloves on right now but I dont have the time . . . .   I pick something heavy up from the bottom of a breast pocket.

A cold sweat completely envelops me. I know this object. I have held one before, in a past life. I raise the heavy metal badge up to the light. Upon inspection, I discover that . . . if this is legitimate . . . then these two men . . . are U.S. Marshals. Mother-fuck-ing-Marshals?!

Fuck . . . me.

I hear one of the tarts climaxing, or at least giving the poor fuck a good show. I decide it's time to vanish. Easing backward out of the room. I quietly shut the door (a sheet of plywood fixed to refrigerator hinges).   I amble easterly down the street; in the direction of the **Citadel**. I pass an abandoned car, just as I hear the door creak open behind me.

The Bone Awl track "You're Late" instantly becomes much louder. Slap. The door slams shut behind me. Someone noticed my exit. I continue down the lane. Never looking over my shoulder.

Time
To
Reflect

Back in the box like a jack in the box. My tiny metal coffin of vertical transport. Taking me in and out of reality as I go up and down, down and up. My coffin is currently playing Marquee Moon by Television. Title track.

Meanwhile, on a thirty two inch plasma, a tan and shaved man bangs a shaved Indian girl. No hair anywhere but for their heads. Fitness models in the throes of "passion." Thrusting in and out. Not with the romanticism of soft core either. Full penetration close-ups of cock inside of cunt.

It makes me realize that I may have a weakness for Indian girls. East Indian I mean, not Native American. Because, who doesnt want to make it with a squaw? Both cultures are beautifully exotic.

Dont get me wrong, there are beautiful women in every single remaining modern pedigree. All I am saying, is that . . . recently . . . I have come to realize that I have a desire for cow kisser porn stars. Cow kissers in general.   Most likely, it is the taboo that attracts me.

Especially when you know that thousands, maybe even millions of men from their homeland wish them dead for such a performance.   For driving men mad with passion.   To unmask their entire culture with one public carnal act.   Thereby raising the stakes to an entirely new level.

These girls probably find a greater sense of freedom through public copulation than through any other act on earth.   Raised by a sexually repressed patriarch who, perhaps secretly masturbated to the very thought of her.   Perhaps worse.

This is one instance in which a pornography career could actually be legitimized.   Same could go for the Japanese, blurred crotches aside.   Both cultures want their girls to remain forever young, and like concubines . . . they lust after them.   Conflicted to the very core . . . .   Hypocritical.   These women are rebelling against an oppressive and overbearing culture using the one weapon they still possess.   I respect that.

As I recall, this Television song is a perfect match for the act of copulation.   The entire album works well, in such a situation.   Yes . . . album. Remember those?   Fuck your ISod.   And your playlist, and your fucking sixty-fucking-four tera gigs, and your dog damned shufflepod.

When a musician or group writes an album, believe it or not, they actually put a lot of thought into which songs are included and where each one works best. Everything is done just so, and for a specific reason. You come along, just snatching up this one and that one. Mixing it all around with other non-related styles and subject matter. With complete disregard for the sound and feel that an artist originally intended their masterpiece to have.

Fancy yourself some sort of pirate radio disc jockey do you? Do you even play an instrument? Self-entitlement has become a plague upon the human condition. Know this, Wolfman Jack-off, Morrissey would string you up like Ian Curtis, and today could be the day.

When you read a book, do you tear out random pages and insert them wherever you please? Do you rearrange art at a museum exhibition? Or watch the end of a film first? Do you instruct a chef to alter a prize recipe when preparing your meal at a restaurant? What gives you the right? Hmmmmmmmmmmmmmmmmmmm?

The modern sexual appetite is a ravenous one. It all seems to be about multi-penetration any more. This is the only thing any girl can do nowadays. The ratio of men with regard to women is way, way, way off . . . something like ten to one.

Modern women always travel with at least one midnight cowboy in the arsenal. As her sexual appetite is insatiable, and must be . . . to satisfy so many hungry men. Usually a volcanic glass dildo, powered by an internal rechargeable core. It reacts to body heat, static electricity, and movement.

Generating a natural vibration without the need for batteries. These spiraled glass phalluses are capable of more harm than good. Merely the result of a society supersaturated in pornography and starved for physical contact.

Drugs didnt help one bit either. Yet drug addicts need to get high, and sex on film pays well enough. And the weirder the sex, the better. Most modern porno being much like the legitimate modern cinema. We have tame, safe, near featureless depictions of romance within an unattainable, sophisticated lifestyle. Everything is nonchalant and casual. Nobody means anything to anyone, any more.

Ever.

So . . . if some degenerate formicophiliac wants to massage the inside of their asshole with a live cockroach . . . masturbate to footage of mating spiders and listen to cheap audio recordings . . . of adolescent Japanese teens discuss fucking while on their period . . .

. . . certain members of society are eager to pay for a chance to see it. Seemingly, there is no shortage of applicants for this type of deviance. And for such instant gratification, who could blame them. They never had a chance.

Tame porno becomes a waste of time. After all . . . I only find myself critiquing the aforementioned style and composition against an actor's believable facial expressions. Always asking myself, is she really enjoying it? Does she cum for real?

Modern cinema has long been a two dimensional medium.   Once upon a time, it was challenged by the third dimension.   But the technology was never perfected.   Inevitably, film returned to its natural, and more comfortable **2D** state.

I am more of a purist, and many others are too. Vintage film is quite the obsession these days, and rather difficult to locate outside of the **PS**ynaps network.   Most likely our newfound fascination is only a response to the many years spent using the **PS**ynaps **3D** interface. I can only dream in **3D** as a result, and it may be permanent.

On the upside, I am able to use my **PS**ynaps link to search the **Junction** while unconscious. This way, I may conduct research while I rest.   In search of information, my oldest addiction.   Which saves me a lot of time. I appreciate that, because time is always in short supply.

Film has become an escape from daily obligation.   No one wants to memorize reality.   If a modern film is shot realistically, no one takes the time to see it.   We watch old movies to escape.   The few that have survived

I adore films with subtitles because it allows me to view punctuation in its natural state.   Many of my fellow survivors do not read or write.   Video instruction has replaced the manual.   Icons and pictures have replaced descriptions. Who needs them anyway?   Why read the book when you can watch the film?   Right?

Long before now, it has been proven that every line has already been conceived. There exists no combination of words or phrases not already found in pre-existing film dialogue.

Reality television let the world know about all of America's little imperfections, which made us more vulnerable in the eyes of outsiders. The meth, crack, heroin, gambling, pornography, food, surgery addictions were on full display. America became less and less appealing, and immigration nearly halted altogether. Misinformation, the civilian war, rioting, and domestic terrorism helped put the final nail in tourism's coffin.

Writing and creative arts were soon regarded as generally obsolete. Except in the hillside compound. In this modern world, there is no need for them any more. Certain genetic features are now removed during any governmental birth. Creativity and independent notion are two worth mentioning.

The majority of men are born sterile. If not, then sterility is induced. Procreation is a privilege, not a right. Women are so scarce and usually kept within an agency compound, safely underground. Or they find an existence on the hillside.

The regurgitation of film began around the turn of this century. Reality television was first sired, and the film industry became stagnant. It did nothing but remake films originally shot only twenty years prior.

Top silver screen actors were then forced to accept meager television roles, in order to survive. Or risk detriment to a respected film career via uninspired writing and execution within the corporate film industry. Independent films were slowly edged out of existence due to lack of distribution. Then the high definition digital era took hold. All satellite cable feeds were soon converted. Then all actors truly began a life of self-consciousness.

It was then that we, the voyeurs from home, could see every enlarged pore on some thespian's goofy face. We discovered that they were just like us. Only, lucky enough to know certain people. And well trained enough to remember someone else's dialogue. It was then that the world learned the truth about imperfections. We discovered that everyone has them . . . but some people are lucky enough to have them removed with the click of a button. One click and that unsightly zit/wrinkle/scar goes the way of the Dodo.

And we realized that stand-up comedians were simply high or drunk or extremely damaged and simply saying every little thing that popped into their twisted minds. Random astute observation forced us to double over with side-splitting guffaw. Spewing practically anything into a microphone for our enjoyment. All of our favorite comedians were high as fuck when they were at their best. Then they died from it. Or they got clean or happy . . . and lost their edge.

Music, on the other hand, has somehow become better than ever by comparison. Many underground karaoke lounges have materialized due to the audio prohibition. A few of them host live music.

Now generally outlawed, music is only socially acceptable when used within the context of a film. Only after the appropriate permits were obtained. But the soundtracks are never released, the songs may only play during the screening and only if they are used in some justifiable way.

I find it strange that music has been so ignored by PSynaps. We embrace the audio world at the **Citadel.** I contact 8 and tell him to meet me in the "office." Which is code for meet me on thirteen. I will shoot, while I wait.

"En route," he responds.

Float
The
Ocean

Smoking a Chester, I lean against the wall of the what used to be the shallow end of the pool. Oceanic storms bring rain with regularity now. A rarity for California in the past.

A meter of water has collected in the pool. I watch as small two headed turtles wade through the stagnant sludge that has accumulated at the deeper end. They wrestle amongst themselves, each one jockeying for the best position in the sun . . .

. . . I recall a dive in Maui I experienced many years back, exploring a sunken ship. Once you get down far enough, it's darker because you are so deep. I found enormous sea turtles floating about here and there. One hanging a flipper over a railing atop the sunken vessel, apparently waving at me. Another swam in close, to check us out.

Reef sharks hunt in the distance. A tiny shell moves slowly but surely on its way below me. I hover above the ocean floor. She was there too, collecting anemone for her collage . . . I talked her into an oceanic fling . . . .

Feeling the effects of my most recent injection, I cap my rig and put it back in my pocket. I can use it at least twenty more times before the puncture site becomes too painful to bear. I would install a permanent IV, but I just cant bring myself to admit I am so strung out. I smoke while I wait for 8.

I used to smoke Bali Shag, but it became impossible to find. As international imports typically are. So I was forced to make the switch. Chesterfelds are not so miserable, of course, but they are a bit different than a filterless roll-your-own. Sometimes I have to break the filter off.

The problem with the mainline lifestyle is that it truly takes up most of your time, if not every second of it. There is only one way to remain truly content. That is to sit in a room with nothing else to do but load and shoot the next shot. Perpetually jumping the gun. Always wanting more, never content. In the past, I have set up rows of full rigs on a table and shot for days . . . .

But in the end, you will wish for something more. Something different. Something that doesnt leave your soul at the dry cleaners.

You can take a pill for pain, but you still want to drink wine, and smoke a joint. The pill is not enough on its own. Neither is that shot. Contentment becomes your newest challenge. I want it all at once, but that will kill me quick. And no matter what you do, it's never gonna be enough. No exit, not ever.

Not from this. The next day and every day after, it's going to force your sick and tired ass out of bed. Make you do it all over again. Or else.

Or else you're going to be really fucking sorry. Better safe than sorry, right? Why would I quit if the drug has become my only friend and ally? Drugs are the most reliable source of affection for most survivors. Ding. 8 has now arrived, how lovely. I work very hard to get to my feet because I am made of lead.

"What did you learn following them to the Peterson building?" I ask him.

"Nothing really, just kept my distance while the chicks made small talk about her fuckin' Pomeranian's giardia. Gross really. I waited for them to enter the building before I contacted you. That's all. Then I contacted you . . . . What is it? What's the big twist?"

He asks me with his dull, grey eyes consumed by his bright round face. But dont let that fool you, I have learned that 8 can deliver pain with the best of them. I assume the weight gain is all part of his cover because I can still see the strong build beneath his fatty tissue. I have seen him toss a man like an ant. And why would someone choose a cover that is so difficult to maintain?   Such an increase of caloric intake must be cumbersome, to say the least.   But these are questions survivors do not ask one another. Privacy is always preferential in modern times. I let it be.

"You know what you are, man? The personification of a spastic colon. I went there to check it out . . . and what did I find?! Marshal badges! One badge to be exact . . . . Are you certain you didnt hear anything useful along the way?" I needle him.

"Nope," he replies.

I draw on my cigarette while watching a small group of maniacs, who surf the break at what used to be Beverly Blvd. It's actually a really nice left. The bits of the buildings that remain below the sea level act as a man made reef. Dog help you if you fall. You will find yourself tumbling around inside of a washing machine full of glass and rusty nails. No bus for you. They'll call you a fucking hearse. If they call anything at all. Maybe they let the sharks sort you out.

"So what the fuck is going on? Couldnt have attracted this kind of attention ourselves. So who is it? Who's inside that could command this kind of response?" I inquire as 8 stares blankly and breathes from his mouth.

I debate throwing him off the roof for a moment. It could look like an accident. Really . . . it could. It has before. I work better alone anyway. Not today.

"I want you to organize a garden for the roof. Work with what space remains next to the solar panels but keep your distance from the wind turbine. Use the rain collectors as an irrigation source and be sure to create enough shade for quinoa. Build whatever you need in the workshop. Have the Engineer set you up. It's your project. A new hobby for you. A past time," I delegate.

I snatch his binoculars out of his hand with fanatical intensity. My stomach grumbles audibly and 8 notices. I havent eaten a bite since yesterday morning. Now being noon on the following day. Not to mention, the rocked cocaine has been murder on my appetite. Now I've got heroin in my blood, and I am fucking starving. I havent been home in weeks because there is too much going on at the moment.

"8 . . . why dont you run out and get me an avocado, tofu, and tomato on wheat . . . . And one for yourself, not that you need it," I smile.

"Thanks," he replies as he shuffles toward the elevator.

The practice of a vegetarian diet is not emotional in any way. It has become increasingly difficult, if not nearly impossible to raise livestock. Due to the widespread outbreak of disease (airborne and water contamination) and famine. Livestock is, of late, killed by one thing or another in a very short time. Always. So no one wants to deal with it.

Over fishing and pollution left every oceanic ecosystem devastated making seafood inedible. Soy, wheat, vegetables, fruit, grains, and nuts . . . are grown instead.

A constant harvest strategy is used to cultivate hardy seeds from quinoa and chia. Chia is already indigenous to the western part of North America. And quinoa is so adaptable to this environment, coming from south America. Cultivators must be careful not to supersaturate with sun or water, but seeds are self-sowing and relatively low maintenance.

I will grow them on the rooftop here as well. Cucumbers and tomatoes, too. Once I receive the clones. Perhaps some herbs, as well. I recall many months, surviving solely on a tonic comprised of chia seed, chlorella algae, and mineral supplements. Comfort food for the apocalypse.

Headless palm trees number the edge of the boulevard as a river of septic waste flows past. Windows of buildings punched out and broken . . . like the eyes, teeth, and eyeteeth of America and its dream. I look out toward Griffith and see vultures circling over what must be a carcass. Of which species? Vertebrate, human, cannie, alien? I will never know . . . .

Returning my attention out west and I notice someone catching a perfect barrel at the Beverly break, lucky bastard. I flick my Chester over the edge, hoping it will land on a brand new hat, purchased not an hour ago. Only to light another one.

Using the binoculars for a better view, I watch some lucky psycho catch a powerful twenty footer and ride it out. Then swerving wide around a twisted metal antler protruding from the briny jade.

Out beyond the break, far out, on the horizon line, I notice a ship. Then I notice it is burning. A tall plume of black smoke juts upward, into the sun. The sun, in all its glory, hangs low on the horizon.

Looming like some sad eye that weeps for a lost cause. I would later discover . . . that the ship I saw in flames was my pirate radio station, **K N I L . AM.**

Broadcast Medium Frequency (1370 KHz). The last remaining shortwave radio frequency in the wasteland. Until now.

Pink Thing

Making my way down, I hop in the box and hit the greasy button with an "L" on it. The car stops on the eleventh floor and a small, blonde faggot hops in . . . flustered and upset. His little face reddened with frustration. Whining about some asshole, in the lobby, not allowing more of his cocksucker friends up to the gay fuck party, currently ongoing in room eleven ten.

"Oh . . . my . . . dog . . . . What a fucking asshole, *right*?! I mean what the fuck? We put up nearly ten-thousand for the night!" He says. Then noticing my suit, along with my general lack of interest. "Oh my, do you *work* here?! Could you *possibly* help me out?" Putting his hand on my arm he says, "I'll make it worth your while!"

Inserting my key into the elevator wall. I turn it and the car ceases its descent, suspended mid-air. Dangling. I inhale and exhale long and deep before I say,

"First thing . . . never . . . fucking touch me . . . unless you want me to touch you back."

I brutally shove him into the corner of the elevator. His frail body bouncing against the full length digital screen, nearly cracking it. His shock slowly turns into a weak attempt at seduction. Making me sick to my stomach. I continue.

"Second . . . should I decide to help you, I wont be accepting any faggot tricks as compensation. Cash only. Now . . . what's it gonna be?"

He continues to cower in the corner for a moment. Then responding with,

"Well . . . I have two thousand euros and an eight ball of cocaine to get me through the weekend. Saving it for a special occasion."

To which I reply, "Done . . . now put it in my hand . . . let's go!"

He gives me the offering. I inspect it, a silver cellophane bag containing a golf ball sized rock of flakey, yellow cocaine. Probably Peruvian, the largest cartel in operation outside of the United States.

America is not yet involved in the manufacture and distribution of cocaine. Here we only produce heroin, marijuana, tobacco, and alcohol. I open it and dip my finger in, tasting it . . . yes . . . it tastes right.

The human receptacle also hands me two rolled notes, one thousand euros each. Complete with blood stains. I shove the bag into my coat pocket.

Then I unroll each bill and slowly wipe them off onto his "shirt." Which would actually be better construed as a girdle or corset.   Disturbing all the same.

"Good boy," I continue, "now let's go fetch all your queen friends from the lobby and take them up to the little faggot's ball. We wouldnt want them to miss the mass gaping."

As the elevator car approaches the lobby . . . already I can hear the fey, whining voices of his compatriots.   Before the doors open, my eyes roll involuntarily. Ding.

"That little faggot's got his own jet airplane, that little faggot, he's a mil-li-on-aire!"

Echoes throughout the staunch white lobby, courtesy of Dire Straights, for whom I have always maintained an affinity. A stadium rock trio possessing a fuck-all attitude.   Coupled with the ability to appreciate -and put to good use, a stylish sweatband. But not in the ironic way in which hipsters would come to wear them.   Not as a costume.   Mark Knopfler was as much the genesis of the sweatband as he was of his own band.

I am instantly assaulted by the intensity of the anal assassins. Which only seems to increase as the doors yawn open. Revealing a distressed lobby lizard (Johnny Knickers, I believe) in the act of fending off a group of aforementioned beaver leavers.

"Stay here," I instruct Mr. Blonde Ambition.

I peer out into the bright lobby. Allowing my eyes to adjust, I see that it's everyone's favorite international-gay-celebrity-pornstar. Of course, I am talking about Richard "The Dick" Dong, with his entourage in tow.

"Let em' up if they've got medical clearance," I bark.

Each one of them, touting a reddish complexion from overexposure. They really love to tan. Groundbreaking insults pour into the car. Ranging from,

"Who the fuck did your hair, anyway?" to "What the fuck is your motherfucking problem?!"

They promptly overwhelm the sardine can. Johnny compares their retinal scans against the medical clearance files.

"All clear," he replies.

The gaggle of epicene stool punchers pile into the tiny car. Leaving a plump one, on a leash, who refuses to move from the lobby. This one is pulled against its will by a tall, skinny one.

He says, "Come on piggy, let's go to the party."

With a little more resistance, the plump swine is persuaded to come aboard. Close quarters. I wait for the doors to close, and I begin my dissertation. Before I am able to commence, one of the Lolas sounds off with,

"What the fuck is with your boots?! Are we at war or something?! Who the fuck wears combat boots in the middle of summer?! Are you fucking mad? It's forty-seven degrees centigrade outside! Your feet need to br-ea-the! And that suit . . . " He drones.

Dick Dong tongues another one in the corner of the ascending car. The most common footwear of the day consists of thin flesh colored socks with a pink rubber soles. Often with webbing between the toes for amphibious capability. All nine of these fecal freaks have on the same fleshy pink slippers. Modern garb is limited to a scant array of synthetic fibers, typically dyed in neon colors and nauseating patterns. Like a clown suit, only worse. Cutting it off with,

"And what should I wear exactly? Sandals? Fucking webbed slippers?! Listen up, you male cunt! I will grind your soul into that linoleum if you open your dick sucker again . . . . How the fuck is it that nonbreeders even maintain a foothold in modern society? You dont have anything to contribute."

S/he shuts its mouth, swallowing hard. Just like any other day in the life of a cocksucker.

"Right . . . all of you fist-fucking party monsters, listen up!" I continue. "Several of you-super-silly-sassy-sodomites have been granted a temporary access to the **Citadel** and nothing more. Do not make me regret this. Because if I do . . . you certainly will . . . . This world will never miss such a colorful collective of cum carousers. Rest assured, we have an excellent disposal system on site, and I am not afraid to use it. Even if you are considered famous in some circles."

I take a brief pause for emphasis. Then I finish my thought.

"I dont want it to go bad any more than you do. It would create more work than you fucks are actually worth. So do us all a favor and be on your best behavior. Remember the rules while you fuck each others' scat, okay?!"

One of them begins to ejaculate in the mouth of another, oblivious to my rant.

"Whatever you do within the room is not to spill out into the hallway at any point in time. Consider this is your final warning. There wont be another like it, I guarantee . . . ."

I then return my attention to the aforementioned concerns regarding my attire.

"As for your inquiry about the suit . . . it is constructed of fine Chinese silk. It was assembled in Metzingen, Germany at the turn of this century. I was my father's first, so it has known a long life. I have made modifications to it. Done with found materials: leather . . . kevlar . . . canvas . . . . Each one infixed to conserve my life."

The shocked shemales are wrestling with the eternal internal struggle of this century: pride vs. existence. Grappling with it, for what seems like hours, as they trade appalled looks with one another . . . . Their mouths hanging agape . . . as if patiently awaiting a cock, that might throat-fuck them back toward reality . . . .

I am enjoying every second of it. They seem to make a unanimous unspoken decision, that self preservation is the best option. Securing their tongues for the first time in all of their happy lives. All except for "The Dick," who proceeds to sloppily kiss the young boy in the corner, never once reacting to my words.

Ding. Take out the trash, one more time. I usher the runny noses out of the car and onto the eleventh floor without making any more eye contact.

Averting my gaze downward, fearing that one more glance may steal my pussy-loving soul forever. Once the persnickety maggots have cleared the elevator, I recall sighing deeply. Then I head down . . . deep into the earth . . . into the safe rooms.

Thickening Agents

The same old story, no factual glory
I against I against I against I against
And I say I don't like it, and I know I don't want it
I against I against I against I against
Almighty watching, almighty watching
I against I against I against I against
And I say I don't like it, and I know I don't want it
I against I against I against I against . . .
H.R.

I must mention that a few weeks earlier, the **Citadel's** punctilious Engineer came to me with a rather attractive proposal. Offering me a significant sum of money to incriminate, or at the very least, discredit one tenant in particular. One who happens to be an incumbent during this year of election.

I did some checking up on this particular marked man, and discovered that he is encouraging a bill. One that would increase state funding for further control for our state borders. Making travel a near impossibility for non-California citizens. No longer would they come and go as they please.

Most of the employees here happen to be non-American citizens, let alone non-Californian. Texas recently managed succession once again. The first time since its previous bout of complete independence, in preservation of slavery, in 1836.

This laid the path for our state to form a single liberal democracy, run by elected representatives. If California gains independence, the perimetric fences are sure to be erected soon after. Just like the hillside compound. We do not want those barbed wire boundaries in place any sooner than necessary.

Many current tenants and employees have escaped certain death. Only to end up at the **Citadel**, in a last ditch effort to trump fate. Yet, they do not wish to be indefinitely marooned. I deduce that they all contributed a little money to this cause. A little scratch to eliminate the common itch. Similar to tithing the church.

If the bill passes, these wayward souls would be cut off from their families on the other side of the fences. The **Citadel** then becomes a permanent home. **PS**ynaps, a luxury amongst only the highest survivor classes, is not an option for an illegal immigrant. Nor is it an option for any of the lower classes. No more visitation . . . . Even interstate messaging would become difficult, if not impossible. And forget about going international.

This is what the people want. The registered citizens. But mainly, it's the wealthy landowners, the studio executives who want it the most. It makes their investment all the more sound. Allowing them to make more guarantees, thereby raising the value of their product. Still free to travel wherever they please via monorail.

After the uprising we recently had, we can get what we want out of the system. Instead of just getting what we get. There's only so much we will take, and we are more in numbers than the governing class. When the rats in charge were faced with their own certain death at the hands of a new America, they bent over backwards.

The exorbitant cry-pussies kissed our rosey fucking asses faster than we could drop trou. Knowing that if the political rats continue running the machine, though now under our watchful eyes. They could still earn a prominent stipend. Even on a shorter leash, the possibilities are endless.

All the power, perks, and bloody buzzards to be made on all the backward dealings of the world, still available. Black market trade involving weapons, precious stones, and metals. Even what's left of the failing energy market, its stock is still up for grabs. But you already know that or at least you should.

Getting back to this particular statesman, he is a frequent guest of our exquisite establishment. And a casual participant in numerous evil deeds while on site. Me? I hate politicians. Always have. Civilians are now fully wise to the fact that a dead puppet is better than a talking one. This is why no statesmen ever leave the sanctity of D.C., and its subterranean development. However, sometimes I hear rumblings of an interplanetary settlement, safe within a neighboring galaxy. For those who can afford such a permanent vacation.

Back on earth, the deal was this, I provide hard evidence of the Senator's inappropriate behavior and the Engineer handles the rest. I remain a silent partner. Total anonymity, with the utmost immunity.

Some video . . . some stills . . . color . . . night vision . . . thermal. I got the Engineer plenty. He was happy, I was happy. That's it, that's all.

And now we have Marshals sniffing around. Two of them. Sodomizing street whores in unison. With their cocaine engorged cocks. Marshals who enjoy the heart arresting stylings of Bone Awl . . . . On the other hand . . . it could be entirely unrelated.

Smile On A Dog

Need a shot.   Heading down to the office for this one . . . my actual office.   Seen enough of the roof for today.   8 is making steady progress on the garden, wooden planter boxes line the edge of the roof on the north end.   Once the soil arrives from Northern California, we can plant seeds.   Surfing has concluded, on account of the sunset. Feeding time. I leave my binoculars in the shed with my rifle and walk to the elevator.

Ding.

I punch the basement level after entering my security code.   On the way down, the car stops at the eighth floor. A fertile and muliebrous brunette enters. Socialization does have its perks. I make small talk. Recognizing that her accent is Swedish, I say,

"I thought most Swedes were blondes . . . you're a fucking knockout of a brunette, go figure."

She laughs, dog knows why. Good sign either way. She states that she is here on "business." I'm pretty sure that isnt code for sexual deviance. I feign interest . . . rather believably. I assume she is with the champagne magnate occupying the entire eighth floor. On her way to a "business" meeting, so I inquire as to her plans after.

At the lobby level, I get off the elevator with her. She tells me to leave my number on her command center, room eight-eighteen. Instead, I offer my contact coordinates and ask her to reach me whenever she's ready. Polite goodbyes ensue and I am back in the box.

Basement level, please. "Broken Glass" by the Murder City Devils plays on the speaker while I lean against the plasma image. Which displays a brunette coed blowing a well known, well endowed professional athlete. As the elevator descends, on the screen the well oiled male is jamming his cock deep inside of a younger, greasier actress. Saliva dripping from his fat sausage link knuckles, as his clenched fist tightly grips his throbbing member in a glorious, yet unconscious effort . . . to keep hope alive.

"I like the sound of you strut struttin' on that big stage. On that big stage. I like the sound of you on that metallic 2 K.O. Oh . . . oh oh! Iggy . . . baby!!"

Seems that leaking a sex tape is really big business nowadays, everybody is doing it for the fast cash. Which is so funny because you know this motherfucker hired an expensive crew to shoot this garbage. Just to make him look good. Not a sex tape at all, really. It's self-financed self-deprecation in the interest of self-promotion. Ding.

Exit basement level. The only sound is the dreary drip drip drip of water that has made its way beyond our perimeter. I stroll down the winding hall over the granite tiles. Thinking to myself, *this is gonna be the first level of the building to go . . . .* One day.

They say it's fully disaster proof. Complete with a **CBRN** detection and defense System. **C**hemical **B**iological **R**adiological **N**uclear. Structurally re-enforced concrete. To withstand a direct missile hit, as well as the daily earthquakes. CO_2 scrubbers and O_2 generators pump in over-pressurized air, allowing 500 plus hours of safe submersion. That's nearly three weeks.

But it's a stinking load in my opinion. Nothing can divert Nature. Gonna have to move my office to the roof one day. I pass through a security checkpoint, the first, where it audits my heart rate, scans my **P**Synaps, also checking my pupils for dilation. Retinas are verified.

A few years before I arrived, a dead man was used to access the nerve center of the **Citadel**. Nearly shutting down the entire operation. The investors vowed, never again. So, now there are **P**Synaps upgrades with heart monitors and retinal scans.

Every person's **P**Synaps is unique, tied into one's DNA. Powered by the human body's electrical current and static electricity. Making impostors few and far between. Though I must scramble my identity through a series of dummy accounts created through dead men. This allows me to use the network without allowing my name to materialize. Another username will appear in place of mine. A virtual balaclava.

Then I continue down a few steps, to the hardwood flooring of my very own place in hell. Through one more checkpoint, the last, and I cruise toward my office door. Placing my index finger on the scanner and I unlatch the door with the key kept around my neck. The same one which operates the elevator independently.

PSynaps handles the rest. Disengaging the secondary bolts, followed by the primary. The bolts extent vertically and horizontally into the door frame. Both door and frame are steel core, coated with ballistic plating. Airtight, gas, and blast-resistant. **E.F.P.** proof. **E**xplosively **F**ormed **P**enetrator. The entire basement facility is certainly explosion ready . . . but is it waterproof?

I shut and triple lock the door. I must check on my kombucha cultures because the **S**ymbiotic **C**ulture **O**f **B**acteria and **Y**east layer is nearing a centimeter in thickness. Which means it is about time to harvest. Then a new culture will be made from the mother in another week. The tea of which, I will drink.

I'm feeling a little excited from my work day, so I project a vintage bootlegged copy of Roadhouse on the wall, to help me relax.

Then I break out the supplies, tossing the white baggies from 909 on my zebra wood desk. A '69 Hermes era. The **Citadel**'s previous owner happened to be a collector of vintage cars, motorcycles, weapons, furniture, and much more.

Upon his eviction from this property, the current owning entity, absorbed the majority of the assets already on location. It was a bitter farewell to say the least, but it left the basement levels full of vintage gear. The Engineer and I spend hours on end restoring motors or fabricating various modern necessities for survival.

I open my bottom drawer and retrieve a brand new, sharp rig. I attach the new silver point to my trusty glass syringe. This, I procured from our medical technician on retainer, as my usual supplier has been unreliable. Then carefully draw some water out of a glass resting on the desktop. I set the syringe on the top edge of the glass. Pulling my spoon from my pocket, I take a lighter to it and briefly sterilize.

Add the fairy dust, add the water. (Because the vodka is leaving red marks on my arms.) And stir with the plunger. I pull a small plug of cotton from one of my Chesterfeld filters and drop it in the spoon. Drawing the cloudy liquid through the cotton and into the reservoir. Remove the air and tie off with a rubber band I find on the desk. Who's the lucky one? Which one of you blood ducts wants it?

Got it . . . smoothly releasing the poison into my arm, my head rolls back with my eyes . . . . Fade to black . . . .

When I wake, I find the needle in my arm and the rubber band still tying off my veins. I remove the rig and the rubber band because I see the junk collecting around the rubber tourniquet. Causing hives and a dark brown rash to surface on my bicep.

Releasing the secondary hit causes my knees to buckle and I go black again but not quite as deep. I bang my head on the desk. Laying my head down . . . and soon after . . . my body walks out the door on its own accord. I follow it on down the hallway. Beyond the peace I have created, and the solace I enjoy . . . I recall this happening . . .

I remember a time long ago . . . days spent caressed by warm sand, wet within the sea, carving in the liquid. A story from my youth. I may have been sixteen at the time. Everybody loves a good time . . . you know I do, and this may be the oldest and sweetest sentiment that I possess . . .

Before the dawn broke, I left my future behind me as I drove far away from and into darkness . . . . A slow day for traffic, so I made it to the coast in about forty minutes. Great time of day for this town. Weaving through a pass which connects the 101 to the 1. Passing numerous lookout points but driving right on past. I was late for a massive swell, I saw the camera feed on the internet. This was before I lived right on the coast, of course. Back then, I would always check the camera before making the drive. Good insurance. This was, also before the advent of **PSynaps**. *Before the game changed entirely.*

Along the way I dropped down the canyon next to Rocky Oak Park. Nearing the Mulholland intersection, I happened upon an overturned minivan. Its white exterior scraped by the rusted shoulder barricade on Kanan Dume. Large boulders blocked the opposite side of the pass. I eased my coach into second from third, pulling over on the shoulder. I walked across the asphalt, toward the carnage. I heard a dog, whining and saw him limping in circles.

Must have been a rockslide. Common on this road. Common . . . random . . . and fatal. A few bystanders were looking on and murmuring, while inside of the van remained a family of little people. None of them moving. Seemed they hadnt made the proper upgrades necessary to safely fit within the seat belts. The centrifugal force had bounced them all around like tiny lottery balls. Losing lottery balls. I asked a squinty eyed caucasian if she knew who the dog's owner was.

"In between owners at the moment," she quipped.

"Someone's gonna be late for the jubilee!", another onlooker began mouth-breathing.

I picked the mutt up, fingering the collar . . . which said "Russ T." He looked like a fox mutt with black and brown hair. Purple or reddish, if sunlight caught it. The lightest part of his coat, ironically, was the fur around his asshole. He furrowed his brow and cocked his head. I smiled, noticing that his eyes are different colors, one green and one brown.

I heard sirens in the distance, most likely alerted by a cellular phone call. I must be on my way. I was late for an important meeting anyway. I slipped out the back of the small crowd, slinking over to my car with Russ under my arm.

"Taking you to the beach," I said, silently shutting the door of the coupe.

Releasing the parking brake, coasting away silently for about a hundred feet before I start the engine. I rolled off slowly, inconspicuously. Everyone else too busy eye fucking a family of dead midgets to notice.

A plump cop passed me heading toward the wreck with siren wailing. Upset, sweaty, and anxious to be on the scene. His one track mind was too full of dead sugar plum fairy tales to care about me and mine. I'm nobody, that's who. Nobody to you. Nobody. I sped off toward the sandy, briny coast . . . third . . . fourth . . . fifth gear.

Pulled up to the dusty parking lot which belied my favorite point break, across the street from my favorite seafood shack. I stroked Russ and opened the door.

"Your new life."

The waves crashing down with emphasis. He watched me, looking for an answer. I was struggling with my wetsuit . . . finally getting it over my heels. Right, then left. Smoothing the sweet smelling wax over slick epoxy. Releasing the true smell of summer into the air, regardless of the month. Russ watched, tail tucked and confused. I finished my second coat and pulled the other half of my wetsuit on zipping it over my torso. Touched my toes . . . seven . . .eight . . . nine . . . ten.

"Come on, Russ."

The waves were peaking up about twenty yards offshore, plenty deep. No rocks waiting patiently like tombstones. I set Russ loose on the sand and watched him tear after gulls, literally scaring the shit out of them. Limping but seemingly oblivious to the pain. I paddled out, leaving him to his wares. I went gliding out over the green glass pulling myself between two breakers then moving into position for the first ride.

Long sturdy strokes, I pulled myself into the path of oncoming Nature. I saw it about fifty yards out in the deeper shinning blue, rolling in at me, forming the perfect pocket. I felt it absorb my energy and lift me up, my feet falling perfectly beneath. My board carrying me far away and beyond. Dashing around whitewater and over and down finding my line, my path. Walking on water had nothing on this cruise.

Once the joyride was over, I pulled the nose back out, toward the deeper north end of the beach. Looking over my shoulder, I saw a lone figure standing there. Looking back again, it had changed position. Someone was petting Russ.

Funny thing, I also saw this boat way out on the water . . . but there was someone waving me down. My eyes must have been playing tricks. Funniest thing. The guy looked exactly like me. Just like me, only older. But I was at least seventy meters away . . . so, who can be sure? Next set was starting to gear up, so I ignored the boat, settling into position. Caught that one and the one after that, and the next one, and the next, . . . eight, . . . nine, . . . ten.

Suddenly, I was famished. Had to eat immediately. I caught one more in, and stepping off, I loosed the leash and walked on land again. A woman was sunning topless next to the natural rock bluff adjacent to the highway. Bless her ever-loving heart.

A surfboard rested beside her and I noticed we drink the same bottled water, Antrice. I looked for Russ but saw nothing so I went to my topless goddess to get some answers. First stripping back the top of my suit so I too was topless. She would be more at ease, I thought. Although she did seem more comfortable in the flesh than Annie Sprinkle. Covering her sun-glassed eyes with a hand, shielding the harsh sunlight.

"Afternoon, gorgeous. Dont get up, just wondering if you've seen my mutt?"

Her lips cracked to say, "Lost your little doggy, Dorothy?"

To which I replied, "Yeah, just gone for a bit, figured maybe you'd seen him. Cute little thing, collar says Russ T."

She shifted and sat up a little. I would be staring at her goods directly, if only I had some shades, but I didnt, so . . . . Eye contact, looking at her green eyes. Focus now.

She eyed my surfboard, "Name him after your board, Jack?"

I replied, "No I just acquired him today. Lost him already . . . . Fuck."

She wrinkled her nose and said, "You've got a filthy mouth . . . even for a sailor."

I countered with, "Thanks, I think, . . . well, I better go and have a look around. Thanks again."

"You're welcome, I'm sure," she said, as I sauntered off looking for my lost, stolen dog.

I looked around the trash cans along the side of the P.C.H. but he was nowhere to be found. So I relented, returning to the coupe for nuts, banana, and fresh Antrice water, breakfast of champions. I dug my key from my wetsuit pocket to open the trunk, resting my board against the open lid. I moved my beach towel, revealing my food stash; keeping cooler in the trunk. I was just about to feast when I heard a whimper, kind of a squealing . . . weak like a guinea pig. Russ T.

I searched my feet for him to no avail, so I followed my ears which led me to the passenger seat where I found him shivering and shaking, curled up in my t-shirt, now soaked in piss.

"Hey little guy, been looking for you."

I picked him up, squealing a little. Traumatized. I continued to calm him down, cleaned him up a bit, rinsing the piss off him with Antrice.

One thing continued to eat at me. I was driving a convertible . . . and I did keep the top down when surfing . . . . But I dont understand how a small pup could jump into a coupe from ground level. Something was beginning to stink. I had a feeling that it was the nudist bitch on the sand with her hand in this particular cookie jar.

I wrapped Russ in my towel and gave him some food and water. I wanted answers and I happened to have a trusty form of interrogation with me. So . . . I twisted one up and walked on down. I left Russ T. in the car to relax. He was having a rough day already and it wasnt even noon.

I carefully descended the dusty path down toward coarser sand below. Avoiding a bottle cap, some broken glass, an uncapped syringe, and heading toward my newfound, fellow early-riser. I walked up to her and smiled to say,

"thought you needed to relax just a little more, and I have just the thing."

I produced the giant cone-shaped spliff. Complete with a cardboard filter tip. She rolled her eyes behind her shades, she affectionately wrinkled her nose.

"Come on," I said, "it's a beautiful day and you're at the beach." I lit it and passed over. "It's kush," I continue.

"Thought it was Rusty, like your board, sailor," she chirped.

"No, dummy, what you're smoking. It's kush. Nevermind. Forget it."

Awkward pause. I couldnt decide what I wanted to do more . . . would I rather fuck this girl? Would it feel better just to bash her in the face? Wallop! I decided to wait it out a little longer. See what developed. The least she could do is tell me what happened with my dog.

She hit the joint three or four times. Enormous hits. Must have been a stoner in a previous life. She passed it to me and I hit also.

"For what it's worth, I really want to share my gratitude for what you are doing here," I said.

"What? Showing the world my tits?" She responded.

"Exactly. You probably do it because you dont want tan lines, but you also like the attention it gets you. The excitement from being a little taboo. And you possess a perfect specimen as well, thank you." I finish.

"So now what?! You need a fuck?! Is that it?!" She inquired.

I replied with, "Perhaps you are the one in need."

She rolled over onto her belly dismissing me, while exposing a world class ass. It was as if each cheek were its' own magnetic field, pushing like forces against one another. Defying gravity.

Continuing with, "What's a little thing like you doing out here all alone, anyway?"

"Trying to be alone," she answered.

I sat and smoked some more. The sets rolled in and I wished I was out there right now. The sexual tension was excruciating. On my end, at least.

I broke the silence . . . asking, "Wanna paddle out?"

"Sure." She replies.

And we did. As a courtesy, I gave her first crack. A decent surfer. Good for a girl. Excellent style. Not all women can surf with style but this one could, and I liked it. I caught one after, but was reluctant to show off. No cutbacks or pumping the vortex, no aggressive posturing. Not if I wanted to get anywhere with this one. Just a cooled out, sea foam green magic carpet ride.

She looked good in a rash guard, too, her nipples showing through. Nothing I hadnt seen before, but still, I was wanting to give her a black eye less and less. While wanting to do the other thing more and more.

Her brown hair wet and matted on her back as she paddled back toward me, a true smile on her face. Not the fake shit you see around town. Real, honest, genuine, pure happiness.

That beach, to me, was the happiest place on earth. And now it was my turn to ride again. I felt intact. To the point of spontaneous combustion, so tightly wrapped and perfectly tuned that I could splinter wood with a glance.

We wore out the old point break, or maybe it was the other way around . . . and headed in to rest a while. I needed to check on Russ anyway. My body felt heavy again, as gravity began to pull on me with full force. Making me realize just how spent I was. Trying not to show it, but feeling as tired as a whore at six a.m. Sunday morning. I dropped dead on the sand next to my board, next to her.

"Wish there was an In and Out nearby," I said.

"How quaint," she remarked.

I felt a film quote coming on, "A little of the 'ol in out in out?"

In my best Alexander DeLarge. She seemed to get the joke but showed no appreciation. Cunt. Why should she, she wasnt the one searching for a lay, now was she? And even so, I would have been too tired. Not even able to wave a white flag from my limp member in retreat. She'd probably end up fucking me instead.

"How about a taco truck? Roach coach? Street meat?" She suggested.

"Funny," was all I could offer.

I was a level headed type, still am, but it's a little hard to make heads or tails of some funny talking brunette I found nude sunbathing on the beach. And I really wanted to know what the fuck happened to my doggie. And what was he up to? Resting, dreaming of a wide open field lined with bitches and bones.

"I've been told I resemble a character in a Kubrick film. . . . Would you agree?" I break the silence.

"What? Strangelove?! You more resemble Malcom X over Malcom MacDowell, if you ask me," she says.

"Charmed I'm sure," is the only retort that readily came to mind.

Fuck me . . . . Try a little harder. I elevated my mind and created what she wanted to hear. I can be a real red devil in a blue dress, if need be.

Eventually adding, "I am an exceptional lover. . . or at least that's what I hear. Very attentive. Thorough."

"Maybe that's what you hear from the voices in your head. Or what your mommy tells you, but not me." She said.

"Well maybe I'll have to prove it to you!" I offered.

"Maybe you should! But not here, I dont want sand everywhere." She accepted.

"My place or yours?"

"Well, I am fucking starving, so let's get a meal for me, you, and your little dog, too. And then we can worry about all of the rest."

"Agreed," we agreed.

Driving fast, southbound down the PCH. The wind was blowing through our scalps, the three of us rapt with anticipation, feeding on every hair-raising curve of the road.

Until, finally, we arrived at the preliminary destination. Which happened to be a nice family owned restaurant that I happened to know, called Thai-Mi-Down. A place from a past life that I was forced to give up.

I played a track from my demo album, though I said it was some new British import I found taped to a bomb found under the hood of my car. She seemed truly impressed by the music. So much so that she didnt even notice my backstory about the bomb. Which did actually happen but is a story for another time entirely. I played her my self indulgent muzak and she liked it. Which is all I could ask for . . . I was in contention.

We tried two dishes recommended by our waitress, while sipping iced Thai tea. I couldnt tell you what the dishes were called but I do remember that they were more than edible. Our waitress was attractive, bilingual, and friendly. While the food was sweet, spicy, and filling without the sense of heaviness. She received a twenty-percent tip. My new found friend received a whole lot more than that. As much as she could take. But it was my agency that would give her the most . . .

. . . I come to and . . . I begin sensing that my
PSynaps is notifying me again . . . with another urgent
message . . . .

*"Hey . . . hellllOOOoooo! What the fuck is going on with
you?! Hurry up! Open your door! I got your food out here,
you fucking prima donna, hurry up, had to piss like an hour
now!"*

It's 8 . . . whining like a blunt cunt as always.
There is something banging viciously at my door.   I
can hear the dull thud through a foot of protection.   I
attempt to pull myself to my feet.   Then falling back
into the chair.   I spend the next five minutes trying to
get out of the chair and over to the door.   Another five
attempting to unlock it.   Then I actually imagined
opening it but was just drooling on myself while
leaning against the wall.

By the time I actually get it unlocked, crack it
open and peer out . . . he's gone.   At my feet lies my
sandwich.   Delicious dog damned sandwich.   Good
work 8.   He's good for something at least.   I re-lock
the door; tossing the sandwich on the desk.   I flop
heavily onto my couch and take a moment to think
about how lucky I was . . . lucky that I didnt get the
band off in time.   Would have overdosed for sure, had
I taken all of it at once.   Better be more careful.

If I die in here, and they wont get to me for
weeks.   It's a verifiable fortress when locked from the
inside.   I'd be a mortal coil stinking to high
heaven   . . . Careful, careful.   Hot damn this shit is
strong.   Drifting willingly into that place between

sleep and coherence in which so many modern slackers live.

I drift farther off . . . to visualize a tall man in a black leather biker jacket wearing a horse mask walking into a bar. The doorman stops him and checks his identification. Which is, a picture of a horse, of course. He walks up to the bar and the nurse asks him,

"Why the long face?"

He orders a Pabst Blue Ribbon. A tall can. And he pays two euro for it. A live band plays a fantastic cover of "Ladytron" by Roxy Music. I am dancing a slow one with Prudence, she's gazing deep into my eyes. I actually feel her caressing my soul with them . . . .

. . . I come to . . . again . . . drooling on my three-hundred dollar shirt . . . . I notice a dried stream of blood running from the puncture on my forearm to my wrist. I am extremely grateful that it didnt ruin my pink button down. That wasted cunt fucked up my suit a few days back.

I walk to the bathroom to wash up, then apply sunscreen. The sun burns brighter than ever now, it isnt safe to go out unprotected. Just thirty minutes of raw exposure could produce second degree burns. But with a little sunscreen and you can get up to two hours of pure vitamin D.

As I stare at my reflection in the mirror, I find myself replaying the events of that day in nine-oh-nine. There is something eating away at me . . . what was it? The hairs in the shower drain? Maybe. Something else. I use my **PSynaps** to replay the event, using the **Cognizant Recall** feature. I watch as I enter the room . . . then 8 arrives . . . .

Staring at myself, I see that my hair is getting long, almost time to tie it back. My beard is coming in full-ish, too. I tried cutting it myself, only to fuck it up. No such thing as a salon any more, so I let it grow. Stylist house calls are for the elite. And razors? . . . . I havent seen a razor in three fucking years now. Not a real one at least. You know, with a posable head and three blades sharpened with laser precision. Not a chance. I grew tired of shaving with the kitchen's butcher knives, it was painful. So I am letting it cultivate now.

. . . . I continue to watch the playback as 8 and I attempt to wake Reevus from her sleep . . . and the paramedics are called . . . and we wait . . . patiently . . . .

I did come across a straight razor. Took it off a Persian hit man I crossed paths with about a year back. He was in town to murder a witness of the state, who happened to be a tenant of ours. Mafia related bullshit.

A boss was iced while his granddaughter was hiding in the closet. Witness to the entire thing. Not only does the poor thing have a dead grandpappy to contend with, but she also has to fear for her life, every second of every day. And for the rest of her entire and quite possibly, short existence.

Though time is always shorter than we think. I found the crafty camel kisser creeping about the child's safe room here. I kindly asked him for credentials . . . as I always do. He quickly produced a straight razor, I assume for silence. I withdrew my Mosquito loaded with smokeless shells. It only sounds like an air gun when it goes off; completely muted, no silencer necessary.

I put three bullets in his face, then taking the razor from him and opening his throat with it. He was still alive and struggling while I cut him . . . and no, I didnt utter anything clever about bringing a blade to a gunfight.

Afterward, I dropped the body down the incinerator chute, and I kept the razor for myself. Tried shaving with the razor a few times but it takes so dog damned long. I found myself doing more harm than good. A straight razor shave is an hour long process, requiring a patient and steady hand. Too much for me. So now I use it like the Persian once did. As a silent back-up partner to my silent Mosquito.

. . . . And the damn useless paramedics finally arrive in nine oh nine . . . and I watch through my own **P.O.V.** as I brush quickly past the two broke dick quacks. I realize what was bothering me when I suddenly notice that neither of them are my usual dipshits. New recruits, I suppose. But I would have been briefed. And as I am nearly past the second medic, I see a tell tale sign of deceit on him. A greasy moustache squats on his upper lip but it is not a natural one.

As I slow the recording down and magnify, I can make out a little bit of adhesive left around the edges. Sloppy boy.

No telling how long the Marshals have been corrupting our perimeter. Time is short . . . I have much to prepare.

Waste Not Want Not

You ain't no punk, you punk.
You wanna talk about the real junk?
If I ever slip, I'll be banned,
'Cause I'm your garbageman.

Well you can't dig me you can't dig nothin'.
Do you want the real thing, or are you just talkin'?
Do you understand?
I'm your garbageman.

Yeah, somethin' from the garage and down the driveway.
Now get outta your mind and get outta my way.
Now do you understand? Do you understand?
INTERIOR/RORSCHACH

If I wasnt wearing a suit worth three-thousand euro, you'd think I was a drifter of some sort. My patchwork three-piece is often complimented by a three-quarter length cashmere overcoat. Also the victim of numerous repairs.

Shooing me away should I ask you anything, because you are so positive that I only want your money. And yes, my suit has seen better days, but I do my best to stay on top of all necessary rejuvenation.

I mean, it's not so easy to just pick up a suit any more. I take what I need, if I can find it. I have been repairing this vintage silk lounge suit for roughly two decades now. The silk has long been reinforced with kevlar lining. (I found some old tactical vests while looting the abandoned sheriff's department.) The waistcoat is kevlar. Overcoat, kevlar. This suit is surely my favorite. It has nearly become a part of me.

I was forced to learn how to sew. Which is actually not so difficult, assuming you've got the patience for it. As a result, I can even stitch myself up in a tight situation. I had plenty of practice with sutures at the agency, practice makes perfect after all. Never on myself back then; injuries rarely happen to me. I generally shoot first and ask questions never. That way, I manage to avoid most trauma. What few nicks come my way, I can easily mend. Simply do a job. Just get it over with and everybody's happy. End of story.

Well, not this story, not by a long shot. I eat my sandwich. Contrary to popular belief, heroin will make you very hungry at times. Even zorcos tend to make me ravenous. Aside from that, I havent eaten in over twenty-four hours.

The sandwich is from Thundercloud Delicatessen, right across the street. My favorite for a few years now, open twenty-four/seven, three-hundred-sixty-five. Gratifying sandwiches. They serve you through a metal grate. But the smell is divine, even overpowering the reeking river of shit that flows down Sunset.

I ate a sandwich as delicious at a little place in Venice Beach, before it was immersed in saline. America's version suddenly became more like the Italian original (more so than the tiny man-made canals off of Carroll and Eastern). Forcing my little sandwich shop to close. Along with everything else that wasnt equipped with stilts. Some high-rises are partially functional, as I mentioned before.

Needless to say, California's notoriously elevated land value became astronomically elevated, practically overnight. And in the valley . . . . Shit . . . . Real estate doubled, even tripled. I heard one story of a guy selling his condominium and retiring on the profits. And dont even think about moving into the Hollywood hills, Bel-Air, Pacific Palisades, Malibu, or up to Santa Barbara.

From Laurel Canyon on west, all the way to the coastline. Even extending north to Santa Barbara County, those upper-class Scientologist bastards unionized with haste. Erecting the giant walls which outline their compound. Manned by psychopaths packing guns and very itchy trigger fingers. They are encouraged to kill. It all began with private roads and fire departments. Which lead to more and more gated neighborhoods and then . . . it spiraled out of control.

LifeCredits are paid to a sentry for any righteous kill. Verified via **PSynaps Cognizant Recall** feature. As the creators of **PS**ynaps, they possess the most current technology available. Admission is granted by invite only. Simple as that. The same went for all motion picture lots, especially the dry ones like Paramount and Sunset Gower. As well as Universal and Warner in the valley.

Adopting a fuck-off kind of business strategy, nearly over night. Protecting their investments, their livelihood. Just solid business . . . nothing personal. Got to keep the machine making the money, no matter what it takes. On the up side, if anyone ever wants to make Waterworld the prequel with the newer, younger Costner . . . it should be a lot less expensive to pull off now.

Water themed films are, of course, all the rage these days. Catering companies are undoubtedly yielding ridiculous profits now, but they arent the only ones. Shit, I bet these powerful studio executives make in twenty minutes what the average senator nets per year. Now that's kind of beautiful, in a fucked up way.

The only other high paying government position is that of the rubbish sorter. The custodians of the government owned claptraps are the true kings of this modern frontier. I find most of what I need at the landfill. Most things . . . except food and water. No gas, no guns. No love, no drugs.

All you find are used toothbrushes, bicycle chains, rusty file cabinets, car doors with broken hinges and deep gashes, busted microwaves, hubcaps, cracked stun guns, broken hangers, filthy couches, paint cans, flatware, cockroaches, old computers, busted windows, their panes, and dented picture frames.   Retired cable boxes and cable cars, microwaves, sandwich bags, cardboard cut-outs, cans of hairspray, collar stays, electric razors, gaming consoles, used Klennexx tissue, tampons, and razorblades.   Cut up credit cards and three ring binders, busted slippers, photographic slides, krazy glue, sporting equipment, tarot cards, and scotch tape dispensers.   Plastic scotch liquor bottles inside of black plastic bags. Single use. Dog shit. Dog shit . . . more dog shit. All of it in plastic bags and piled sky high like some stinking tower of babel. Cockroaches. Plastic cups and bottles by the zillions . . . never questioning where it goes once it leaves the curb. Never knowing that it goes just miles away, thrown onto a heap with no effort given to break down, scrap, or compost any of it.   We prefer not to ask . . . . Empty cellophane wrapped cigarette packs, sporks, more cockroaches, cologne bottles, plastic film wrap, cereal boxes, rats, milk cartons, and gum wrappers, more used toothbrushes. Any toothbrush is of value to me. As no one manufactures them on a large scale and plasma torches are so unreliable. So it's actually easier to find old ones and sterilize them in bleach or boiling water.   Combs, too.   More hamburger wrappers, plastic lawn chairs, television sets, coffee mugs, swing sets, gear shifts, buckets, bedpans, laser disks, hockey sticks, pissy pregnancy tests, tapes, remote controls, tennis balls, and old semen filled magnums. All found their way deep into the water table with the help of hydraulic fracturing and other types of crustal destabilization.   Plenty of old manuscripts, magazines, bibles, and reader's digestives clutter the ground.   Along with trashed library books with brown pages and worn edges. New books never opened or read.   Printed before the elimination of paper altogether.   Now rotting in the sun, still wet with last night's rain.   Trees became far less sustainable.   This coupled with the digital age made parchment obsolete.   Garden hoses, lamp shades, broken baseball bats, old tires, used diapers, food containers pock and mar the land as far as the eye can see.   The landfills (those that have not yet burned) have consumed our modern countryside, our stinking treasure chest.   We mine them when in need. Gold, silver, platinum, copper, lead, titanium, palladium, indium, tin, and zinc have long been gleaned from remaining discarded electronics. Aerosol cans are often made of steel.   Even staples from old documents can be harvested.   Although stainless steel wire staples are ideal.   One must be an exceptional scavenger to hack it out here in the west . . . .

Everything else you could need and more, oh, so much more.   The mountains of refuse tower to the heavens, clear to the naked eye for miles.   Japan, destroyers of the oceans and home to nearly four-hundred million tons of refuse per year, saw its survivors attempt turn a quick profit.   Taking a cue from Dubai, they constructed drossy ski resorts with artificial snow, near Tenzan in Saga, but it was a deathtrap in the end.   The refuse was far too unstable to support the snow's weight; let alone the pressure of the resort.   In America, the cold, elevated location in Tahoe was selected to control the stench.   Because nobody was willing to live in Tahoe by that point, no one could protest the decision to dump there.

The state received some hefty pay out, of course. Though not as generous as they used to be. What would once net private island money, now it gets you a down payment on a vacation home. If you can find a vacation destination, that is.

Most have regressed in the most primal of ways. Too little tourism to maintain the influx of euros it once produced. Now you are more likely to become a snack. Although, there are some Hollywood bus tours still in operation.

Giant rolling rooms, reinforced with electrified steel bars and a cow catcher for any renegade cannies. You can hear them coming for miles with megaphone blaring stories about old Hollywood, and you smell the trash burning engine's putt-putt sound.

All of this to say, the statesmen have nowhere to spend their money but outer space. Interplanetary destinations. And for a steep price, no doubt.

Not that any of this helps you or me in any way whatsoever. I still laugh knowing that the shit eaters in D.C. used to have summer homes and yachts in the Hamptons, Miami, Key West, and beyond.

Now, they are a little more like you and me. Now they know what it's like to survive. To truly work. To earn a hard day's wage. It hasnt even gotten so miserable for them . . . yet. Some still hide a summer home or two from the public. Maybe even a vintage sports car.

Now they are scared and looking over their shoulders. One day, it just may be the Revolutionary Tribunal's Reign of Terror here on American soil. Bring on the guillotine. All is fair when dealing with a bunch of corrupt non-performers. They always get what's coming to them in due time. And we get a clean slate.

My PSynaps alerts me with a warming sensation, a slight brightness in my eyesight, accompanied by a soothing tone of my preference. One of my sometime musician pals is attempting to contact me. Probably looking for dope.

PSynaps is a remarkable addition to the planet. Connecting the user to most, if not all personal electronics. Users can also link directly to loved ones, even feeling their virtual heart beat from across the planet. Which must be nice considering the fact that travel is so expensive, and often fatal.

I cannot use this feature to contact her because it could lead them to me. More importantly . . . it could bring them to her. And she has been so safe for such a long time now.

Born within the armed forces. PSynaps was a gradual mutation that first began as the Semi-Automatic Ground Environment. It grew into the internet and progressed toward the DNA of mankind.

With research, development, and testing complete, the PSoldier technology was conceived. It metastasized throughout the military's many agencies. Eventually gaining ground within mine.

Tiny transdermal microchips gave upper management the ability monitor and track all of their worker bees round the clock. Not only that, it monitored a unit's health, both physical and mental. The entire central nervous system was tapped. Raised bulges appeared on the spinal chords of any PSoldier from the nano computer implant.

PSynaps was the condensed version introduced to the public after years of testing throughout numerous top secret missions. Used in high stress situations. Created from DeoxyriboNucleic Acids then united with fiber optics. A subject's central nervous system is linked to the implant.

Allowing the user access to and support from PSynaps AIRborne. Available from nearly any global position. Free from any external devices because every feature is subcutaneous by design. Every year, the new models become more compact.

This provided commanding officers with an advanced warning regarding any decline or improvement in a GI's disposition. Offering them enough time to intervene if necessary. If someone exhibits the signs of, say, going rogue. Or of suicide. Handlers could monitor this person via PSynaps feed, to determine whether or not a contingency plan was in order. Eventually they would be able to watch us through our own eyes.

Now all worker bees receive an implanted kill switch, as well. The kill chip is much smaller nanotechnology. The kill switch implantation procedure is also risky because the explosive is attached near sensitive jugular tissue which can tear easily.   Once PSynaps was introduced, the commanding officers then wanted to actually control muscles via remote console.   Turning the human computer into human puppet.

All of this took place after I left my federal position.   So, thankfully I managed to dodge the kill switch movement.   My locator chip has long been deactivated and removed. I left it out in the ocean, so deep.   About a mile outside of what used to be the county line between Malibu and Ventura. There's an underwater shelf that drops off for miles.   Cold and deep. Never to be found again.

I get my things in order: some clean points, two of the three baggies from 909. Both boy and girl drop into my pocket.   Then I unlock my safe room, secondary and primary locking mechanisms.   Via PSynaps, of course. I leave the office . . . making for the elevators.

Simple Human

As I ascend to floor nine, I notice that a song by Secret Machines from *Now Here is Nowhere* plays on the speakers. Instantly inducing nausea. This only due to the fact that, in the past, I shot far too much cocaine while listening to this album. It's not a pleasant memory for me . . . riding the crazy train. Had to get off that motherfucker **ASAMFP**.

Banging coke is a whole other psychotic ride that a normal person never need take. I used to kneel at a table in my living room, this particular album on repeat, loading shot after shot, of what I refer to as, **heart-stoppers**. That's a shot of blanca large enough to buckle your knees and stop your pulse dead. Dangerous. Really fucking dangerous shit.

All you do for days on end is peak for two minutes and instantly jones for more. Repeat, repeat, repeat, repeat . . . .

Nowadays, I only smoke or sprinkle it over some dope to keep me awake, to balance the opiates. I'm so overwhelmingly repulsed by the physical recall induced by the music that I exit the elevator on the fourth floor. Taking the stairs for the next five.

A little exercise never hurt anyone, not that I keep on much weight anyhow. But I am . . . well I was . . . a boxer . . . in my younger years. Fought middle-heavy back then; now I'm more of a middleweight. It has served me well in countless situations. That, and the fact that I've always been a strong swimmer. Swimming is a now a crucial aspect of modern survival. The ocean gets angry and a city drowns. Better learn now, if you dont already know how.

In the service, I used to swim from one beach to another. I'd round up some action first. Taking action on whether or not I could cross this canal or that lake.

Sometimes I would have a zoomy deposit me a few kilos off the coast in the middle of the night, so I could swim to shore. Every fucking time, I pulled it off. Cleaned up on the winnings. A natural born supernatation. Eventually, when my reputation began to precede me, I had to find a new racket.

So, I began running guns and ammunition to the local militias, well, nobody that fucked with us anyway. They only waged civil battles that we couldnt even begin to give a fuck about. And I could make some money on the side.

In Baghdad, Beruit, Cape Town, Dushanbe, Homs, Kabul, or Karachi my munitions were in high demand. I got the best weapons grade missiles, mines, rockets, rocket-propelled grenades, AK-47s, and M16s. (Though Sig Sauer and Walther rule the current arms market.) Back then I got plenty of good ordinance, too. Working in unison with a few other moonlighting servicemen to systematically monopolize the market. Capitalizing on any up-and-come-lately revolutionaries.

If there was a demand, I had an unending supply. The dog damned U.S. of A. always had deep pockets back then. Uncle Sam was far too busy sniffing blow off a transsexual's saline filled a-cup inside of a Thai juice bar to notice anything was missing in the first place.

I just took care of all their little problems and they leave me the fuck alone. And they never run out of little problems. Shit, I was so busy with my dual lifestyle that I barely had any time to punish pussy or spend what I was making.

The indiscernible manilla envelopes filled with non-consecutive hundreds just kept on coming. My Venezuelan bank sure fucking loved me. They got a healthy cut at twenty-two percent, and I had sanctuary if I ever needed it. An out. My little mirage. I spoke the language already. It was all going so smoothly. Well . . . it was nearly perfect . . . but I'll get back to that.

I am finally on the ninth and barely out of breath. Pretty good for a geezer like me. I mean, the new life expectancy is fifty-nine years of age. That nearly cuts the old one in half.

It also means I'm closing in on my final ten years or so, twenty if I'm lucky. Though I last longer than most. Due to modifications made in the past . . . when I was federal property.

Okay, room nine-eleven, his moronic request, I wave my hand by the lock on the door and push down on the handle. Stopped short. Nearly breaking my newest nose because he's engaged the chain latch. Paranoid fucker that he is.

"Let me in double-quick!" I shout into the black hole behind the door.

No answer for some time. No movement. I knock loudly. Waiting in the hallway for what feels like hours . . . . .

Rock 'N' Roll Nigger

"Aaaaaahhhhaaaaaaaaaaaaaaaaaaaaaaahhhhhhhhh, the infamous Doobie Gillis himself." A familiar voice spouts from the darkness within.

I respond with, "open the fuckin' door Rambeaux, or I'll huff and I'll puff!"

I see that familiar smile through the crack in the door, and I must admit, it's good to see him. He appears to be super geeked out on either speed or coke which is why, I expect, he called on me for some horse. To come down fast.

"How ya been old buddy?" He asks.

His rattletrap of a hand lovingly outstretched through the opening. He manages to unchain the door and let me inside the chamber.

"You appear to be in desperate need of some rest and relaxation, my friend, and I have just the thing," I say.

"Hey man, where's your hairlip?   What happened to it?" He inquires.

Ignoring his question, I survey the room instead while removing the baggies from my coat pocket. Tossing them on the coffee table made out of a vintage pong arcade game.

The room is strewn with eight and ten stringed vintage Griffon guitars, candles, books, recording devices, used rigs, dirty spoons, cracked mirrors, and some soiled condoms on the floor near the bed. The maid has not been allowed inside for quite some time. I pity the one who is ultimately charged with the task. He asks me to prepare a shot for him, on account of his unsteady shakers. I gladly oblige him.

"Is this couch safe to sit on?   Got anything pointy hiding in there?   When was the last time you fucked on it?   Hmm?!" I interrogate.

He simply replies, "Easy man, . . . my heart cant take it."

I cautiously sit and prepare two shots at once in a spoon laid on the table.   Then I help my drug buddy with the messy bit also. He has what appears to be gangrene forming on a hole in his arm.   He quickly suggests that I inject it into his cock.   I decline.   Suggesting that he see someone about a permanent intravenous dock.   And that we use his external jugular for temporary access instead.   In honor of instant gratification, he accepts my offer.

Just one junkie doing another a solid. The word oxymoronic comes to mind, but we have always been there for each other in the past. Once I get him sorted out, I get myself there, too. As I lounge on the sofa smoking a cancer and listening to "Baby's on Fire" by Eno, I take a minute to absorb the room around me. I drag long and deep on the Chesterfeld, then exhaling audibly.

The carpet consists of a dark paisley pattern with rich purple, sky blue, sea foam green, and gold accents. There are a few blood stains, mainly in the corners near the running boards. The wallpaper is pure white and three dimensional with a raised paisley pattern. Nothing I would notice it from a distance but up close, you can enjoy the detail. Around the ceiling, I see crown molding the very color of ice. In front of me sits the bed with covered with a silver duvet cover and burgundy pillows. I slowly realize that we are not alone.

There is a mass beneath the duvet. Maybe a robotic humanoid sex apparatus? Never one to wonder, I get to my feet, straggling in the direction of the bed. Where I rip back the covers with drunken intensity to reveal Graycie, fast asleep. Dead to the world.

I admire her soft curves in the blue light. Accented by jewelry. A piercing in each of her nipples, her labia, and clitoris. Black X shields are attached to the barbells, one penetrates each brown nipple, each of them also outlined with a star tattoo. Beside her lies a wrinkled vintage t-shirt of our old band, **hatchetface**. People just love putting holes in themselves these days.   I do as well.   The only difference being, that I prefer smaller gauged needles.

Graycie and I used to do the twist, it's no big thing. Havent heard from her in a while. I guess this is why. She's into sex on camera, but I cant fault her for that. It is one of the last remaining occupations for an uneducated modern woman. She's got a gift.

"They said you were hot stuff, and that's what baby's been reduced to . . . "

I watch her sleep a moment.   A supine Rambeaux begins mumbling to himself while fumbling with his belt buckle . . . but I think I . . . can make this out:

"Hey . . . hey . . . hey . . . if you want to . . . want to . . . get it on . . . 'an shit with Graycie, I mean, it's . . . totally exciting to me 'an I wouldnt want you . . . to feel . . . you know, like . . . upset 'an shit 'cause of some old bullshit shit . . . from way back in the day, 'cause I'll do 'er with you if you want, man, we can totally . . . double up . . . she fuckin' loves that, really she does . . . it's cool . . . it's a good thing . . . to share, you know . . . like in kindergarten . . . when they made you share an' shit. Share and share alike . . . . Come on man, it's jus' for old times' . . . jus' think about it . . . 'kay? An' what is it about doing a single spot on a talk show that has everyone in a twist? Huh? What is it . . . ? You get one song to put all of your energy into. Right?! What's so wrong with that? National coverage . . . terror on the airwaves . . . mass hysteria, man . . . ."

I feel a twinge of jealousy, but really I shouldnt. I dont participate in three-way intercourse anyway. With such a shortage of females, most have resorted to multi-penetration. I've heard stories of girls who can take on six at once. That's two per hole. Seen footage of five. Heard a rumor about the utilization of a tracheostomy hole, but I wouldnt believe anything that I wasnt personally allowed to witness. Doesnt matter any more anyway. She's his problem now, good riddance, and I am grateful.

I make my way back over to my old pal, Rambeaux. Who once had every Outlaw Motorcycle Gang on the continent looking for him and out for blood.

Some misunderstanding about a statement 'ol 'Beaux made in the press. It was eventually smoothed over through private donations and public apologies. This was back when I was initially secreted into the band with an entirely different face, to serve as a bodyguard. VIP detail.

We lazily reminisce of better times before the natural catastrophes of the present day. I'm pretty sure he's dreaming this whole conversation but I dont mind. At least we got to see the world before it completely went to hell. Japan was so unbelievable prior to nuclear meltdown. Stockholm and Amsterdam made for life changing experiences that we'll never forget, regardless of the current situation. "Dead Finks Dont Talk" is flowing from the speakers.

"OH NO, OH NO, OH NO, OH NO!"

Eno yelps from beyond. The room is lit with tranquility bulbs that are so easy on the eyes. Divine as hell. This black velvet couch is rather womblike. I understand why no one ever seems to want to leave.

Sometimes we have to throw them out on their ear. When the cash flow eventually runs dry. When it's over . . . no amount of tears will suffice.

While the world continues to fall apart out there, our clientele come here to forget about the truth. At the **Citadel**, one sits at the zenith of luxury. People will pay dearly for the comfort and security this building has to offer. Strangely enough, they dont seem to pay me quite as well. So . . . by default, I am forced to create certain other enterprises (some of which you are already aware).

We finish listening to the album, and I offer him some xanadu for guaranteed sleep. He declines. I cant even give these away. I leave him with another shot all ready to go. I quietly slip out of the room while Graycie snores and Rambeaux nods in and out of existence.

While walking to the box, I jam my hands into my coat pockets. I find three crisp euros inside. Rambeaux, you sneaky bastard.

The creation of a successful band is quite a unique achievement. You (and possibly a few others) are solely responsible for creating a successful concept out of thin air. Whose success and rivalry can only be equated to that of a professional sports team. So instead of a few hundred employees and millions in start-up capital, artists opt to work with only a handful. In some cases, it may be you alone getting the hypothetical fledgling off the ground. And with little to no pre-existing income.

Later on, long after rock 'n roll's golden era had past, many music groups were in fact trust fund babies. Wealthy at birth by famous mommies and daddies. With little else to do than spend all day sipping margaritas by the pool. Writing clever introductions, witty lyrics, catchy hooks, and habit-forming codas. Of course, no one respects them in the end because they only used the family name to get their little feet inside of the many open doors.

The bands who had nothing, who came from nothing yet became everything and more. Those are the ones worthy of your respect and mine. Unfortunately, the well respected musicians are the only ones who die young. Ask Billy Joel. Every hack in the dog damned universe gets to live one hundred years and peddle a shiny new turd of an album every three-hundred-sixty-five.

For **hatchetface**, it all began a long way back. Longer than I can believe that it actually was. Rambeaux and I would run strong for hours and hours on end. Feeding on each other's high. He played stage after stage high on life. And whatever life offered to him. I was beside him through the lot of it . . . the worst of it. I cared for him, and he cared for me. No sex mind you.

There was never any shortage of action on the road. And he never hit on me, which I respect. My second cover, as band member, was a bit effeminate and could give off a certain vibe, I guess. I embraced both the feminine and the masculine qualities of human beings. I still try to be enlightened. I try. I try and fail and try again as any person does in this ride.

Why do you think roller-coasters are so popular in our country? No other country in the world boasts such ridiculous theme parks. Yet America, at its best, touted over six hundred such rides in existence at one time. Perhaps the roller-coaster ride is the American dream personified. Perhaps its popularity lies within the rickety ascent, the triumphant sensation felt once atop the climb, with the world at your feet. Or maybe it's the downhill, helter-skelter ride sure to follow.

But the ride is not over yet. Not for me, and certainly not for you. Volunteers continue to line up, height requirements be damned. The ride runs continuous on a track controlled by man. Not one man, but many. A team of men built by other, more evil men. Men that hide in the shadows, never showing their faces. This ride offers a cheap thrill upfront, followed by inefficacy. Extreme disappointment. To ride requires payment. Either by blood or cash.

But I digress, the point is the tour. Many a tour we took together, myself and Rambeaux . . . and the rest of the group. The best tours were always the European ones. No one in Europe stresses over the drug aspect. The fact is, all performers get high on something. Be it boys . . . girls . . . drugs . . . booze . . . goats . . . Christmas trees . . . whatever it may be. Artists get high. The Europeans understand this . . . they are apathetic to the need. So, naturally, the Amsterdam tours were the best of the best.

Arguably, Nirvana gave their best show in Amsterdam, and there is legitimate cause for it. Why? You may ask. Because Amsterdam is such a nonpareil. A city often passed over due to its dark undertones. A city that offers the best night life on the planet, if you know where to look.

The absinthe bars are always a terrific start. But with an open mind, a night in the city can take you into far off places you'd never think to find. Places you'll never forget. If you think Los Angeles is a scream, well then, Amsterdam is your mecca.

We usually wake around four p.m. to pump and dump, we then evacuate the hotel premises, to consume a solid meal at a nearby cafe. The Cafe Palais usually. The Dutch offer the absolute best in commissary. Fresh ingredients have been delivered that very morning from some nearby rural setting. Grown with care but without poison. Fresh ingredients make for the cleanest living.

When you are banging loads into your arm at a quarter gram a shot, it's good to have something wholesome going into your body. I usually ordered an egg sandwich that came on country wheat bread sliced two centimeters thick. A Grolsch, fresh from the brewery. Just eight ounces will get your attention and have you feeling fine. Once recharging, we would return to the hotel, which was just a hop from the Paradiso.

After each band member recharged, shit, shot, smoked, snorted, swallowed, sipped, and slugged whatever it was they needed . . . we would proceed to that night's show. And there were oh so many shows.

On that particular tour, the Dirty and Vacant Tour, Rambeaux had the novel idea to mold dildos of each member's member.   We included them in a limited release of our latest album entitled *Tar in Lung, Plaque in Heart*. A quick stop by a coffee shop, to pick up some local blonde hash and we were on our way to play.

The line was around the block, and no one noticed but me.   Maintaining a slow, deliberate pace. I'd jammed my hands inside of my pockets in order to conceal my weapon.   If any silly fuckers showed up, wanting to play any funny games, I was ready.   But the idea was to blend in.

At this point, I had been secreted into the band a second time as a touring guitarist.   To better gain his trust and get even closer to 'Beaux without him knowing.   Then the mission changed, as it usually does.   It then became about breaking up the unit slowly.   They gave me until the end of the Dirty and Vacant tour to accomplish this task.   If done correctly, I would remain undetected . . . even to this day.

I became one of the thirteen notorious maniacs in the confederacy known as **hatchetface**. At that, I was a natural.   One of the band.   I even played the chainsaw some nights.   But most of us traded instruments throughout the show.

Back then, I was only killing proletarians in my spare time.   For the fuck of it.   To blow off steam. This was before I worked **1369** missions.   When I was primarily a guitarist with weapons, combat, and reconnaissance training.   However, I was good with music.   Any reputable musician can contribute something to an ensemble, on virtually any instrument.

When you play an instrument, you put yourself on display, and allow the music to possess you publicly. This is why I respect a talented rock star. I respect anyone who can make an entire stadium jump.

Sometimes fans got a little too drunk and belligerent but still, I wouldnt draw on them. Only if absolutely necessary. I was a safety. A guarantee. Not to say that I couldnt rough someone up. Those were the perks. Sorting out the jerks.

We never initiated anything. We werent hiring the Hell's Angels for security. But if you got pushy, you got smacked in the eye/throat/mouth. And we were never sorry about it.

We were caged animals on tour, and I was the unofficial animal trainer, with a license to kill. To kill the corrupt. I was maintaining the balance. Balance is necessary. Around midnight, we would eventually take the stage. Barring any unforeseen delays . . . .

Like a hungover speed dealer who missed the train, and thereby could not make it to the red light district until well after midnight. And when the lead guitarist had the need for speed . . . well, there's really no other need in the world that compares, is there? Cant play a show without our lead guitarist, can we? . . . So we waited. And the crowd waited, too.

The fact is that rock stars, true rock and rollers are extremely hard to kill. They are like cockroaches. But sometimes a cockroach will make a foolish bet. Sometimes, I was made to collect on certain promises made by the aforementioned rocker. That is why rock and rollers die suddenly. The Keith Richards, Adam Ants, Perry Farrells, and Alice Coopers live long lives only because they were allowed to do so. Because they played ball just enough to survive.

Often I was worked into a target's life as a studio musician playing guitar, drums, keys, and occasionally the trumpet. Whatever was needed. I was inserted for up to one year in advance. Sometimes to be used more as a mole. I would gain trust and destroy from within. I had to get on the tour so that when the time came to end the madness, I was there to kill the pest. Perhaps, that makes me an exterminator, as well.

A rock and roller, however, is also a shaman. One who congregates with the masses in the collaborative appreciation of seminary knowledge to induce catharsis. Watch Nesta Robert Marley perform live and tell me I'm wrong. Church. Yes, you are actually going to a type of worship. Even when you defy your parents to see some band they hate. Performing live at your local basement venue. They play songs and you sing along. Church.

Defective Defector

I roam restlessly around the **Citadel** just to see what kind of trouble is waiting for me around here. You would be surprised by what you find by walking around this place. Just by the smell. I know when a body or body part has been secretly dropped down the incinerator chute during the darkest hours of the night. That smell is unmistakeable. Unforgettable.

I know when a body has gone ripe inside one of the rooms, yet another unforgettable scent. I have previously mentioned some of the less prestigious occupants of the building. If ever I discover evidence of foul play, I always react swiftly. I have no qualms about silencing demons. I take some pleasure in it actually . . .

. . . *One of the most pleasurable "malcontenants," to date, was a Ukrainian defector who had been inside the* **Citadel** *for roughly a month. When one of our masseuses went missing. Again, the local military would not touch it. So it became my problem. Our records showed a suspicious number of rubdowns for just one man. So I began surveillance on the subject. His comings and goings seemed normal enough. I inquired as to how long the* **DND** *or Do Not Disturb, placard had been hanging from his doorknob. Approximately nine days* had passed since a maid last saw the inside of the room. Strange enough for me.

So I waited until he went out on his morning run, east down Sunset then north up Laurel Canyon. I entered room four-seventeen, which was smelling most foul, due to the collection of refuse inside. Definitely not the reeking stench of a dead body, although the stench of human excrement was prevalent.

The room was surely a mess, but there were no obvious signs of a struggle. I checked the bathroom, dirty but empty. I looked in the closet, nothing. I looked around for any kind of strangeness but there was none to find. Then my eye caught a reflection of the bathroom counter through one of the bedroom mirrors. Massage oil. About seven different bottles of massage oil. The same brand endorsed by the **Citadel**. My interest was thoroughly peaked.

I inspected the nightstand and inside its drawers, not a thing. I pulled back the satin sheets to inspect them for blood or anything at all. Just a couple of dried wet spots via sex or some form of it. What the fuck was he hiding? A gimp in the closet? A machine under the bed?

I replaced the sheets and pulled the top cover back in place. Frustrated, I slumped down on the bed's edge shifting my weight. And then I heard it. . . a muffled cry. It reminded me of Russ T. Forcing me stand up, as straight as the hair on my back. She was inside the bed, I thought. Not in the mattress but inside the large wood frame.

With my heart racing, I threw off the mattress, pulling up the support boards, to reveal our masseuse bound and gagged. And apparently blind. I raced to remove her gag, cutting her restraints with my razor. She was making an awful sound. Not a scream at all . . . it was a choked, ruined cry of some sort. I quickly carried her to a vacant room two floors down, alerting the paramedics, the sick fuckers that they are. I contacted Unit 8 and instructed him to stay with her.

I would later learn that the Ukrainian had been injecting her eyes and throat with bleach and other household agents he swindled from our closets. We later uncovered that he was attempting to make her a sex slave. Perhaps sex slav would be the accurate term, considering her former nationality.

He injected her with poison for five days, repeatedly strangling her within inches of her life. Also brutally raping her. Apparently she reminded him of some unrequited childhood obsession, and he simply could not help himself.

Had I known this at the time, I would have simply gassed up the Galaxy, and run him over on Laurel Canyon. But . . . not knowing this . . .

. . . I opted for patience instead. Climbing inside the bed. Which proved to be a much more exhilarating experience in the end. I replaced the sheets on the bed, just like it was. I climbed deep inside, and pulled the mattress back over the bed frame. I waited for about an hour.

The air was in short supply under there. I imagined how hard it must have been for her to breathe. Must have felt like being buried alive, and after enduring torture to the brink of death time and again. The minutes slothed by like years, and the smell was furious.

Finally, I heard the door open and slam shut. I felt a weight on the mattress only briefly while I imagine he removed his shoes. It smelled foul. She had been using it as a toilet for obvious reasons. He said something that was muffled by the mattress, then he beat it savagely with his fists. A little intimidation technique I assume. The intrigue was getting to me and my heart began to race. Like when you fall in love.

I heard him turn on the shower. Debating whether or not to snuff him in there or just let him find me. If I allowed him to discover me on his own, it would prove to be far more engrossing, of course. So I waited a little longer. Like a cobra shoved inside of a mailbox. I waited. He took a very long, final shower, and I discovered that he was a baritone. Chanting "Kiss Me Deadly" by Lita Ford. I waited in patience. The water stopped. I prepared myself.

He began to yell in his native language, and I knew it would not be long. He was psyching himself up for the act itself. What a fucking pussy, just get to it already. Get the thing over with, who needs such anticipation? Just get it finished. That's what I always did. What I always do. It would be a day for which I would gladly pay twice over.

He was pounding the mattress like an ape beats its chest; getting himself worked up for the main event. Little bastard, picking on unsuspecting women and still he's doubting himself. Finally frenzied enough, he tore the mattress away. The malevolent look of rage crawling all over his face.

I grinned, stripping him of his nerve, and I sprang into action. Which was rather difficult, being that most of my body had gone numb. Awkwardly resting inside of the bed's frame for the past hour or so.

He literally screamed at the sight of me. And I was just laughing . . . laughing and slashing. I cut that fuck to ribbons in there. Room four-seventeen.

Lopped off his ears in two fail swoops. Watched them flop down onto the hardwood by his bare feet. The toes of which, I consecutively crushed under my heavy black boot.

Followed that up with his nose, then the eyes. Like two over-ripe grapes. Spilling forth an opaque fluid as the razor opened them. Also closing them forever.

I gave him a permanent smile. All the while he was just pleading. Begging in his native tongue as the masseuse must have. He did so quite convincingly. Yet . . . it was not quite enough.

He gathered his strength and tried to run, so I promptly cut his left achilles tendon. After which, he began hobbling away from me. I followed that up with the right one. Call it co-dependence, call it what you will. He was trying to walk out on the tab while I was enforcing house rules.

Nonetheless, the grand finale would truly make him howl. I pulled a garrote from my sleeve, slipping it around his throat. I dragged him toward the bed. Fixing the other end of the noose to the headboard. There, I proceeded to snip his smallish manhood off at the root. Leaving no chance for regeneration. Then shoving his prick down his choking black throat.

He made such horrible sounds, but it was nothing like the caterwaul of the masseuse. I have numerous bite marks on my hands. The result of his vehement protests. My hands have slowly become covered in scars of protest over the years. Each one telling its own version of the past. A chunk missing *from my right ear . . . near the top. Also the tip of my nose, now a little shorter, from a quick kill knife fight in Rio de Janeiro. It ended in my favor. My arms and torso bear testament to many other close calls.*

In the end, I did it right, I took my time with him and enjoyed every fucking second. It was perhaps, my finest performance to date. Room four-seventeen, I will never forget it. Once I had opened him to my liking . . . I sent him on his final mission . . . . To roast.

Opening the balcony doors, I got a running start. The limp Ukrainian rag doll sailed through the air head first with a kind of clockwise arc. Sprawled arms loose and tossing in the wind. Then the sound of the implosion on the driveway below. Knocking loose his final breath.

The happy dispatch more resembled abstract art from where I was standing. He popped from within. Then I contacted the cleaner via PSynaps and went to do a shot. To steady my bloody, shaking hands.

The room was sterilized, flash-renovated, and re-listed the same day. The driveway was cleaned and the Ukrainian ruled a suicide victim. No police, no judge, no jury . . . just good old fashioned justice. Not that the masseuse sleeps any better for it. Even from beyond . . . he still manages to haunt her dreams . . .

. . . She does learn to speak again with the aid of a tracheostomy. PSynaps has two models available on the market. Both are hands free, and entirely implanted. She works here still, as a masseuse in our spa. Her days of making house calls are long over.

She refers to me as her black angel, whatever that means.

I look at my scarred hands.   Time has been hardest on them, perhaps.   As many times as I change my face, my hands are still the same.

My PSynaps emits a warm sensation accompanied by a slight low ringing in my ears. Before my vision is a call impulse that I do not recognize.   Similar to an unknown telephone number. So I let the caller leave correspondence.

I later find that it is my Swedish infatuation from the elevator.   Sounding drunk and apparently just out of her "meeting" and wanting to "say hello?" I've got nothing going on, so I return the call.

She's in her room and in the mood as well.   So I tell her I will be there in about twenty minutes, however long that actually is.   I will be late.

Fauxgasm

I head to thirteen for a shot. "Three Days" by Jane's Addiction softly plays through the speakers while I bob my head to the rhythm. I'm not even looking at the wall screen. Check my pockets for my white drugs, locate them, and then exit the elevator.

The wind is really ripping and a red sun slowly setting behind the horizon . . . . It gives me an eerie feeling. City lights are so sparse now that when the sun sets, it is downright fucking dark. Not the best time to be on the street, but a splendid moment to be on the roof. I set up my next big hit by candlelight, inside of the abandoned closet. Having forgotten about the shot in my breast pocket, I find a vein, register, and blast off.

Then I smoke a Chester and watch as the sun slides down low beyond existence. Allowing blackness to consume the city once more. Horribly beautiful, to say the least. I can hear them in the distance. The killer hippies whipping themselves into a frenzy. Over to my right I can see the colony of bonfires; I see them gathering in what used to be Griffith park. They are gearing up for the hunt. On the menu tonight, any unsuspecting mammals left unprotected and fending for themselves in the all-consuming blackout.

Flicking my butt over the edge, I give the driveway one last glance over before I head for the elevator. It seems quiet down below, so enter the car and select the eighth floor. I will roll by and have a drink on the Swede. The end of "Three Days" plays as I exit to the right. I knock softly at the door. Let's call her Stella. Moments later, her bright face appears in the crack, and she invites me inside.

Her chamber has a much different theme than the one belonging to my rock and roll drug buddy. More light hearted and bright. Though I fucking hate it and wish I had my sunglasses.

Yet, I politely make both conversation and a drink for myself and her. Unfortunately, Grand Marnier and seltzer are the only two things stocked at the bar. I suppose it's popular in Sweden this year. It actually tastes quite delicious.

Some atrocity, not worth mentioning, plays on the loud speakers. Prompting me to say,

"Look . . . if we're going to be mating . . . or even considering the possibility . . . I cant be forced to deal with whatever shabby sheik consummate bebop bullshit it is that you may presently tend to prefer. When I am here, I want ultimate sonic excellence. I want to associate you with something beautiful and classic. Not some spur of the moment, spunk rag bugbear! All I am really trying to say is . . . set a harmonic standard or two."

I ease the tension by making a silly face, forcing her to smile. She asks me if I party and I try not to laugh. So she breaks out a joint of what she considers to be strong shit and sets it ablaze. We dance to "Do the Beng Beng" by Derrick Morgan. Then 'Fatty Fatty" by Clancy Eccles.

"I really love you, fatty fatty ... I really want you, fatty fatty!"

Comes partying out of the obnoxiously loud sound system. At the **Citadel,** we always welcome the sound of music and the makers of it. Provided you are not infected and pass our rigorous entrance exam. And you better have cash or a proper stash. Once it's absolutely smoking inside the room, bop-bop-bop, yeah. I break out my baggies. Oh yeah.

"How do you feel about this kind of party?" I ask.

"Thought you'd never ask. Girl or boy?" she inquires.

"Whichever's your pleasure," I answer.

I decide not to break out any syringes because I am running low. I dont want to press my luck anyway. So I just cut some lines on the mirrored coffee table instead. Using a recycled aluminum business card. One I received the previous day from some up and coming producer-asshole-fucker. I shape four lines of blow and two of horse. I offer her my titanium straw.

"Now those two are heroin so be careful there, little heroine," I warn.

She puts down half of the blanca, then a third of the heroin. From what is left of my reflection, I finish what drugs remain. Carefully watching my beard. Tucking my bangs safely behind my ears, as I lean in to take my hit. Then I lay back and let the drug reach my heart . . . my soul.

"Dont worry, it's clean shit, no hangover, practically zero physical addiction," I offer.

I lean into her a little and I begin to stroke her brown locks. I move in closer . . . and soon we're passionately kissing. Our tongues rolling around one another. I'm sucking on her lips, opening her shirt, and playing with her stiff pink nipples. Then I am removing her pants. I go down for a taste, and I am not disappointed. A clean pussy is a rare and beautiful thing, especially in these times. Something she will be rewarded for and . . .

. . . I reward her for roughly twenty minutes. Stabbing at her wet hole with my tongue. I dont go near the asshole, it's like an armpit with shit on it. Nothing good can happen there. "All Women are Bad," by the Cramps drones from the speakers. She comes twice on my face.

Proud of myself, I whip my cock out and make her suck it. She does so, and sloppily but with a tenderness. Telling me that she loves the way I taste. Good girl, soft yet firm. Emoting all kinds of shit in her native tongue. It's all just dirty talk to me. So I resort to jamming my dick down her throat. Then I get slightly creeped out because she seems to enjoy it a little too much. So I stop the face fucking.

And maybe you are thinking, how can he be so cavalier in such dire times, with virus and disease so rampant? To which I would respond, *"an extensive health screening, background research, along with a full physical examination from our own robotic physician . . . man hours are put into the safety of our tenants here. If she got in at all . . . she's clean."*

I hope so, at least. This better not require a bore punch. She pulls out a rubber guarantee, putting it on me with her mouth then I ease the head of it inside her wet gash. She shudders, coming almost instantly. This girl is fun to please. I give her at least three more reasons to love me the most.

After nearly an hour of severe pounding . . . smack, smack, smack. The brain of my cock butting against her **Ernst Gräfenberg**. Wet and deep. She gets on top and begins to ride me awhile.

Realizing that my sexual interest is waning and before I go limp . . . I roll her over and pound away. Then I fake a shuddering orgasm and pull out. Not before a brief convulsion of the corpus cavernosum, of course. Once convinced, I roll off of her and know that she will not feel unattractive due to my inability.

I . . . for one . . . cannot climax on heroin. An unfortunate side effect. Coke can make it difficult, but a heroin orgasm remains an impossibility. I can always get hard, and I can fuck 'til doomsday. But I simply cannot cum on her face like she asked. It's the impossible mission. The true dragon to chase. As we lay, smoking a post coital butt, she tells me that she leaves tomorrow but must see me again.

Typical. . . . I am unamused. I just tell her what she longs to hear, that I cant wait to see her again. That I will spend every free moment obsessing about her. Adding,

"Thanks, I usually have to pay a girl hard earned cash to treat her that way."

"What?" She replies, not having heard me.

"No . . . nothing. I said I need your tight ass to cum like that these days."

I get up, walk to the black marble bathroom with chrome faucets and cashmere hand towels, and I turn on the shower. It has probably been a full ten days since my last one, and there is no time like the present. So I wash the scum off and redress. It is much darker in here and feels better on my eyes. I am preparing my goodbye when she says,

"Wait, I wanted to give you something. To remember me by . . . a haircut. If that's alright, I mean. You sure could use one. Maybe the beard could go, too. It was a little rough on me down there."

"What a lovely idea."

I mutter as I feign a smile, trying not to feel insulted. She pulls out a chair and motions for me to sit, then she heads to the bathroom. Returning with scissors and a comb. She drapes a soft white towel of unknown thread count over my shoulders.

I insist that we hear "Hairdresser on Fire" by Morrissey, over the sound system. She agrees and I manage to relax. I tell her she can do whatever she pleases. I drift in and out of conversation for about an hour. Sometimes on autopilot, other times I am in the moment.

She takes off most of my hair, even shaving my face. First trimming away the long whiskers with sharp scissors, followed by a shave with a real razor.

"I picked up some razorblades in Japan. They're radioactive . . . and sharp as hell. Paid a pretty penny for them, but they're probably the last ones available for public consumption. A woman's got to shave," she informs me.

Secretly, I am appalled that she managed to get them through our security check. I take a gander at my reflection and barely recognize myself. I must look twenty years younger.

"I cannot believe how long it's been since I- . . . . Thanks." I offer my gratitude.

"Now let me feel how close that shave is," she welcomes.

Opening up again . . . inviting me back inside. We copulate for another twenty minutes, and upon my "second coming," I depart as usual. We then say our heartfelt goodbyes and I slink away humming a jingle I used to know from a land before time forgot.

Down the narrow stinking hallway, toward the lift. The poor lighting sputters and ticks. I jab the downward button and head for my office. This old man needs some rest and relaxation.

I clear the many checkpoints and unlock my office, primary, then secondary bolts. Then, listening to "Contrapunctus Four" by Bach I sink into my soft leather couch, which is, maybe a seventy years old. Well broken in and deeply worn. Also, lately doubling as my bed. Because I rarely make it home any more. Once Russ died, I began sleeping at the office.

It was considered an enormous faux pas to have a dog in my line of work. It's the hair. The telltale hair. It gets into everything, the car, your clothes, the bed. Everywhere.

Making it virtually impossible to perform a hit and leave it completely free of trace evidence. A hair of the dog drops from your coat and onto the crime scene, and investigators have material evidence putting me in the room. If I become a suspect, and they sample my pet's hair . . . bang bang goes the gavel. I remember locating one unlucky mark using the tracking chip that was implanted in his dog's thigh.

When I worked for the agency, the local police always hated us for stealing their thunder. So, if ever they could nail a government prospect, that would be all the better.

This, of course, was way back when the police gave a shit. Back when they were still collecting paychecks. Back when a police department still existed. Now, it's like the wild west again with some remaining technology.

My line of work is a lonely one, so the only way to stay sane is with canine companionship. Call it an occupational hazard. Russ T. was a loyal friend and he will be missed. I only return home to check on my apartment every month or so. Aside from that, I remain here.

Although, to say that he died is not all together accurate. He was dismembered. Tortured to be exact. Not that he could have told them anything . . . but I am certain that it was personal. Which means, that whoever the sick fuck was . . . they knew me and whatever they knew . . . they surely did not like.

American Afterlife

THESHOW I SO
VER   THEAUD
IENCEGET   UP
TOLEAVE   THE
 IRSEATS   TI
METOCOLLECT
THE I RCOATS
AND GOHOME
THEYTURN AR
OUND   NOMO
RECCATS   AND
NOMOREHOME
WOOL

Watching the ceiling fan go round and round from my office couch . . . I drift off to dream . . . . I sink deep down . . . . Down low . . . lower into the abyss of cerebral subconsciousness. I find myself floating face down in a sea of black water . . . though I do not struggle to breathe. The water is warm, . . . natal, even. I feel an utter sense of peace as I drift round the world within my mind . . .

. . . I remember her face, that hauntingly beautiful face . . . as it would grimace . . . and distort . . . with pain and shock. My soul mate, a double agent. Or at least, that's what they wanted me to think. I bought every little lie they ever sold me, and maybe, somehow, I even fucking liked it.

By this point, I was so far gone with spooks and their head trips, that I didnt even know what love was. Let alone, what it felt like. Or even which direction was up, for that matter. Merely a puppet in the hands of damnable men; as I happily danced from one assignment to the next. Ever grateful for the opportunity to serve my country. What a crock. According to my handler, she had given me up . . . and I had no choice but to retaliate. Nice and neat.

The government owes everything to fear. Fear induced by repeated terrorist attacks, which led most of the sheep to vote a gamble into the white castle. Soon after, we all witnessed a steady decline of international appeal. Not only the destruction of foreign relations, but the environmental status quo. The gulf became a shambles and once that went to hell, the rest of the ecosystem soon followed. Within the next twenty years . . . we would see America dealt many blows.

The earthquakes and volcanic eruptions in the west, tornados centrally, and hurricanes from the east and the south. No one wanted to lend aid. As a retaliatory measure, a U.S. embargo was enforced, forbidding any foreign trade whatsoever. This, compounded with the execution amendments, led to our current violent lucidity.

Now, I have seen a lot of things in my time . . . I have watched the world fall apart before my eyes. Even had the chance to experience this world during its heyday. I was lucky enough to thrive along with it for a while. Right up to the point where it began tipping in the other direction. And it became plunder rather than free trade. And the people who ran the political machines were taking more and more. Never concerned about the repercussions. About the blow back.

It has been recorded that nearly seventy percent of the U.S. was sold to foreign investors at one point. Which created a bit of contention once the foreign embargo was enforced. The general public fell complacent. Ordering in and shopping online. Sedate and warm inside their homes. Docile and devoid of defenses. Going into debt and wasting away.

It was a slow process, but soon enough the change was more than evident. The energy and water became government property. Soon there was an end to petroleum in sight. The final drop for public consumption was barreled and sold to the highest bidder. Bought up by the most wealthy and stockpiled. We were forced to walk, bike, or use public transportation.

Everything was working out so well for the puppet masters that they almost pulled it off. The timing was right, it was perfect, resistance would have been minimal. Guns were outlawed years before, which meant that most private militias had been disbanded by this point. Food had been restricted to mild rations in order to keep the citizens weak of mind and spirit.   The press release they hid behind was,

"A lack of agriculture caused by drought and pollution resultant in an anemic yeild of crops and livestock."

It was all exaggerated fabrication.   A ruse. And we . . . you and me both, we bought it willingly. Our plots were sold right out from under us, and because we thought it was the end of the world anyway . . . we didnt care.   We didnt believe it was actually happening.   We never put up a fight.   But other forces proved to be more in control of our planet, more than the tyrants in office.

The greedy bullies were attempting to pull off the biggest heist in American history.   And the most hilarious thing . . . they were all **elected** officials.   Had we been more aware prior to voting, we might have been able to weed out the shitstains.

As it was . . . we were all much too busy to give any attention to it . . . whatsoever.   We were practically begging for it.   Touting little white flags. But Nature had other things in mind.

I have worked for numerous men who only prey on fear.   I have long been an inducer of fear myself.   The fear that resonates from a country in times of war.   In this case, in times of immutable Natural destruction.

A little song and dance to distract us, while the slight of hand is working to the **Nth** degree.   The plan was to overtake the country, and the rest of it would follow.   Ultimately, sights would be set on the entire continent and everything beyond it.

The most corrupt industries in the nation's history had joined together.   Somehow self-appointing a crooked commander-in-chief, a man drawn from all of their resources.

Buying elections and swaying the public with a fervor never before seen.   In the wake of ultimate ecological war, famine, and drought, we were simply trying to survive.   In more current times, citizens have considerably improved their standing.   However, it may still be too late.

Back then, a person had no real say, citizenship was no more than a rental agreement.   We never even saw it coming until it was far too late.   The double-cross.   I had become a pawn like so many honest countrymen before me.   Cheated by my very own guardian, sold out to the highest bidder.

When I became resistant to the agency's suggestions . . . they issued my death warrant. Medical discharge on account of mental instability was my prize.   Severance.   I worked long and hard for it.   But that would not be the end of it.

Once I left the agency, I had a constant flow of fly-by-night visitors.   All of them patiently waiting for me to make a fatal mistake.   Offering them the opportunity to tie up one more loose end.

To be the property of the government is a rather compelling existence.   Having invested so much time and money into my training and all of my upgrades.   Once I became an independent, they wanted revenge. They felt betrayed I suppose. Some kind of futuristic Frankenstein . . . to turn on my master. Who, in turn, desired my soul like some old, jealous flame.

Though not before they had their way. Not before they made me destroy everything that was beautiful in my life. She was as much a victim as I was, and I should have listened to reason. I was unable to do so at the time. Call it brainwashing, or mind control, whatever feels right to you.

While under the care of the agency, I was experimented upon with intensity. I was taught how to kill all living creatures with expedience. My targets ranged anywhere from civilians to cops, even other spooks.   Maybe even a senator.   Governmental celebrities, if you will. Even standard celebrities are at risk, Lennon, Cobain, Ledger, and Herzog to name a few. Sometimes it was a female. All targets were those who "deserved it."

Even in times apart from agency work, and as a method of relaxation, I would often target a town where a rash of violence was currently ongoing. During my mandatory month of R&R, I would secrete myself into a sickly town, in order to stalk and locate the bloody root of a problem and eliminate it.

Yes, the cases remained unsolved, but I know there is little chance of resurgence. Like a cancer permanently in remission. These things would cleanse my conscience and allow me to return to my day job at the agency. For a time.

I prefer low profile work. Usually a little shot from a vagrant in an alleyway will do the trick. A little shot that stops the heart but leaves barely a mark. Between the fingers or in the armpit with a small gauge needle. Inside of the nostril works, too.

The mouth is a lousy idea because any coroner will thoroughly check the oral cavity. Standard procedure. If it happens to be a woman, you can always go deep inside of her, between her legs with a pin prick. Drug addicts are the easiest, because everyone expects them to die young anyway. Especially I.V. drug users.

Not a pretty existence, of course. But an existence, all the same. "Natural causes" is the goal. If at all possible. If not that, then "suicide" works just as well. Suicide has become so common in present day, that the medical robotic technicians refuse to resuscitate these so-called "victims" any more.

I have conducted so many "suicides" in my time, that I am practically ordained a priest of demolition. Setting many evil souls free, into the night, and out of our world. All of the elements seem to work in concert with me. In my journey toward salvation. I will not ever . . . not for nothing . . . stop for . . . anything.

My superiors affectionately referred to me as "the suicide machine." And hey, if the money's right . . . I can do anything you want to pay me for. Except children, of course. The world needs children. Now more than ever.

I was all too practiced at the art of deconstruction. Of human demolition. All it took was a little bait and a bit of hate, and I was a good little doggie, hot on the trail to never-neverland. A trail that lead me right to her.

Imagine my surprise when I finally realized that everything was . . . well . . . what a fucking fool I was. Following every puny breadcrumb down many rabbit holes, like the apt pupil I was. In the end, even though I seemed to choose their side over hers, they still found me expendable. Fucking figures.

At least I had the forethought to hash out an escape route. That was the one and only thing that saved me from myself. Too bad I couldnt take her with me, what a waste. I had no choice. The first available flight to Venezuela had me nervously sipping bubbly all the way to my little piece of paradise.

Trying with all my might to forget the horrible atrocities I had committed in the recent past. My one man escape plan. What a fucking pipe dream it all turned out to be.

I had it all figured out, the lack of extradition to the U.S would buy me a little time. But instead of taking the time to try me in court and throw me in some underground military prison, they conveniently marked me for termination. Because it's just cheaper that way.

The sand in the hourglass was moving and at a rapid pace. Western civilization's wicked witch was pulling out all the stops. Up to this point, I actually believed that they needed me. Respected me. All of these things, silly things that a career man strives for; things I thought I already had. I was so certain.

Unfortunately, I was prompted to wake up from that diluted hallucination posthaste. Funny how being the subject of an international manhunt can do that to you. To call it a burn notice would not do it justice.

I should have seen it coming and I should have done something about it. I should have been formulating a solution. I wanted to fix it all. I wanted to, but I could not. Back then I was not the man I am now. I did not have the conviction then, that I do now. Nor the discipline. Instead, I found a nice place near the beach . . . and I retired.

Mojitos were pleasant enough, for a while . . . but soon I wasnt sleeping as soundly. Soon enough, all of those voices began calling my name once again. I had lost my peace, and required something heavier to fill that hole. It was there that I had my first romance with heroin.

Before then, I would only use it as a tool of interrogation. Or as a cover. It was there that I lost a piece of myself. I had to go blank for a little while. That's all a habit does for you, it gives you tunnel vision. Focus on nothing else but that tiny little point.

All of your hopes, needs, fears are right there in that spoon. Not that my retreat lasted very long. They found me within a week. I figured that I would be safe in Venezuela because of the very limited extradition policy with America. Actually, this fact made it a primary location of interest.

I thought I was protected. I merely took a weeklong vacation that I desperately needed. What did they do? They sent spooks to kill both my doctor, along with the lovely woman who was helping me recover from my facial reconstruction.

First, his car was rigged with Albanian C4. A remote device was enlisted. They waited until he was leaving the church with his wife and family. Six in all.

Then they went after Chelsea, another woman who was helping me recover in other ways. Her body was found in a back alley, hardly recognizable. A police contact assured me that she had been brutally raped.

I barely managed to escape just hours after my surgery. Experiencing terrible premonitions, supposedly brought on by cheap anesthesia. I managed to get myself underground just long enough to heal.

Spent the better part of two weeks inside of a basement in a shantytown just outside of Barcelona. As soon as I was strong, I got the fuck out of Venezuela with most of my cash. Boarding a cargo ship in the dead of night. La Rosa Negra.

Stowed away inside the hull, with my cash in a canvas duffle bag, and a pistol in my fist . . . . Time slowed down and it felt like weeks in there. Just waiting for it to go completely snake. But it never did. In less than a week, I was back in my homeland.

Passing along the Caribbean Sea, beyond La Bahia de Corrientes, and into the Gulf of Mexico.

Then north, past Key West. The boat was due to dock somewhere in Marco Island . . . so, about a kilo offshore, I had to part ways with it. Luckily, my sutures had already stopped weeping because Florida, even then, was notorious for hosting over twelve different species of sharks.

After my swim, I slowly meandered west across the states. North up the 75 until catching the 10 west. Hitchhiking primarily. Careful not to pop up on surveillance at any bus or train stations. Laying low at gas stations or rest stops. Not that they could recognize me with my new face, but better safe than sorry.

Passing through The Big Easy, Bat City, and of course, Sin City. Ultimately landing in Kill City. Also known as Edge City, depending on whom you ask. I had a newly crafted face and a nice bit of start-up money. So I promptly began doing deals with all the dog damned devils I found there . . . .

Here, I mean. And pretty soon, all those devils had me right back in their pocket, just like it was before . . . with big brother.

They knew exactly what they were doing. They also taught me something valuable about myself. Something that would shed more light on my path than anything before it. They taught me about struggle . . . that without it I am nothing. I simply do not exist. The agency was always inducing stress and strain. Perhaps, I enjoyed it. The journey is the only thing we have, after all. Once you are at its terminus, that's all the time you get.

The earth begins to quake, pulling me from my thoughts, my memories. A horrible feeling grips me. I fear that it will soon be time to sleep, once again. Fear.

The fear of what I may do in my dreams. Fear. The fear of waking up to this. The fear of being left alone, the last man alone. Fear. The worst thing in the world is fear.

Promotion
Beyond
All
Recognition

I

I awoke today, my mind on her again, as always. Like a bad joke. A killing joke. My mind constantly obsessing over her beauty, her strength, quiet solitude. Those eyes. Eyes that could scratch the moon with so much as an upward glance from this pea of a planet. A face that was clean and smooth. Free of anger, with encompassing soft pink lips. A neck like flowing gold, diving down her soft bosom . . . and perfect breasts.

Torture.

Eventually, I put all of my retirement money into my arm, (roughly five-hundred thousand euros). So, I needed a job. Badly.

The savages found a job for me. The drug lords, the arms dealers, tobacco barons, drug cartels, and even the pharmaceutical syndicate. The fucking louts had a problem investment, called the **Citadel**. Which had recently become overrun with undesirables. A **severe clear** detail. I was to be the cleaning agent. The garbage man . . . .

I got a little team of delinquents to help me with the all of the dirty details. Anonymously farming my talent from contacts made during my time in Pakistan and Lebanon. During my work with a private international security firm, one that shall remain nameless.

My crew was mainly ex-military. Some were government celebrities, murderers and thieves. All with a severe degree of fatalism but a proficiency in combat, none-the-less. The team was extremely effective.

Major League Doorkickers, if you know what I mean. Sharks and gorillas, going abso-fucking-lute-ly **FISH** and **CHIPS** and in the worst kind of way. **Fighting In Someone's House and Causing Havoc In People's Streets**.

No rapists or pedophiles though, I made that very clear. The **Citadel**'s original **Family of Noise** consisted of seven different Johns. We had Johnny Patches (due to his terrible patchwork uniform), Johnny Longhorn (from Marfa, Tx.), Johnny Wayne (who did a dog-awful impression of the Duke), Johnny Two-Cocks (once a force to be reckoned with on the straight pornography circuit), Johnny Hondo (from the Texas town of the same name), and of course, John Sinclaire (the Brit). Also, the Mexican, we called him Juan Wayne. Which he loathed. Fuck him if he cant take a joke.

I told them that I was an ex-marine (true) and that I had been honorably discharged (also true). Then pursuing a "career" in "private security," for lack of a better term (true again). I claimed to have fallen on hard times in Karachi. That I was in need of a change after nearly a decade in the combat zone (not exactly true). The reality of the situation was far more complex, as you well know.

While clearing the **Citadel**, we also partnered with some severely pitiless canine. Mostly shepherds and chows. Angry little fuckers. Which is what happens when you starve them before a long day's work. A hungry dog is much more effective than a well fed one. Some of members of the infantry were adding cocaine to the water bowls for increased intensity.

After much rumination, it was decided that we start at the twelfth floor and work our way down. Standard eviction procedure, forceable entry followed by a coerced evacuation of the premises. It didnt matter to us if you were in the shower fucking your sister. We moved you out. If you fucked with me . . . . Well . . . I carried a cattle prod and a Mossberg, and I wasnt afraid to use either. The entire clear took us a little over a week.

I remember, the Saudi princes were the absolute worst. Motherfuckers come to America, to the **Citadel** specifically, to shoot drugs and fuck all of the young boys to their little heart's content. Having more money than they knew what to do with, and they had a reputation back home to consider. So what better place to cut loose, than from inside of this fortress? Over eight-thousand miles from home.

Gaining initial wealth through oil production and sales. The Saudis were also at the forefront of the **PS**ynaps development in 2021. It amazes me that Dubai has been the hotbed for fiber-optics since the 1980s.

Once mass production oil drilling came to a screeching halt around 2026, **PS**ynaps became the answer. Converting the world to another way of life, the hardwired way. Melding technology with flesh. They say,

"It's not cyborg . . . . It's the future. The human computer."

These pampered little shits came to the establishment, booking an entire floor at once. They would proceed to party and fuck their way into oblivion. Just imagine how the self-entitled silver spoons reacted to me telling them what's what.

Always so proud of their pre-market upgrades, that they have to flaunt them all over the lobby. Projecting the absolute highest pixel resolution from the palm of their hand. Yet it excited me, having next year's upgrades, right here in my building (which is why we let them inside in the first place).

They are our only connection to the world to come. They always have the necessary finances. Credit being a thing of the past in this uncivilized world, the wealthy travel with vast amounts of cash, precious metals, stones, information, or technology. Even the best drugs. The **Citadel** is a candy lane.

Fucking cow-kissers, with their own team of big, bad, motherfucking bodyguards, they didnt take kindly to me one bit. I always told them,

"Know what?! I dont give a shiny shit about who you know . . . or who you think you know! There are hundreds of mazuma junkies out there and itching to take your place. Begging for a section of Shanghri-La."

Continuing with, "I only want to complete a simple task and you only get in the way. If you dont meet our requirements, you must vacate the premises. The shortest distance between two points is a straight line. If you dont like the stairs, it's always more efficient to drop you out of the window, if that's what you prefer."

I have not ever needed to utilize the window option, yet. The powers that be were so damn impressed with my team and its prowess that they offered us a full time position. With salary. Paid in food, gasoline, drugs, and tobacco. That's what they gave me for being too effective, a lifetime spent to rot in purgatory. Still, I havent managed to crawl my way out. But one day soon . . . I am certain . . . .

The **Citadel** will definitely miss me when I am gone. But as it turned out, their biggest complication ended up being a supernatural one. Those things do not care about a dog damned shotgun. That wasnt part of the deal anyway. I'm no priest . . . to say the least. No shaman here.

So I focused on the tangible issues and ignored the rest of it. Or rather, I ignored what I could manage to ignore. But somehow, someway, it developed a taste for me, or perhaps it was an affinity. I honestly could not say. The only thing I know is this . . . I respected it, and it seemed to leave me alone.

What purpose do any of us serve in the first place? All we ever seem to do is take . . . and take . . . and take some more . . . like a dosed infant with no short-term memory.

I recall Mildred Montag from Fahrenheit 451. How she repeatedly ingests sleep medication. Time and again . . . until finally, the paramedics are called and her stomach is pumped. The only problem, Guy Montag is not around to discover us and kindly inform the authorities.

Leaving us to our self-induced pharmaceutical haze. We continue into excess like so many before us who have slammed handfuls of pills with tumblers of scotch. Lighting our own fuses with blowtorches, and always in such a hurry to do so.

If we cannot learn from the past and move forward, then we deserve to perish. Here, in our little remainder of hell. Where every element now seems to conspire against us and our new found glory.

To exist in this modern world is to partake in the slow and certain sabotage of the simple human race. A decline which has been pre-approved by dog. Executed by the faceless relentlessness of broken Nature. A new Dodo bird has materialized and we are it. You and I.

Lately, I am ashamed to be an American, I am ashamed to be from this planet. I think I am ashamed to know anyone any more. You see a problem yet ignore the solution because it requires a little too much effort. Or worse, a little more money, or fuck . . worst of all . . . a sacrifice.

As if you have a lifeboat, which requires a little cleaning and a little fuel. You are more inclined to put holes in it than give it polish. You see it at the bottom of the ocean already, and you're saying,

"What's the point?!"

Well, the point is obvious, the point is survival. If you had but one tree from which to feed, would you not provide it water and offer sunlight. Would you nurture your only means of survival? Would you take the time? You wouldnt . . . would you? Keep on taking. Continue stealing every breath you get.

You no longer see the beauty in Nature. You only see that it is going down the drain, and it isnt even worth your precious time. No need to reuse or reduce.

Throw your trash onto to the pre-existing heap and simply watch it burn. I wonder how many dollars you will have in your account when the entire financial system is crumbling before your eyes. When all of your paper money is suddenly rendered worthless . . . how hard will you be laughing then?

Flash
Fire

Knock knock . . . the door raps. Without moving, I tap into the building's security feed with my PSynaps Level X upgrade. I see a taller male subject, cloaked in a dark flowing overcoat and wide-brim fedora. I raise myself from the couch, with extreme effort. Unlocking secondary, then primary bolts. Cracking the door slightly to peer into the dim hallway. A silhouette of a man slowly comes into focus. I smell spent matches in the air.

"Did somebody send you?"

No answer. The sound of water's drip drip drip drip drip drip drip drip drip . . . .

I continue . . .

"Just standing in the hall, playing with matches, are we?"

Still no reply, so I offer,

"Did you know phosphorus was accidentally created by a German while attempting to render gold from urine?"

"I was sent down from up above. The boss thought your operation could use a shot in the arm." The fuck replies with a wry smile.

"Who sent you . . . from way up in the sky?" I counter.

But within seconds, he's bulldozing me with the one name that always causes me to tighten and go a little paler than usual. Aleister Mehloi. I find myself trying hard not to show how distressed I am.

"Er, . . . uh. Um . . ." I falter. "Well, uh, . . . come in. I guess. Just give me a second."

I say while slamming the door in his face. I envision the heavy black door exploding his pointy nose. Crushing the intrusive proboscis. I should be so lucky as to win this battle with such ease. The stereo begins playing "Two of Us" by the Beatles.

As I race to the desk, I sweep all of the exposed paraphernalia into the top drawer with my forearm. A couple of needles, one spoon, some cotton filters, and a few baggies containing a familiar white powder. I survey the remainder of the room for any other SNAFUs, Situation Normal All Fucked Up.

Once content, I race back to the door. I hope to find him writhing in pain on the ground. His nose open like a faucet. I arrive at the door and open it with haste, welcoming him to my headquarters. But I greet no one.

I peek around the threshold to the right, then the left, and back to the right. Nothing and no one. I call down the hall.

"Hey match man, where are you? We were just getting acquainted. No need for hard feelings."

But I am talking only to myself. I feel something behind me in the offic, but I am afraid to turn around. As if the air conditioner has kicked on, but it feels more like a punch to the gut. Because I have encountered something like this before, during our **severe clear**. I only say this for the sake of self-preservation.

"I meant no harm. Come back whenever you like."

I attempt to close the door, but the task is too difficult. Finding that my equilibrium is bit off kilter. A ringing in my ears slowly creeps in, nothing I have ever felt from **PS**ynaps. Accompanied by a sickness that consumes my body and mind. I feel a pressure on my heart.

"Hey, I dont know what I did to . . . insult you, but I'm sorry."

I gasp, choking. I hear a voice in my head. Which tells me that I should be open to new experiences and new people. That I need to venture outside of the **Citadel**. That I must move on from here. I must go to higher ground. I agree with the voice, but the pressure continues, and I still have difficulty breathing.

"What?! What can I do?! Please!"

191

I scream into the darkness. The grasp tightens around my throat, making my eyes roll back. This must be it . . . . The moment I have been waiting for my entire life . . . .

This is . . . the end? . . . . So unforeseen . . . .
. . . .
. . . .
. . . .
. . . .

. . . And with a severe convulsion . . . I am released. I fall to my knees in throes. Choking for air. As I regain my composure I hear,

"The hillside is your fate, let all of them burn. Every last one."

The door claps shut with such a force. I fear that the security of its frame has been compromised. The room shakes as a result, feeling like another earthquake. Two of them already today and more to come.

I collapse, curling into a fetal position, stars circling my head as I am trying my damnedest to hang in there . . . to hack it . . . to Fuck It, Drive On. I ease my breathing down, slowly, controlling my inhalation, this will cause my heart rate to slow.

As I lay there shaking and hugging myself, I feel a stiff object in my breast pocket. I finger it frantically and yank it from the pocket, tearing it slightly. I hold the syringe up to the light, as I inspect the contents. An opaque liquid floats within. Lying prone on the floor, I tear the cap off with my teeth, spitting it into the corner of my office.

I dont even bother to finding a decent vein. Even a simple skin pop will do. Jabbing wildly at my forearm, and finally I'm registering with a shaky hand.

As quickly as I release the drug into my bloodstream . . . I too, release all of my fear. My struggled breathing subsides and my heartbeat slows and for a moment . . . every . . . thing . . . seems . . . to . . . go . . . . black . . . .

When I'm high, I'm not there, and you better keep those dirty fingers off my filthy heart . . . . I come to . . . inside of a funk lingering from a life before . . . as someone I no longer recognize.

I feel sick and my heart's thrashing with adrenaline. As if someone was wearing me around town while I was off . . . on vacation. I feel used. Used once and destroyed.

Forgive me for all of my transgressions but I do declare . . . I am a saint in my own right. I slowly notice 'Good God's Urge" playing inside the room.

My sound system has not let me down, and in fact, has guided me through my violent episode. It now gently eases me back into my reality.

I pick myself up off the floor to make my one-millionth shot. It certainly seems to lose its charm over time. I never seem to get as high any more. Increasing the dosage is futile. I would sooner stop my heart than feel a difference.

I'm Dirt

For a genuinely spine-tingling and hair-raising experience . . . or on a special occasion . . . like tonight . . . I always prefer to shoot the extract of a human adrenal gland. Rumor has it, the donor in question is high on the purest cocaine, and in a life threatening situation at the time of extraction. I can only hope this is true. I pull a nice C.C. into my rig and find a vein.

The drug is smooth and pure. I am happy with the result, intense focus . . . without the tension. Much better that the stuff I once took off Cavie Lester.

Now, I am ready and willing, I descend to the parking garage level. I will be taking a ride tonight. I locate my coach, affectionately referred to as the "Time Machine," on one of the underground parking levels and drive it up to the street.

I ferret a cigarette out of my pocket without extracting the pack. Put it to my lips . . . light . . . and drag. I reach underneath the dashboard and locate the wires connecting the brake pedal to the taillights and cut them with my stiletto. Twisting them off. I turn the engine over and let it warm. Then I slowly idle my Challenger out of the garage and onto Sunset, heading east toward Griffith. Away from my Forward Operating Base. Pressing onward, into the black veil of nightfall.

I never drive without run-flats. If the tires are vulnerable, then I am, too. I only burn petrol in an extreme situation, and this is beginning to look like one. If she's still alive, she will be at the Observatory. I roll the window down and exhale a grey cloud into the dark night.

The engine hums as I run every rusty, ragged, and rotting red light I reach. "Dirt," by Iggy and the Stooges plays over the speakers; the song begins slow and deliberate. All the while, steadily working into a heated tension that gets me singing the chorus before I know it.

Local militants are at home protecting their castles. Only evil people with evil deeds to do, travel at this undogly hour. The roving gangs of cannibals are a primary deterrent. Along with the pissing rain and pop up electrical storms that only seem to roll in during the sloe hours of life.

The smallish wipers of the old '69 work to excess. Reminding me of past times spent dwelling in the surf. When your little arms are jelly and the breakers just keep rolling in . . . hammering you endlessly as you dive beneath them, only to be pushed down into the deadly deep by their overwhelming force . . . stuck in the washing machine.

The note I found is still crumpled in my fist, and I'm driving with the other. Fumbling with the radio, I attempt to locate a strong signal. I tune to **1370 AM**. Which has been the only remaining broadcast of consistency. Although, it was under repair for a while. Seems that a fire broke out in the control room one day, claiming most of the ship.

All other pirate radio stations have tapered off in recent years. What few contenders remain, leave much to be desired. **K N I L . AM**, now stationed somewhere off the coast of Baja, now under new ownership, is the one reliable entity in this time of doubt. Broadcast from a freighter, way out on the wet, and occasionally subject to extreme weather restrictions. But on this or any ordinary rainy night you can catch a golden oldie shot out over land and sea.

I blow through the decayed hanging light at Western, taking a left and then curving to the right; heading east again. I close one eye, my right, so it becomes accustomed to the darkness. I roll past a bum slowly loping along the sidewalk. Walking evenly, with his rolling suitcase in tow. The note said,

"Want to dance?"

"Dance?" What could it mean? I fucking hate to dance. Lying next to the bloody pillow was a molar resting on top. The note was written with lipstick on an off-white piece of cloth in what I assume was her handwriting. Though I have never seen her handwriting.

The note was sealed with a bloody kiss. The transmission she sent me . . . disheartening, to say the least. Just begging and begging for help. Just like the good old days. Like a blast from the past, and . . . I . . . . feel . . . . fine.

Nearing the park entrance, I switch off the radio and the lights. Opening my left eye. I take a left into the park. Cruising for a moment, then I switch off the engine and coast. Drifting down the path, I toss the note onto the floor of the passenger side. Picking up my Sig Sauer .44, I found a large enough mold to make my own cartridges, thank dog. I cock it with one up the spout. Holster it. Pick up my AB Coltellerie stiletto and stick it deep in the ankle of my steel-toe boot.

I am losing momentum as the uphill grade becomes steeper, so I let the car stop on its own. Then quickly throwing it into park.

As I brave this briar patch set before me, I need all the help I can get. The taillights have been disconnected because on a night this pitch, a little light goes a long way.

I exit the car but not before grabbing a tactical Mossberg. Weighing in at just under seven pounds and packing a punch that lasts a lifetime. A bandolier with another twenty rounds will ensure a successful mission, as well as a six-count sidesaddle on the piece itself. Add three grenades to the mix, and I finally feel prepared, for the first time in a long time. It's a far cry from my days in the green zone, weighed down with full body armor, assault rifle, and at least ten stripper clip mags.

Long Range Reconnaissance Patrol . . . **LRRP**. Picking up a large branch along the hike which I will use as a club. It will work better than the butt of my Mossberg. I shatter the knee of the first canny I come across. Surprising him from darkness, I overtake his position with requiescence.

First the knee . . . then the face (make it personal, make it remember you in the afterlife). Most importantly, make it fun. Savor every second of your remaining moments. I enjoy the entire experience. His brethren, unfortunately, did not take very kindly to my intrusion.

He had four mates camping with him. Which is what they tend to do, being too disorganized to go it alone or with some type of majority rule. They just gang up in groups of three to as much as twenty cannies, to group hunt in the dark. Sleeping during the day.

Dont go telling yourself they are just zombies, or some type of vampire. They are more evil than anything the Stoker or Murnau could have imagined. Like Nosferatu, these children of the night do not rest unless they taste blood on their black tongues. Constantly moving like landsharks. Gasping at the air for want of something else, . . . of blood, or worse. Fucking their victims violently, prior to inevitable execution via mastication.

I have personally witnessed many horrific deaths, yet I cannot fathom one worse than that. I cannot. The other four, they see me kill the first one, and actually seem to envy the way in which the task was carried out.   As a professional obligation, I take the time to convert the remaining three into believers.

First disposing of his mate, with, of course, the immense branch I had picked up along the way. Two down and many more to go . . . I throw down the limb and pick up my .44, silencer in tact. I hand pick the remaining two.

Seems they were hoping to ambush me in the brush just below the Observatory's remains, but the rain covered me, hiding my scent. These animals have an elevated sense of smell that would make Russ T. jealous. It's how they make ends meet, so I wouldnt fault them for the adaption. I actually admire it in a way.

This mission is more or less a crap shoot anyhow.   The odds of finding the Swede are razor thin and shrinking by the second. It's the least I could do for a woman so kind as to give me an "orgasm," a haircut, and a shave, all in the same happening. I owe her this much, the least I can do is try. Marshals are enemies of the hillside compound dwellers, so I figure, they'll take her to cannie land.

The fucking rain inside my boots begins to squish as I walk. A matchstick in there is scratching hard at my achilles and I am trying not to notice. But now the pain is beginning to bleed, so I stop and remove the thorn.

I notice an owl nest on my left, illuminated by the moon. A sliver appearing like a magic trick, only for a second. Displaying three baby owls resting on a nearby branch.   Life in transition clinging to a survivalist instinct. Nothing more than a dream on a breeze. I press on, toward the observatory. If she's anywhere, she's there.

I can see a candle burning in one of the windows and I know they must be inside. Cannies hate light. I come upon another tent grouping before reaching the shattered remains of the Griffith Observatory.

These grotesque specimens are in the process of feasting on what appears to be the body of an adolescent girl. Its face having already been cleaned to the bone, yet the scalp remains. A long mane of prolix blonde hair. Her skinny body rests lifelessly on the lap of the vicious scoundrel currently cleaning her forearm of remaining meat.

I take out my switch. Other envious, nervous watchers await their turns in the shadows. Like me. Before they have time to enjoy their catch, I streak out of the darkness and eviscerate the feeding canny's jugular.

Returning to the blackness before the others can blink. They stir and follow me out, into the darkness, where I can truly have my way. The obvious advantage being, I am not as passionate. I am capable of thought before execution.

With them, it's unmitigated instinct. Silence is my companion, so I enlist my stiletto once again to dispatch the two other killer hippie grunts. Really just pawns sacrificed to the greater good.

My fingers stick to one another with the syrupy crimson. But for only a moment, on account of the heavy downpour of mildly acidic rain. Constantly washing away the dirt, making every day a new start. It gives me a reason to press on, though it stings my eyes. Goggles would have been useful, but I cant think of everything.

I hear movement in the bushes behind me, and I continue on in the direction already chosen. Set upon my goal like some suicidal fuck crazy salmon. She lies just beyond the tree line, inside of the east vantage point. Where the candle burns. Iggy drones inside my head.

"There's a fire .... Well, it's a fire ..."

Negative Creep

Peering through the window, I see an older Marshal laying out every one of his little threats on the table before her. Bound and gagged in a chair. A dead cannie on the floor beside her, probably a scare tactic. Clearly, she has never found herself in this type of situation before and is understandably capsized.

The noise from the storm must have concealed my approach. I seem to have the element of surprise in hand. Not to mention, two large speakers blare **K N I L . AM**. Now playing one of my personal favorites . . . the "Kill All Hippies," single by Primal Scream.

Slipping in through an open hole that was once a window facing old downtown. Now most of the L.A. Basin is underwater. The other Marshal sits at a desk in the far corner of the room. He looks like a brakeman to me. The relaxed one who slows it down when necessary. An architect of tension.

I plan my attack on the fly. First pulling my Mossberg around front and silently cocking it. Safety off. I then remove my Sig and cock it . . . removing the safety and replacing it in the holster at my ribs.

This is when ambidexterity comes in handy. In my youth, playing a drum kit improved hand eye coordination and ability to isolate each limb. I tap at my kevlar vest and feel a bit more secure. Good enough to survive a knife fight, in case I run into Jimmy Dean along the way.

The switch is back in its proper place at my ankle, I pick the shotgun back up as it hangs across my shoulder on its strap. Ready as I'll ever be. I move forward, hearing the grenades jingle, and it's a good feeling let me tell you. One. Two. Three.

I flash into that stinking, musty room. Kicking in the wooden door like a jumping jack on hot coals. I exorcise the first and younger Marshal before he can pull his sawed-off from his lap. I squeeze the trigger of the Mossberg. Perfectly tuned, breaking like a small glass rod. Though it kicks like a mule.

The explosion distorts his face in such a way, that I stop and recall Picasso's *Dora Maar with Cat* for a split moment. Over my right shoulder lies my destiny and I turn, dropping the shotgun to my side and picking up an iron pineapple in the same move. I hold it up above my head. The cherry bomb in my right, pin in the left. With my left, I pull out my Sig. Fixing its aim on the grey Marshal's right eye.

"Now, sheriff, just leave the lady be, she never meant you any harm. This here is between you and me. She doesnt even know my real name." I offer.

"You dont even know your real name?" He smirks.

"She walks out of here now and we can talk. Otherwise it's the fat lady for us all." I say.

He fingers the Colt Single Action Army in his lap as she eyes me wildly. As if to warn me of something, but her gag hides exactly what I need. I notice the old man's eyes drift to my right, and I catch the movement of a shadow in my peripheral vision.

Must be a third Marshal now joining the party . . . still too shy to come inside. I will deal with that one later. Holstering my .44, I pick up the shotgun hanging on my side with my left hand, maintaining the grenade in my right. Its pin, still a ring around my finger.

"I will change you, if you go for that shooter. Now, let her walk and we'll talk." I warn.

"You havent got a clear shot . . . you'll blow off half her face from there." He answers.

"Shooting from the hip can feel as natural as pissing with your dick. I dont aim at a toilet, Why aim to hit a turd like you." I reply.

"Did you talk to the spectre? Give him a piece of your mind did you? Or did you crumple like a doll? Did he tell you what you feared was true?!" The Marshal asks.

Tiring of the goose-chase I say, "Told me jack shit, just like you! Give me the girl or it's on your conscience."

"Go to the hillside," the Marshal finally says.

He motions me to retrieve her, seemingly submitting to the standoff, and I move in quickly. Dropping the Mossberg to my side and replacing it with her warmth, we back out of the room silently. He goes for his pistol, but I remind him of my insurance policy. Just as we're out the door, I toss the hard charger back inside the observatory.

Cccccccccccrrrrrrrraaaaaaaaaaaaaaaaaaaaaaaaaaaacccccccccccckkkkkkkkkk!!!

When I peer through the window, and it looks like a cat caught in a microwave. Chunky salsa. Crispy critter. Now, to face the hardest part of the journey . . . getting home.

Outside, where the rain is waning, I encounter the owner of the aforementioned shadow. It belongs to a raggedy old devil whose name I never caught. Not a Marshal at all.

Someone whose name has not existed for a very long time. Creatures of his calling know nothing but blood and fear. His peers only call in times of need. When they need to feed.

Just an ex-teacher-mechanic-postman-transient-antichrist out in the dark, looking for a good time. Here we are, walking on this moonlit night, searching for a way out. A way home.

This antichrist, let's call him Zap. Let's say 'ol Zap is going on . . . oh . . . maybe his fifth day without a proper meal. Let's say that his neighbor is looking mighty delicious at this point. So it's either become Cain, or kill us instead, the outsiders. What would you do? Well, I know what I'd do.

Here he comes around the corner, reeking of shit, because all antichrists shit themselves. He's covering good ground for a pants shitting human predator, who runs like a pissed off five year old. After little chase, I relieve him of his duties and his mind. Mossberg.

Everything . . . and I mean everything . . . mortal and immortal . . . dies when separated from the head. No one makes that cut and lives to tell the tale. Medusas, vampires, zombies, aliens, Frankensteins, Marie-Antoinettes . . . the list persists.

The rain is letting up and the sun is creeping over the horizon. We will be more visible now. Moving down an overgrown path toward my parked Challenger. Running as quietly as two adrenaline charged adults can. Breathing is labored and unyielding, but we run faster and lighter than ever before. Escaping from unseen demons at our back.

Then, I hear a snap, my right leg trips a line. It releases a swing arm that pulls taught a line connected to a net beneath us. I should have noticed the bending tree. Sloppy. As we struggle to get free, it only hugs us tighter in its bosom.

Must be a booby-trap set by some enterprising cannies, determined to ensnare unsuspecting tourists, immure the evil rumors about Edge City. Cannies generally lack the resources and intelligence required to lay a snare. It seems they are learning. Further adapting to survive.

Resistance is futile, so I wrestle free my stiletto Then push it out of an opening in the twisting net; pressing the button to open the blade. I pull my elbow back toward me, and with the blade I saw through the netting. Eventually creating a hole in the bottom; I release us to earth's gravity once again.

No sooner than we pull ourselves together than I hear something galloping down the path toward us. However, curiosity would not get the best of us this time. Instead, we dodge out into the forest and away from impending danger. Toward the Charger . . . . Toward the **Citadel**.

Dead
Wax

  The creaking hull haunted me throughout my dreams. The vessel's upward motion was followed by the rapid dips that made my stomach sink into my bowels. Again and again. No relief from my fate. Not even in my sleep. Haunted. Hunted.

  My dreams were of warm beaches and long rides. Instead I rose, inside of my domestic quarters. Instantly reminded of the cold. The fuel in my heater had burned up long ago, and a deep set chill had long been encompassing the room. Me along with it. The waves beat and thrashed along the starboard side. My side.

  The boat has been a useful tool within my agency for many years now. Interrogation chambers, far out on the high seas. Internationally unclaimed waters near the Bering Sea. A Bermuda Triangle type scenario. But in the North Pacific Ocean via Kotzebue, rather than the Atlantic.

  The vessel was another one of those places that doesnt exist and never has. If you ever found yourself here, on the boat named La Verdad, the time you spent would be unforgettable.

  As I shook off the cold grey morning, I stood up, already dressed. Having slept in all of my clothes for warmth.

Stomach empty and bowels full, I shuffled around in my boots and lit a Chester. Heading to the latrine for a pump and dump. Once brushed and washed, I made for the commissary and a quick bite before embarking on what was to be an overwhelming day. In the commissary, I made my breakfast and ate solitary. Eggs and beans. Powdered eggs. The worst. Still better than monkey dicks from an MRE.

Wasnt exactly the Queen Mary . . . was it? More like the Titanic. Washing it all down with hot coffee. Which burnt my throat as I swallowed, drinking it too quickly. As I was finishing, an announcement came for me over the intercom (this was prior to the advent of PSynaps). My day was to begin.

We were questioning a man who allegedly operated a prostitution ring. This ring was the pride and joy of numerous deviant and powerful men. An ongoing investigation brought us to him. The purpose of the interrogation was to extract information regarding the whereabouts of a missing girl.

A girl who happened to be the daughter of a well connected cocaine and heroin baron with whom the agency had a pre-existing symbiotic relationship. Columbia had recently become the new leader in heroin production. And much closer to America than the Middle East. Less gasoline, fewer checkpoints. The man's daughter was ten at the time. Now missing for days, although believed to be alive. But for how long, we couldnt know, because her RFID chip had been removed.

We picked our man up, regarding his suspicious involvement. This involvement was determined by a sting enacted by my team. One of my best was able to infiltrate this particular human trafficking syndicate, posing as an interested party. He was involved with that sex ring for a solid month before he laid eyes on the man currently in our holding cell. We dont know how our agent maintained his cover for such an extended period of time. Those are questions you simply do not ask. One thing we were certain of, we had our man. **Cavie Lester**.

I opened the hatch which held our prisoner. I told him to take off his clothes and throw them out to me. He did so, reluctantly. Mumbling insults under his breath in German while I patiently waited in the blowing wind and foam. He took his time. I too will take it slow when I have my turn. A solid five minutes later I was inspecting his clothes for any signs of correspondence, weaponry, or explosives. He was clean. Smelly and covered in filth but clean of contraband.

"Follow me," I said, "time for a shower, you've earned it."

He looked at me with confusion, and I realized then that he didnt understand the language. Cavie was German by decent but had been hiding out in Columbia for a decade now. I dont speak nazi. And even if I did, I wouldnt spew that aryan filth to anyone. So I told him in Spanish. I only spoke to him in Spanish from that moment forward, though it will be translated.

He followed me into the belly of the ship. The halls were dark and wet. Dim lighting surged brighter . . . then darker . . . then not there at all . . . then back again. There were many steps that led us down deeper . . . to that room. A room which never existed. The room we occupied for what seemed like an eternity.

Continuing our prolapse into the pitch, I could hear his breathing becoming labored. I assured him that the shower was near. He wasnt buying it. Where else could he go? No escaping me. There is no place in the world he could go . . . to outrun me.

His frail body was shivering in the stinging cold. We were close, I could see the light of a lantern peeking from beneath the doorway. I knew the room would be ready for us. I was getting excited. He began hyperventilating; spewing out great gusts of vapor into the chilly air. He tried to collapse on me, so I dragged him by skinny ankles, down the hall and into the light.

Slowly, I muscled the door open, it being mostly rusted. That, along with its sheer weight, made it a cumbersome task. I managed to force it wide enough for passage, dragging the Gerlumbian inside. Toward the inevitable.

My abettor waited patiently inside, he had prepared the room just the way I preferred. A chair occupied one corner in the room, the room roughly ten meters square. Diagonal from the chair sat a desk with a second chair, on the other side of the room.

I told Cavie to take a seat and wait for his shower. He sat . . . slowly. My little helper strapped him in. On the desk sat a record player. No way to tell what had been playing on it. One side had ended, and the needle scratched endlessly on the dead wax.

A few candles burned on the desk. Everyone else used a running generator during interrogation sessions on the barge. But I dont like the noise. Or the smell of exhaust (unless it is coming from a four stroke boxer). So I collected twenty car batteries from supply. I daisy-chained them together to create one enormous cell. Capable of sustaining a room for well over twelve hours. My shadow can charge the cell with the generator while I am away from the room. Then turning it off a respectable hour before interrogation begins. We must leave time to clear the air.

Next to the record player were my tools of persuasion and my wax stack. My colleague stood in the corner by the desk and said not a word to either one of us. The pedophile was shaking violently. I picked up a pair of jumper cables from the ground and approached the anticipatory ex-living.

Above his oscillating head was a shower head to which I attached the positive current of the jumper cables. The negative current was then attached to the leg of the metal chair on which he sat. The other end of the jumper cables were then connected to a separate thirteen volt car battery. This one, assigned to the guest of honor. So that the daisy-chained cell will not drain too quickly.

I turned on the water, which was barely warm enough to be liquid. I allowed the icy water to rush over the Gerlumbian's pale, nude body. He began convulsing even more violently at this point. I asked him about the girl. He decided to play innocent.

Thirteen volts may not seem like much. But I assure you . . . it is more than enough. As the frigid water poured from the ceiling it was positively charged, our man in the chair completed the circuit. Setting him on howl.

The plastic restraints began to tear at his wrists, and as the charge consumed his frail body, they began to bleed with ferocity. I wanted him to taste death, for a moment. So he knew what was coming for him . . . what was lurking around every corner. I removed the positive cable from the battery, giving him a moment to regain composure, Something he never actually managed to do.

He was pissing down his own leg by that point. No matter . . . all of it goes gently down the drain. The Membrane Bio Reactor will handle the task. I told him he should unburden himself. That I would not stop before hearing all of his sins. Asking him again about the girl. He gave me nothing.

At which point, I motioned my consort to shut the door, which he did. It was the next action that proved to be tremendously effective. Once shutting the rusty valve on the hatch, he produced a torch and proceeded to weld the door shut. All the while staring at the soon to be dead man, so that fear would overcome him.

He wept and defecated uncontrollably. His shit, a watery green consistency, was absolutely reeking for a moment. My shadow and I exchanged glances as the fecal matter ran down the drain at the Gerlumbian's feet. Toss a little sodium hypochlorite and sodium bisulfite in the MBR and discharge that grey water into to deep blue sea.

"Whooooaah . . . easy there buddy . . . careful you dont go freaking out all over the place. Try to relax . . . take a deep breath. Now I want to introduce you to my shadow in training," I explained.

I also told him that he would never leave this place. That I would never let him go. Whether he told me what I needed to know or not, he was mine. Forever.

I told him not to worry. That it would be quick. I lied . . . it would not be that way for Cavie. My shadow began working on him with the blowtorch. The sounds of pain were so invasive, that I decided to play some music.

I retired to the desk. There, I observed all of my tools at rest. So peaceful and shiny. Instruments that would make anyone sing. I picked up a spoon and began to prepare a shot. Mine first. I switched on the record player again, moving the needle back to the first song. It was a familiar one to me, a track from *Dirk Wears White Sox*.

I mixed the water with the horse and drew one cc into a clean syringe. Taking my time to fix, allowing my shadow ample time to work. I took up a glass thermometer from the desktop and handed it to my minion, asking him to check Cavie's temperature.

I told my shadow to keep him above thirty degrees celsius, so he wouldnt slip into a coma. As he checked our man, I shot up . . . .

My head rolled back as I fished a Chester out of my pocket . . . . finding one, I put it to my lips . . . and leaning forward, I lit it with a candle from the desk.

Screams caused me to look over at my colleague, and noticed that he wasnt actually taking the Gerlumbian's temperature. He was indeed using the thermometer . . . but not in the intended fashion. Instead, the evil fucker had forced it down poor Cavie's urethra.

He was shrieking. I sang along with the record. "Whip in My Valise" was playing as I fixed another shot.

"Who taught you-ooh to torture? Who taught ya? Who taught ya?"

Stuart Leslie Goddard echoed along with Cavie's howls. I readied a shot for our detainee, he was certainly going to need it.

215

The inoculation I prepared was composed of heroin and cocaine. More heroin than cocaine for the pain. I walked over to turn off the water. In Spanish, I told him to,

"Give me something . . . give me something and I will give you something."

Indicating the shot. He went all quiet for a second and I knew he was considering my offer. He proceeded to tell me (in fractured, shivering Spanish) about a place just outside of Cabo San Lucas where the girls were housed and trained. Located in proximity to many illustrious vacation resorts.

When I asked him how the children were trained, he was kind enough to enlighten me. Revealing that once they are abducted, they are taken to a safe house where they were dosed with heroin and administered a crash course on male sexuality. Children no more than six years old. Once they were hooked on smack, any remaining desire to run would quickly dissolve.

I asked him for an address and he got cagey. To calm him down, I put the needle into a vein on his arm and gave him .5 cubic centimeters, approximately half of the shot. But still, he would not give me an exact location, so I decided to give him more.

"Hold still now . . . wouldnt want to blind you. Cálmate."

I slipped the needle into his ocular vein. He flinched a bit. I watched his eyes roll back into head as I pulled out the needle. A swift slap brought him back into my world, and we were able to proceed with our work.

In the same way that adrenaline is extracted from sheep or cattle, so may it be procured from man. Inserting a long needle into each of Cavie's adrenal glands, located just above the kidneys. A long IV tube was connected to a drip bag. We would harvest many things from this meeting.

I returned to the desk and instructed my shadow to continue with the interrogation. He was asking him all of the same questions, only with a little more force. The record reached the end of side. Bump . . . bump bump . . . bump . . . bump bump.

I proceeded to hum "Happiness is a Warm Gun" as I prepared another shot for myself. One for my compatriot as well. He was looking tense. Humming the melody. I mixed one for myself first and set it aside. Then I made a strong one for my helper.

"Mother Superior jumped the gu-hu-hu-hu-hu-un . . ."

I continued singing while enjoying the show. I sat, smoking while I watched my partner work his magic. He had the water going again, the jumper cables, too. And still nothing. This motherfucker continually refused to name any person or location.

My little helper reached between the Gerlumbian's legs and began to stroke his uncircumcised dick. It seemed a bit unethical to me, but it was his time to shine. Once his dick was hard, and the thermometer inside, my shadow began to squeeze the shaft. Hard, then harder, then . . . snap.

And that drip bag is beginning to fill with a clear, slightly brown compound. Still a long way off. But we were getting somewhere.

The thermometer broke for the second time and he screamed once again. More deeply than before, my helper continued. Shattering glass within the prisoner's urethra for a good hour. Which, to him, must have seemed like days. He was howling. The electrified water rained down on him, on his broken body. His soul was exiting before our very eyes. We watched with undivided intensity.

"Happiness . . . is a warm gun. Bang bang shoot shoot."

I was singing. I imagined putting two bullets in Cavie's face. I reconsidered. He deserved to suffer long term. Instead, I offer my shadow the loaded syringe.

"Hey, why rush things, take a moment to savor this," I say.

He accepted out of sheer frustration. We had only a general area, from our sting operation, but no specific neighborhood. We required more details regarding location. He sat at the desk fixing his mood with the shot I prepared for him. He began shuddering, mildly convulsing and then slumped forward. He was not effective enough. His training was now complete.

I am the angel of death. I kill all I see. The dose was too high, even for me. Enough horse to satisfy a horse, of course. Hotshot for a hotshot.

My shadow's mouth was wide open, and drooling. His eyes fixed on the ceiling. **DWYMO.** The drool slunk across the table toward the Dual record player . . . still spinning its silent scratching song. The needle scratching the dead wax . . . bump . . . bump bump . . . bump . . . bump bump. Now I had to get myself out of there. Picking up the blow torch, I proceeded to work on the hatch.

As for Cavie . . . his fate would be slow and drawn out . . . . He did not tell me what I needed to know, even while under the influence of **Scopolamine**.

I decided to feed him a steady diet of **Krokodil**, a cheap heroin substitute, first cooked in Siberia. Initially concocted within dirty kitchens using boiled iodine and codeine caplets. This dope was and is extremely painful for the body to process. Withdrawal sets in within hours. Skin feels afire and muscle spasms ensue.

The best part . . . within weeks of this treatment, a user will begin to lose chunks of skin like a leper. Gaping open sores gave way to gangrene which ultimately led to amputation. Using his filthy living body as a fear inducer for any incoming interrogation subjects.

The strangest thing . . . he was always begging me for the next shot, knowing what it was doing to his body. Cavie would eventually tell me everything I wanted to know.

He wanted me to kill him . . . . To make it fast . . . I would do no such thing in the end . . . I do not take requests now. I did not take them then . . . I am an animal trainer. Nothing more.

Once Cavie was used up, and costing more than he was worth . . . we decided to give him the ultimate retribution . . . . I enlisted the help of my friend, Dr. Absolom, who was a magnificent surgeon. I have used his services in the past for facial reconstruction. He removed all infected limbs from him (3 total). He then cleaned and stapled each amputation.

After which, the good doctor went the extra mile. He surprised us with some impromptu work done to Cavie's remaining genitalia.   Forming a rather authentic vagina from the leftovers.   We then placed want ads in local ports. Wherein we cast willing participants for a new film concept. A transgender amputee website, hosted by Cavie himself.

He was used in the utmost of ways by transients and wayward convicts.   Anyone who wanted a quick buck and a place to unload was accepted onto the ship.

A video was shot while a load was shot, and a man was paid for his time.   After which, a pirate video stream uploads the footage into the ether . . . from somewhere deep inside of scrambled anonymity.

Twisting In The Wind

I awake in her bright room, safe and sound. Still wearing my wet and muddy clothes and sitting in a white armchair. The Swede snores gently from the California king. I quietly excuse myself and shoot for the roof to clear my head.

My one-millionth elevator ride yields no door prize, so instead I give myself a little treat. Two of them . . . one for now. One for later tucked in my breast pocket. Walking out onto the bright rooftop, I peer around at the valley before me. Another glorious day in the sun.

Feeling swell now, I walk over to the edge so I can survey the action on Sunset. A familiar bum conditions himself with fervent pushups. Done on the hot concrete next to his suitcase on wheels. His face reddened from the exertion, dripping great beads of sweat onto the pavement.

The overwhelming scent of hibiscus, honeysuckle, and the open sewer lining Sunset Boulevard chokes me as I inhale. The vagrant seems to be preparing for a hunt. When darkness falls again, he will be faster and stronger than anything else out in the void. Capable of chasing down and overpowering even the aptest of night beasts.

Clouds drift by so close that I can almost touch them, vacillating in the gusty wind. A perfect blue sky as their backdrop. Pure white nimbus hovers, then dashes away on its own accord. Gusting at nearly thirty k/pm. The wind is whipping my hair so violently that it begins to stab my eyes. I attempt to tuck it behind my ears but it tears loose. Too short due to my recent haircut. I resign to pull out my shades and shield my eyes. My vintage black out TB-10s do the trick.

I remember that tomorrow is the 113th academy ceremony. Elan Merryweather is up for best director. This year, he helmed a critically acclaimed remake of the Stevenson classic, Treasure Island, starring Hurley Aimes. He is up for a few awards.

True classics from Welles . . . Hitchcock . . . Herzog . . . even Wood are now remade for a quick profit. The money is practically guaranteed if they remake a previously successful film concept.

Elan is a personal friend of mine, and I may be attending the gala as a result. His most recent landmark masterpiece, *Love Not Given Lightly*, won nine awards last year. One for costuming, set design, best proliferation of funds, best same-sex kiss, best intergalactic sexual encounter, best supporting sound design, and so on.

Another man on the other side of Sunset is gently sweeping debris with a dead palm frond. He stands in front of my favorite sandwich shop.

I hear the roar of a two-stroke coming from the west, heading in my direction. I soon see what all the commotion is about . . . a 1978 Airhead . . . red and silver. Petrol being as scarce as it is, only the wealthy can afford to travel this way.

Those who have enough credit with the government are permitted to travel via monorail. The poor must walk. As the motorcyclist passes the **Citadel**, I see that he is wearing a well tailored grey suit with white chalk pinstripes. His brown and gold helmet has something etched on it . . . . One word.

I strain my eyes to read it, removing the shades from my field of vision, resting them on my forehead for a clearer view. I squint and shield my eyes from the sun glaring off broken pieces of glass. In what used to be the southerly windows of a building on the north side. I am trying to make out the words before he gets too far out of view. Straining my vision . . . I think it reads: **"WHAT?!"**

Behind him trails an excessively long scarf blowing in the wind. It is pure white and possibly silk. I am reminded of an airplane at the beach tugging a long sign. Telling everyone to *Eat at Joe's*. I hear him throttle the engine into fifth as he disappears over the hill and around the bend.

I should get mine out of the garage more often. Although, an unprotected ride has become more and more hazardous to your health. The secret is to keep moving, never stop. Like a shark. To keep the cannies away from you.

Always better to have a metal box around your perimeter. Just in case you need to smash yourself out of a tight situation. But who could afford to gas up an automobile with any regularity?

I see a trail at the top of what used to be Nichols Canyon. A trail that I hike upon occasion. To maintain my cardiovascular performance, and soak up a little sunshine. I used to take Russ with me. But even then, I wouldnt be caught dead without my riot stick. A modified street sweeper, designed by yours truly. A Boy Scout is considered a pussy by modern standards. One must fend off blood thirsty mongrels on a weekly, if not daily basis, to keep up a relatively normal routine.

If you dont feel like braving the wilderness, so to speak, then you may find yourself taking the stairs instead of the elevator. A stair exercise regimen works the largest muscle mass in the human body. Therefore increasing the caloric burn rate by two or even threefold. I usually hydrate for an hour in advance. Once beginning my routine, I do not stop for at least another hour.

If you choose to survive in this place, you must be willing to push yourself harder than anyone else. This way, when disaster strikes, at least you were prepared for it. For dog's sake, do yourself a favor and learn to swim. I run my course on the stairs from bottcm to top and back down again. Then up another time. Perpetually crusading. About ten times up and down on average, to maintain an adequate pace.

Naturally, I do not workout while under the influence of drugs. Typically, I train in the morning. Before my first shot. The shot becomes a reward for punishing myself, once I become sick from the exercise.

My heart is strong by now and accustomed to all sorts of torture. I was put on a program in my hyper-intelligence days which modified my cellular structure. Ever since, I feel stronger, faster, and most capable. Could have been a placebo like they said . . . who could tell? But I feel a difference even now.

For instance, last week some rabid street urchin overtook one of our barrier wardens. The others were taking a decent beating in an attempt to contain and remove the parasite. We try not to kill out in the open, if at all possible. While the cannie easily bested multiple guards, I stood back, observing every angle by which to strike. Then I got involved.

Strike, after fluid strike, I continuously rearranged his alphabet. Leaving him with even less teeth than when we began . . . . A few less marbles, too. I assure you, he wont be back any day soon. If he does, he wont live to tell the tale . . .

I hear the amplified sound of a guitar riff coming at me from over the hill. From the direction the biker's destination. Loud, thrashing chords of deliverance sweep out over the street. A tall figure glides along the pavement shedding sound.   Echoing against the ravished buildings lining Sunset.

Son of Harry Perry rolls past, donning a white turban and full beard.   Still singing about,

"A message, a message ... from another world."

His axe, white with red circles.   The Kramer has been passed down through generations, and still . . . it sounds so pure.

From his red sash belt hang numerous cigarette box amplifiers.   Each one of them blasting his mantra into the air.   Sounding impressively loud for their size.   His white robe blows in the breeze as he continues to solo, passing by the **Citadel**.   Levitating above the filth covered ground.   A shrill voice dominates my consciousness,

"We . . . um . . . we need some . . . assistance in the bar, um, PLEASE!"

My **PS**ynaps informs me of a security breach. Notorious for indecent behavior, and once called the Wet Cigarette.   Now, our lobby bar is known only as the Scar Bar.   Due to its negative affect on your liver.

I reluctantly walk from my perch . . . over to the lift.   I would much prefer to stay here watching the clouds, and listening to music.   But duty calls.   I jab the button labeled L.   As I descend toward my duty, I enjoy the peace and quiet from within the elevator.   Nothing in the world could have prepared me for what I saw down there.

As the doors part, I am immediately approached by management. A withered shell of a cold woman who was, a long time ago, born here . . . literally. She will probably die here, as well. Her laugh was the type which reminded me of a demented kid. A demon child. The talking skeleton looks rather distressed. She says,

"It's Ms. Renoir, she . . . well, her . . . monkey!"

I shove her out of the way, making mine into the bar. It seems that our V.I.P. client has a certain fascination with primates, and tends to travel with her pet chimpanzee, Felix. Now, when I say chimpanzee, you think cute and cuddly. Maybe they are sometimes, but certainly not after being fed xanadu and red wine all afternoon.

Approaching the entrance, I notice a couple of blood spots marking the white wooden flooring. Walking further inside, the blood becomes more noticeable. The room, empty but for the elderly woman sobbing in the corner. Saying,

"He's just my baby, my little . . . ."

It is then, that I notice the ape crouching on the top shelf of the bar. The shelf, nearest to the ceiling. A cigarette burning in its right hand and a bottle of booze in the other. Screeching uncontrollably and visibly unnerved.

I step on something wet, crushing it beneath my foot . . . slipping . . . barely able to catch myself. Then regaining my balance. I straighten my jacket.

Upon inspection, I realize that it's a teensie weensie little doggie head. From a chihuahua, it seems.

"So let me guess? The chimp . . . who was clearly over served . . . . Lost his temper and brutally attacked a nearby puppy dog?" I inquire.

"Ms. Renoir there owns the chimp. The dog's owner is in triage. She was clutching her chest, and we thought she was dying." The wax sculpture manager states.

"Fine," I offer.

"We dont really know how to get him down off of the bar. Just do something!" She adds.

"Let me understand," I begin. "You serve this drugged up primate who, as a result, rampages inside of your damned bar . . . and now . . . that the shit has hit the fan, you want me to *fix* it?"

Taking a moment for impact . . . and once I'm certain she's at the end of her rope. I chime in with,

"First off, I'll need you to remove her . . ." pointing to the distressed simian's guardian.

"Mrs. Renoir?" The human sepulcher asks.

From the corner, another old bitch with a dog slurs in with,

"Why dont you throw trash like that out in the street."

To which I reply, "Tobie . . . everyone in this room and abroad knows you are an antisocial ramrod of a cunt. Constantly parading around with your own psychotic lap mutt. Always hassling the celebrities with ancient stories of better days, and your rat-fuck of a dog is forever biting the ankles of passers-by. Or wailing, having been stepped on . . . or just plain in-the-way. Why couldnt it be your mutt in pieces? Torn to shreds?" With that, I put my toe into her pup's ribs.

"How dare you?! That's a **PRIZE WINNING BLOODLINE!** He eats better than you. You fucking mercenary!" She's raving mad and feeling no pain.

"If you insist on releasing her into the streets this night, know that I would be obligated to let you join her. You will keep her warm tonight." Then I focus on the soulless manager, saying, "Get the fucking organ grinder out of here, follow that with yourself. I need total isolation. Everyone out."

I finish. When suddenly and from out of nowhere . . . another little darling of a shaver insists on spewing superciliousness. A dog damned diuretic deluge. Threatening me with the things his father will make happen . . . .

Utilizing fear, in a feeble attempt to socially rape the situation. I cannot for the life of me remember what he said exactly . . . and without drawing my weapon . . . I merely offer him this reply,

"You are but one thing . . . and forever, you will be one thing only . . . a piss poor chawbacon of a cunt. A megalomaniac clod hop. Malodorous and out on the maraud. A local yokel suffering from delusions of grandiosity.   You come here and threaten me with some future day.   When your begetter will walk in here . . . and essentially . . . dance this mess around . . . .   Yet you forget one fact, you pukka shell motherfucker.   Even your paternal inseminator cannot prevent me from lynching you, this very moment. Here and now.   (I pull a garrote from my sleeve for emphasis.)   Perhaps, it was your dear old dad what got you into this place but rest assured, I will be the one to take you out."

He departs quickly as I light a Chesterfeld using my silver Zippo.   The fresh flint makes it difficult to spark, requiring more than one attempt. However, I still manage to look intimidating while doing so.

I sit down and give the room has a chance to clear.   Smoking . . . I remain calm . . . controlling my pulse . . . my breathing.   I finger the syringe in my coat pocket.   One from earlier today.   A doozy.

Everyone leaves and I have that funky monkey all to myself.   I remain seated at the bar for another ten minutes.   I shoot a bit of the toxic shot, setting the remainder down on the bar to relax a while.   I smoke. Some of my blood, now trapped in the reservoir, floating.

The chimp eyes my wearily, still pulling on that bottle and now looking around the room anxiously.   I know that look.   Nicotine fit.   He needs a smoke.   His last one burned out maybe five minutes ago.   And trust me, I know how lovely a cigarette feels while on a xanadu binge . . . especially when you've been drinking all day.   So I decide to offer him one.

Pulling my pack out of my pocket again, I set it on the bar, and take one for myself. I put it to my lips, make eye contact with the chimp, then light it up. Just like in the old commercials . . . I am thoroughly enjoying my drag. Then I exhale the thick smoke, blowing it in his general direction. The stage is set. Now all I have to do is wait.

The chimp finishes his bottle, tossing it carelessly. Not at me, mind you, but around me. Near me. It's a test. I continue to smoke calmly. Blowing smoke rings at him. Waiting for him to cave. The craving, clouding his better judgement.

He begins his slow descent from his perch; knocking down more bottles from the shelves. Which come crashing to the floor at my feet. Then taking an object from one of the shelves. Finally throwing a lump of bloody mess at me. Which, I assume, is the remainder of the chihuahua. It lands on the bar, one meter outside of my comfort zone.

He hops onto the bar, still maintaining a good distance from me. Distrust overwhelming his face. I remove a nail from the coffin. I pack it on my Zippo and offer it to him.

He gives me the horse eye . . . he's not buying it. I continue to smoke with ease. Tossing the unlit cigarette over to him where he eyes it for a moment, unsure. Slowly picking it up and putting it in his teeth.

"Need a light?"

I say more to myself than anyone else. He fucking nods at me. A slow, deliberate nod. I hold out my Zippo striking it, the flame burns orange and hot. I stub out my burning Chester. Offering the flame to him . . . he edges toward me awkwardly. Side stepping the entire way. I make no sudden movements. In fact, I have not made any since sitting down. He's almost within my grasp.

I see that he is hard up for a fag, yet he vehemently distrusts me. Taking his time . . . but eventually . . . leaning in timidly . . . and looking at me first . . . then down at the tip he wishes to light. I give him all the time in the world to relax and he knows it. When I'm sure he's committed . . . and leaning in for smokey relief . . .

. . . I touch flame to fag.

In one expert move, I seize the opportunity. Picking up the syringe, I thrust it deep into the chimp's neck. He tenses up for a moment before I press the plunger. Then looking at me with a gaze ever loving joy and hate.

He takes a lone drag off his now lit Chester then falling backward to the ground. As he hits the floor, a little puff of smoke escapes his lips . . . .

Remember To Forget

Currency of the day is primarily composed of hard street drugs, precious gemstones, metals information, or technology. As for cash, it's euros, but not everyone will accept them. Barter is best.

Ultimately, we did succumb to the international currency movement. Initially introduced as the euro towards the end of last century. No one in America ever truly respected it. Though we were forced to convert, once our banking system collapsed. It was too insecure. Barter is the way we play nowadays. Back to basics.

Internet auctioneers paved the way years ago, allowing the barter concept to take hold swiftly. If you dont have anything to trade like powder, ice, or halcyon, then you can trade water or food. Or services. It's a harder game now, but we always find a way.

Typically I receive my monthly payment in return for services rendered, in the form of a quarter kilogram of white Afgani seed heroin. Which helps motivate me while keeping me calm and focused, all at once. Lately, petrol and tobacco are also more abundant at the **Citadel** on account of the current property owners. They keep me stocked up with Chesterfelds.

It lies with me to budget myself for the month. Using anything extra to trade for other goods or services. Usually parts for whatever I happen to be restoring at present, if I cant find them within our storage rooms.

I'm currently rebuilding an Indian Larry original I found scrapped. It began life as a Harley Davidson Forty Eight, then rebuilt in 1999. Larry exchanged most of the flash for style but maintained, and improved its power.

It was then abandoned for years. I found it in my travels, scavenging abandoned mansions and buildings in the area, then I brought it here. We have a complete garage and workshop, so I spend free time tinkering on diamonds in the rough. Polishing them back to life before my very eyes. If I destroy with my hands, I must also use them to create.

The building's restaurant, the Gate, covers all of my gastric needs. Though I have grown rather tired of its menu and often venture our for some culinary variety. If there is something special I may be looking for, I must forge a deal with the delivery coachman. They like to get high too, everybody does. It's the only way any more.

Those food jockeys are some serious sons of bitches. Crazy and well trained in the art of survival.

They must be, food is extremely difficult to come by for some. When you get that grumble in your belly and it's been there for days . . . it tends to influence your judgement supremely. These chow hacks drive rigs for grocery franchises that offer delivery services.

To offer safety while unloading. The delivery rigs have enormous cages protecting the entire back end. A slick operation, where the driver never need exit the truck. He simply backs the carryall up to the pre-existing loading dock, all of them built a standard ten feet above ground. The cage touches the exterior wall of the compound's collection facility. An electromagnetic lock is engaged, holding the truck in place. The driver simply walks through the inside of the truck and through trailer to the back end, attached to the dock.

Free to grab whatever he may need to unload along the way. Never leaving himself vulnerable, he will continue this process until the order has been filled. These semis come equipped with hard rubber tires, impervious to puncture due to their lack of air. The tires actually deflect bullets, returning them, back toward the shooters . . . rolling right over nails or spikes like paperclips. Due to its height, the monorail makes the convoy nearly impervious to IEDs.

The monorail is the elite way to travel, built and maintained privately by Scientologists to ensure safe passage in and out of Kill City. The monorail deposits the delivery trucks in town. Then they, along with the rest of us, are forced into the streets.

On an average city street, we have what I can only compare to a railway system like trolleys used in the old days. The delivery semis attach to rails after unloading at the local warehouse dock. The rails take them to whichever local compound is desired. Every compound must have its own rail system for delivery and personal transportation.

Once inside a compound, the truck disengages the electromagnetic track system. Lowering itself onto the tires, free to make turns, etc. Should any enterprising cannies lay a pile of decomposing remains on the tracks, or perhaps a steel girder . . . . The enormous cattle catcher on the front of the electric freighter easily removes such debris casting it to one side or the other.

One truckload can be worth hundreds of thousands of Lifecredits. Credits are what the wealthy use to barter. Based solely on a person's exact net worth during the moment of purchase. Think of it as an involuntary rationing system.

A household in the hillside compound will be issued a number of credits each day, representing the net worth of its inhabitants. Spending must remain below this figure, or there will be consequences the following day.

A controller makes the daily decision based on work performance. The system serves to keep the families on the edge of desperation. Constantly in pursuit of financial security.

You're almost more free living out here among the squalor and shit, fending for yourself. I choose to stay beyond the electric fence line, out here in the unregulated wilderness.   In the remains of a once magnificent city.

Delivery lorries doles out goodies to the wealthy at a gasp-inducing mark-up, of course.   But they pay, oh, they always pay.   They pay for the same reason others must steal.   The growl.

Go forty hours without so much as a morsel and tell me what you would do.   Now go a week without a bite.   I promise, you'll do most anything for a taste . . . hence the cannibalism.   Plenty of hungry mouths searching for meat . . . driven by hunger . . . it was just the natural evolution of things.   The dehydration can also make you crazy.

Indoor plumbing is a thing of the past for anyone living off the grid, and it's still too expensive for many of the families within the hillside compound. This building offers running water of course but at a steep price.   The majority of the city must use crude rain collection structures to gather drinking water. It's still pretty acidic but safe enough to drink if you filter it once.

Tonight, the sprawling hillside pyres burn bright in the sooty cloak.   Heaps of garbage burn high from within their metal skeletons, a cage constructed to contain the blaze.

Giant metal thunderdomes, contain the conflagrations.   They line the perimeter of the compound.   One burns about every hundred meters or so.   Massive bonfires meant both to frighten cannie hordes and to serve as a marker for aircraft.

Sometimes the food is dropped from above instead of driven, it depends on the size of the order. The bigger the order, the more trucks needed. So why not just send one enormous cargo plane.

Or perhaps it's a life and death scenario. Maybe some cunt producer needs to overawe the next-young-hot clone, so he throws an impromptu soiree. But no champagne to speak of . . . and no caviar! Worst of all . . . no anal lube!!

Well what's a dog-damned-shit-sniffer to do? Airfreight special delivery, of course! And for more money than he cares to admit, but hey, the film gets made and it wins eighteen fucking shitty awards.

Now the academy offers three-hundred and forty-two categories that one may qualify for, including best anal kiss. Now the entire ceremony takes at least three days to complete. It is typically the most extravagant event of the year. People will actually kill for seats. Asses have undoubtedly been penetrated in exchange for all access passes, and gladly.

Those worth knowing, will happily show up . . . broadcast via PSynaps to the entire world. International participation is now heartily encouraged. Tonight marks the 113th award ceremony and as I mentioned, a very close friend of mine is up for a few laurels himself.

He captained a remake of an extremely old book. One so rare that most have never even heard of it before now. A tale of a boy shipwrecked on a deserted island with a band of pirates. For some reason, I cannot recall the author's name at the moment. It was a rather long tale that I surely read in school.

Back when there were public schools, they gave us summer readings. Which must have been when I was exposed to it. When I saw Elan's film, I realized that I knew the story already. But he must have altered the ending a bit because it caught me by surprise. Surely, Mr. Merryweather will lead the judges by the nose.

Americans finally adopted the metric system as well. Holding out until about seven years ago. Having already succumb to China and India's extravagant courtship, nearly every last American corporation sold its rights to the highest bidder.

Foreign investors were easing in too slowly for the public naked eye to see. Aside from Washington D.C., foreigners soon owned pretty much everything east of Nevada.

Vegas refused to crack, nor Hollywood. Vegas became the mecca for Italian-Americans . . . mafia owned once again. Once run out of New York City by the minorities' majority. I once overheard a refugee singing,

"Those of you with lighter skin shall be torn from limb to limb."

Supposedly she and her mother had barely escaped Brooklyn with their lives. Just barely. Her father was not so lucky.

Well, Hollywood has always been full of filthy rich Scientologists. They opted to keep all profits within the state lines, giving the finger to the rest of the world. Along with anyone else, so unlucky as to live outside of their precious hillside compound.

Viewers hungrily awaited with baited breath for every new release. Distributors and on down were making a killing. Everyone involved reaped the profits; the film industry became the last profitable American commodity.

Yet, directly adjacent to the hillside compound, rots the remains of this great conurbation that no one seems to want rebuilt. The cannies help keep land value low. It's not profitable to renovate with those devils right next door. The parsimonious Scientologists wouldnt sell or share their sure thing with anyone. In some cases turning their backs on their own families.

The rest of the globe, more than glad to dicker drugs to our country. Whichever drugs we do not already master, that is. And they always will, provided that Americans continue to buy them.

Dope dealing foreigners are merely cashing in on the American dream while tearing it down. They only want our film. Thank dog for style. It has become the one and only thing you cannot steal. Stolen style is as obvious as that sore on your lip.

Life can never truly live up to a fantasy. Except within one percent of the world. It has become increasingly difficult to legally gain access into the U.S. Once the capital fucks realized they could sell things like "liberty" and "freedom," it was all over. American citizenship has long been big business. The white collars are merely cashing in on one last paycheck before Hollywood becomes Bollywood before our very eyes.

The elements conspired against us as well. Rising up with great ferocity, showering doom and destruction onto the world. By the end of it, the United States had seen the worst, the world said we were cursed. Maybe we are . . . I say we're damned.

Cop Out

In the beginning . . . and for much of its duration, our magnificent country has been host to a variety of agencies. Some were privately independent, but most were supported by a military. Which enforced all of the laws you and I tend to break. There were, of course, other lower militant figures like policemen and security agents.

At least that's how I remember it . . . the way it was in my youth. Law creates order. Order creates peace. Peace creates happiness. I was, in my lifetime, privy to the disintegration of this system.

As the natural world revolted in disgust at what the human roach had done to it . . . the common order and politeness honored among society became less and less attractive to the populace. It simply became too difficult to preserve. Once the food supply dwindled, and everyone felt the fear of true hunger for the very first time in all of their sheltered lives . . . .

It was then that the federal government intervened setting up military states with the national guard. The task had become too formidable a responsibility for local p.d. So, the armchair generals sent in the cavalry.   Martial law set in.   Civilized no more.

That being the exact demise of the police officer.   Of the police force itself.   At which point, everyone became government property.   I already was, so I didnt mind.   To most, however, it was quite a change, and one met with rebellion.   They fed us, so they owned us.   This is what they would tell you.   Or they take you away in the unmarked vans where you were silenced forever.   Curfews were also enforced. All of this before cannibalism was a true threat.

Speaking of which . . . prisons had become a bit messy, as well.   Rioting overtook most of the cities as the national guard failed to get a foothold.   Prisons were even more chaotic.   The wardens ordered guards to execute the majority of violent offenders. Extremely violent criminals or wards of state were classified as non-reformable and thereby disposed of, due to restricted rations.   The most violent went first.

People on the outside were fighting to survive, it was no one's concern about what happened within the penal system.   Eventually, the prisoners were put out of their misery by a choice.   The first option pitted one prisoner against another, in a fight to the death. For the reward of an honorable burial.

The other put them in front of a firing squad, followed by a mass grave.   All of it done before the cold eye of the camera, and uploaded into cyberspace for member viewing . . . at a nominal fee, of course.

This practice was affectionately referred to as Social Cleansing.   Members of the new society were encouraged to donate more and more, to view vivid close-up footage of the action. Thus, having something intriguing to discuss whilst treading conversational water at any future public gatherings.

It was the **fear** that spread throughout the inmates . . . emanating within every cell block. Along with the fact that they needed fresh air, food, and water . . . this caused a massive rash of cannibalism, prison riots, and consequent breakouts.

Ultimately . . . this would leak the disease back into society. Not that prisons ever did much for civilization anyway. But now we had hardened criminals by the hundreds, released back into the primordial gene pool.

Law enforcement, already had their hands full out in free society. So, the elimination of convicted malcontents was a solution widely embraced in both the public and political realms.

Competitive programs were based on vintage movie plots. Always involving a herculean protagonist in a fight for life. All were broadcast on international data streams. Many recognized this practice as vulgar and disproportionate. However, the majority ruled on the matter, and the show was a mainstay. Gaining utmost popularity and earnings within its thirteen year run.

This was during a period, far in the past, when Americans could only remake the films they already enjoyed watching. In order to capitalize on a sure thing. Rather than create new, original film plots; with fresh thoughts and inventive storytelling.

Instead, a golden oldie from before the turn of the century was selected, to become the blockbuster rehash of the summer season. Guaranteed money. Unfortunately for some of these investors, the remake would be far worse than the original counterpart, and dire box office earnings would follow.

The moral is . . . there is no such thing as a sure thing. Ever. Not here . . . not any more. Not even the lowly pig has a place in this slop.

Even the glory day of the top cop became a thing of the past, and many fools rejoiced. The newly ex-cops were simply absorbed by the military ranks instead. All except for the elderly and overweight desk driving pencil pushers. They were put out to pasture and reintroduced to society. Humiliated.

I was never so unlucky as to be affected by this changing of the guards. I work alone, and I certainly do not earn a paycheck. I earn, but, not on paper. Dead men do not hold jobs. Dead men do not have contracts. Best of all, dead men do not have consequences.

It was not one thing in particular that sent the ecosystem into revolt . . . but a culmination of countless variables working in concert to create perfect chaos. The ice caps continued to melt, raising the sea level. This, in tandem with the decimation of the San Andreas fault line via fracking, crude, and natural gas drilling. All compounded to create the perfect storm. The extreme pollution of the planet only made Nature's reaction more violent.

The water choked us while the earth cracked wide to swallow us whole. We werent the only ones falling prey to the big one. Peru, Chile, Brazil, Japan . . . all recorded quakes at over 9.0.

Responding to the movement of oceanic fault lines, most every active volcano on the planet erupted passionately. Pockets of magma were suddenly released. Displacing excessive gas pressure, universally cracking the earth's crust, and lending to the chaotic bane. The newest plague of humanity was Nature's mutiny.

The military states were also established due to the excessive looting. This, resultant of limited water and food. Not to mention, the endless earthquakes that radiated from the San Andreas fault line. Coupled with the ongoing tidal assault that was underway. Affecting the entire western coast of the U.S. continent.

The western coastlines of the central and southern Americas suffered batteries, also. Albeit, a bit less violent. The **fear** spread just as quickly there. In Lost Angeles, massive waves drowned and cracked the pavement of the Basin as far inland as Melrose and La Brea. All of the town's garbage . . . along with many of its inhabitants . . . were washed from the face of existence . . . . Dragged out to a watery grave.

Underwater earthquakes caused vast landslides near Japan and across the Hawaiian islands. The landslides gave way to tsunamis which found their way west . . . to us. So picture it . . . the earth is opening up like a gaping wound as one killer wave, after another decimated our coastline. From

Oregon to Cabo San Lucas, giant water walls flowed for what seemed like an eternity.

Vast evacuations were orchestrated to limit fatalities. Due to constant rising water levels in the preceding decades, the angry ocean claimed over a million lives that month. Over half were lost during the initial aqueous assaults, due primarily to a serious lack of preparedness.

Another five hundred thousand died resultant of injuries sustained during the initial disaster . . . or by subsequent calamity. Many drowned attempting to escape its fury . . . but really . . . no one was meant to survive. This would be our final lesson . . . or so it seemed.

These natural anomalies led to a general panic . . . everyone was scrambling. Many left the coast in search of higher and drier land. Many returned to their homes in the midwest, taking up channel surfing instead. But those who chose to remain on the west coast, especially those in the southern region of California, would get the worst of it.

The rioting began quickly. Typically, they occurred just after an earthquake. Rioting and looting. Gang members along side of cubicle worker bees, stealing whatever wasnt nailed down. Unity. True unity for the first time. Yet the human race was already in retreat.

Lost Angeles was then set ablaze. The origin of which was eventually determined to be Skid Row. The emergency federals along with local firefighters were denied access to the ignition source by a mass of raving transients. The ones taking credit for the scorcher, hundreds of them, easily outnumbered what remaining public officials there were.

Angry civilians attacked the hobo army with what guns they still had lying around the house. Prompting a retaliatory attack from the agitated vagrants. This retaliatory strike dissolved what few vigilantes there were.

The rest of us laid low on higher ground, watching as the city burned before our eyes, filling the sky with black soot. Ash and dust rained down for weeks and no one saw the sun for what seemed like months. That is what actually did it . . . the darkness. Panic was rapidly becoming chaos. **Fear** gripped every citizen as it did every law enforcement official.

After all of this, the soldiery swarmed in to remedy the widespread panic gripping every survivor. Everyone was so excited, I remember thinking,

"This is it . . . we'll be saved."

But . . . no. New laws came into play on a regular basis. Laws that were punishable by death. Or worse . . . deportation. Shunned, banished, exiled from Eden. Although, by then, Eden had pretty much gone fucking mad.

New laws surfaced that pertained to water and food rationing, littering, socializing, breeding, and the aforementioned curfews.

At twenty-one hundred, (that's 9 p.m.) all members of the new closed society were to be home and behind locked doors. The home security companies made billions in this brief period.

The national guard executed people for failure to curb their canines. The shit was contaminating the groundwater then . . . and still is. Nowadays, there are hardly any dogs left at all because they have been mostly eaten by the poor. Or by cannies. Only the wealthy keep pets. They are the only ones who can afford to keep pets alive.

Yet, the law still stands to this day, and there are a few rich cocksuckers I hope to catch in my crosshairs for that very offense. If not for any other reason. Littering is now a fatal offense, too. When I'm bored, I still pick off litterbugs with my CheyTac.

Military presence was reaching critical mass at a rapid pace and pretty soon everyone felt cagey. So we began to act out. The first tantrums being minor . . . random assaults on authority figures. Soon it was full scale rioting again. Another revolt was underway. The fires began again. Smoke too. So much smoke . . . for days, weeks . . . and you think car exhaust is bad? I promise you, it can always get worse. And it will.

Thousands of lives were lost in the name of freedom. It was the closest we ever came to a second civil war. Before long, the government had a hard time finding employees. Thankfully, no one wanted to kill their own kind any more. Not for money, at least.

Then the food dried up and panic . . . again . . . came to town. But the government would not play with us any more. Its pride had been irreparably damaged. So, the nation stood by as L.A. burned once again. If the wilderness gave a shit, it would have chosen that particular week to bombard us with a fifty foot tidal wave . . . . But it did not.

The universe . . . like the government, had suffered too much rejection from us already. When the dust settled, most of this town's inhabitants were dead or gone . . . **Fear** then set in for the long haul.

Those who remained, began rebuilding, once again. The Scientologists aligned themselves with other powerful entities within the film community. Laying claim to the high ground, for obvious reasons. The hills on into Malibu and even Santa Barbara fell under lock and key. Electrified fences hosting gun turrets, manned by trained killers still line the compound's perimeter.

Now, foreign investing has been slowly creeping in, even at the **Citadel,** to rescue the remains of my beloved town. Turning it into the wild west it has become today. In what few parts remain, not already claimed by the hillside compound.

No one is certain what year it actually is, or the actual day of the week. All records have been destroyed, and no one has a parent, grandparent, or guardian from whom to learn the past or present. Most do not have living relatives. Most have been slain.

America lost her soul long before this point, but she had not a hope now. L.A. was only the first to go the way of the Dodo. In the oncoming years, the rest of the world would follow suit. It's pretty much every man or woman for themselves, wherever you may travel. If you are able to travel.

Free-For-All
Feast
Fuck

Rage is what takes you into the unknown. It is the thing that forces you to remain on the outermost edge of society, here in Kill City. Like the cannies do. Like us at the **Citadel**.

I have witnessed to the invalidation of thousands of jobs. Occupations that have been around for a century or more. Some in existence for all time, except for the present. Trades that have no place in modern day survivalism. Professions for which the ancient appreciation has long expired. Only the elite upper echelons of society may partake in such luxuries any more.

Affluent trades only for the bourgeois, like fine tailoring, hairdressing, automotive mechanics, and sales came to a bitter end. The builders of dream homes or dream cars. Even local law enforcement became null and void once the dream finally became our nightmare. These men and women would attempt to find a new walk of life, but there were none to find. No thriving businesses anywhere, but within the hillside compound. Or within the military. The dream was now long over, and no one could do anything about it.

Sure, a few lucky outsiders weaseled their way into the hillside. Put to use behind the scenes of the next new blockbuster. The majority of us have a fate far worse than that. As for the lion's share . . . the average joe . . . the concept of death will seem like a romantic fantasy compared to the horror life will become. For me. And you.

Most are destined for Tent City. Hideous hovels located inside of the abandoned state parks. The state, due to nothing more than ego, still claims the land due to its resale value. So optimistic . . . they actually tell people that it will eventually transform itself. Pipe dreams.

Yet, the state officials never been here to see it in person. Refusing to spend a cent on maintenance or cleaning crews. It must look a lot less dismantled through a satellite feed.

The sties of Tent City are primarily occupied by former blue collar families with little or no higher learning. These people did their best to cultivate from the land. To yield fruits, vegetables, and raise livestock. But by then it was far too polluted. Barren of minerals. Water was ample but extremely acidic. Too acidic for consumption by plant or animal without sufficient filtration. Food becoming so scarce that rations were soon unbearable.

Rations became so small that the infighting resulted in the forming of confederations. Which eventually morphed into battle clans. In the middle of a pitch, algid night . . . there was utter carnage.

Neighbor pitted against neighbor, spilling blood into the street as many blood lines came to an end. Lives were unwittingly lost by the hundreds, in the name of the great cannibalistic war feast known only as, **The Heap.**

A furious assault that saw more casualties than victors. As all war does. In the end, what few surviving tent dwellers there were, decided to form a single alliance. Adopting autonomy against society once again. Autonomous except when feeding. The hunger would draw them in close to the city, and out of the parks.

The new ruling clan became infused with any surviving flesh-eaters. Working in unison, and quickly to preserve the meat of their fallen adversaries. Salt was still plentiful then.

The meat was first butchered, then rolled in salted banana leaves. A mash consisting of yams would be added to the meat for marination, before cooking. Yams were one of the few crops that could grow in modern soil. The flesh was then wrapped again in the banana leaves to be slow roasted. Trust me, you wouldnt even know the difference between brother or beast.

If the flesh was to be preserved for an extended period of time, it was sent to an underground meat cellar. Sixty meters below the earth's crust, in a dry salt chamber. Temperatures sink to just under 3 degrees celsius, cold enough to prevent immediate decomposition. Nasty I know. I have only eaten human flesh one time and only because the situation was terminal. Not my cup.

The meat, however, ran out very quickly and frenzy ensued, caused by an increased awareness of self. Coupled with aggressive tendencies. Rapid muscle gain has been reported . . . as well as a ravenous appetite.

Benefits of cannibalism include: heightened sense of sound, sight, smell, rapid metabolism, increased strength, and endurance. Negative effects include: the loss of family and friends, deplorable breath, chronic diarrhea, incontrollable rage, and dementia.

I know it sounds amusing . . . but really, it wasnt. Because you actually have to eat people to survive. Up close and personal with your neighbor, childhood friend, ex-girlfriend . . . whomever.

I only went that route one time. My hands were tied. Yet many are content to remain in that savage state. Victims of desperation, fueled by a general lack of options. The battle of the boroughs lasted only days, but something most unholy was birthed that dreadful night, roughly one decade past.

Slowly and steadily it has been gaining power ever since. Hand over fist. Millions of lost refugees have gone to the trails of Griffith and Runyon looking for help, finding only hell and death inside. Death . . . and the mass consumption of it.

Nimrod's Son

Our demons are contagious . . . .
Her shimmering hair . . .
fresh from the sea . . .
come across great distance to me.

My heart ever aching with regret,
three little words I never said.

Eyes bright like the sky, like the sea.
Bright eyes, alive.
Enlighten me.
My mind's eye,
watching her mind's eye,
watching me.

And the waves crash . . . endless.
Mindless . . . .

Heavy heart . . . back from the dead.
Three little words I never said . . . .
FRANKK

Hell is only an illusion. Ask any modern priest. It's a mindfuck created by calculating enterprisers. Around the age of three, a child is typically exposed to such things. Age four for some luckier little bastards. Coincidentally, what is the appropriate term for a fatherless female? Is it bastard, as well? Bast-ette? And I am still dreaming . . .

This day, I awake feeling particularly free and vulnerable. Also finding myself carefree and jealous, even smitten, as it were. Emotions rarely found in my repertoire. Now . . . I cannot think of anything else. To do so, would kill me.

The Swede, this fucking female is ruining my life before my very eyes. Worse yet, I think I want her to do it. I certainly want to be wanted. One more time.

Which is the thing I find most frustrating . . . having had the opportunity to fall in love with someone once before. I passed it up. Preferring the company of maniacs and revel devils instead . . . .

Before today, I could have left this place in the dust of my fading memory. Now, suddenly I want to save it. I want to make something out of nothing, like someone did for me, a long time ago. Once upon a time, the **Citadel** was home to so much prosperity, so much affluence. Sickening affluence. I prefer never to see it that way again.

A deal must be struck with the compound in the hills. Forces must join together if we mean to take down the current figureheads. To remove the negative parasitic elements forever.

Mental. Govern-Mental. To govern the mind. It's right there in the title. Other words that require closer examination: manslaughter = man's laughter; therapist = the rapist.

This wasteland needs no national government. In addition to the best cannabis outside of Amsterdam, California now cultivates the poppy, which is refined into heroin and opium. The northern climate is optimal for the poppy plant. State organizations are now thriving and happy to have an export of value, once again.

History has long been sucking its own dick . . . repeating the same mistakes over and over again. Even if you could conquer the fourth dimension, it will only give you the same result. I would simply use it to stay within the same decade, the 1970s. After a little exploration, of course.

On second thought . . . after experiencing the culmination of our existence . . . I would return to my glory days of high school. To experience that a few times over. Then college. Enjoy a normal life, a natural one. One entirely different than the one I chose for myself. Utterly devoid of the agency. A happier one, with a happier ending.

A deal must be struck. The hillside compound hates the fact that they must report to a controller. One assigned by the federal government, to monitor and distribute P.H.V. Lifecredits. Perceived Human Value. Dictating the way in which you will eat every meal, how you will put clothes on your back, and provide for your family. Lifecredits are the new carrot at the end of an exceptionally long stick.

This is the only logical answer . . . no government, no controller, no Lifecredits. The hillside compound will be so grateful for my help. My skills with ordinance are also valuable to them. I will be welcomed, invited inside and treated like a friend. From there, I will learn and obtain leverage from within. Machiavellian warfare.

I continually revel at night, every night, amongst the thoughts of the dead. Surrounding us. They say the same thing in my ear . . . **"live hard."**

Live harder than any temerarious warrior before you. Live to the fullest and harden your step with every turn of the screw. A model citizen must possesses an extreme penchant for performance within everyday life.

Why exist within the same mainframe as some self-pitying, overeating, t.v. dinnering, two-time loser? I dont even compete with these funny shits. Who says the class system is dead in modern America? There is a definite hierarchy. . . a social hierarchy . . . but there's a catch.

Out here, any silly fucker can join in the fun. Anyone. Even you. Yes, you . . . and even me. All you need are two simple things. Two things, as old as the dust on a priest's junk, money and power. In this town . . . anyone can be king. Yes, even you.

I only need to pop up on a few radars. Draw those bastards in close. Close enough to smell their hot putrid breath, paired with ridiculously expensive, yet offensive cologne. A scent most likely procured by a trophy wife, assigned by a government dispensary. Because no one trusts what they meet on the street.

It is time to come out of hiding. I need to set my sights higher. Beyond the senatorial scale and into the realm of my handlers. The man behind the agency's curtain must pay me a visit. A bit of a lead, to whet his appetite. I must gain the interest of the blue bloods, and the rest will come to follow. I only have to waft some pussy in the air. See who wants a piece.

The idea of me, a seed growing here, would be enough to spark an investigation. Either way, contact must be made soon. Room six-oh-eight will receive special treatment tonight.

The two Marshals finally checked in under assumed identities. We allowed them inside, in light of their discrepancies. Now, I can catch them off guard. When they report back about the mess they've found . . . it will bring Horace Lesher out into the open. So he can press the flesh.

Marshals are already busy investigating the mudslinging campaign involving the senator. As I told you, it was organized entirely by the **Citadel's** Engineer. Now, if I could manage to get all of them here together. All at once, with a bow on top. They can get closer to what it is they are looking for . . . closer to me. I can get closer to the answers.

Sunshine Superman

Oh . . . and there we were all in one place.
A generation lost in space . . .
with no time left to start again.
So come on Jack be nimble . . .
Jack be quick.
Jack Flash sat on a candlestick.
'Cause fire is the devil's only friend.
Oh . . and as I watched him on the stage . . .
my hands were clenched in fists of rage.
No angel born in hell . . .
could break that Satan's spell.
And as the flames climbed high into the night . . .
to light the sacrificial rite . . .
I saw Satan laughing with delight . . .
the day the music died.
Singing . . . "This'll be the day that I die . . . .
This'll be the day that I die."
MACLEAN

As I wait atop thirteen enjoying the sun . . . I fly a kite. I watch the gulls. The clouds. This is it. The last hurrah. After this . . . there is no more hope.

No longer any possibilities for this roach . . . still forging ahead. Surviving on instinct and nothing else. Surviving on fear.

I wont miss a thing about this particular detail. About the **Citadel**. Except for this view . . . this bright and shining day. The full moon at night. I removed the Swede from property. For her own protection.

I will miss these things. I have done all I can do. My time here is over. It's up to you after this. Are you ready? Are we rolling? The note I left on room six-oh-eight read . . .

"Tea party begins at noon . . . . Trouble begins at one o'clock sharp."

The wind has slowly deposited enough sand and soot to cover all of my needles left on the ground. Nearly one meter of debris now blankets the roof. I still wouldnt go barefoot on a dare because needles always have a way of resurfacing. Although it would be nice . . . I admit. It has been so long since I last dug my toes into warm silicon granules . . . digging deep with fists of phalanges.

I usually sleep in my boots. Fully dressed and well prepared. Ever ready. My little radio comes in clear today . . . considering the windy conditions. "Who Loves the Sun" by the Velvet Underground competes with the wind in my ears.

I asked 8 to set a table for my meeting. It will take place here. Next to his beautiful garden. He did manage to scrape together a composition of meager production value. But times are tough . . . to say the least. So I decide to cut him some slack. Two chairs and a table. Simple. Minimalist. Best.

The table of vintage formica is three legged and round. At least two meters in diameter. The chairs look even older. Perhaps from the nineteen fifties. I dont actually know what year we are in . . . let alone the date. No one does. So it is debatable. All part of the control strategy . . . implemented by the great authority.

Does it concern you that there are over forty synonyms for the noun "government" in the english language alone? Yet . . . in the Japanese language . . . there exists not one single word for "no." Japanese politicians must have it so damn easy.

I have prepared a treat for my visitors. Tea on the roof. I havent done a shot in over eight days. I need my clarity now more than ever. Besides . . . I want to feel every detail. Intensely. Down to the very last second.

I have spent the last three days smoking cannabis and drinking red wine while listening to vintage reggae albums on vinyl. Safety from within my basement office. While earthquake after earthquake shook the building's foundation . . . roughly six times daily.

I have not used heroin at all. If you are wondering how I can stop so suddenly . . . it is only because I now get high another way, through levitation.

That . . . and all of the purest drug chemistries now come without substantial physical addiction. For the most part. Minor discomfort accompanies the weaning process . . . nothing can be done about the psychological aspect. That's up to you. Physically speaking . . . the homemade bathtub shit made from found household products will get you into the most trouble.

Psilocybin mushrooms soak in hot water. I collected them on my last hike up the Nichol's Canyon trail. The teapot sits atop a solar powered hot plate . . . I gently stir in plenty of mint and honey. Imported from the midwest. I think he said it was from Nebraska. Bees are now endangered. Making honey extremely difficult to come by . . . and so delectable. Nearly all remaining bees are now property of the national government.

I let it steep longer and pull out a Chesterfeld . . . putting it between my lips. Old habits die hard. Although my Zippo is windproof and would have sparked the fag anyway . . . I cup my hand over the flame. I drag long and hard on the Chester. Wont be long now. The vicar will soon be upon me for the rooftop showdown.

I feel my other lucky lighter inside of a pocket that I added myself. Sewn on the inside of my jacket's left sleeve and secured by an elastic band. It is a lighter in the shape of a tiny revolver.

I do not fear death. Never have. What is the point? Live as if you're scared and you will surely meet your match. Live as if you are dead already and no one could ever touch you. How can they take what you do not have? There is nothing to lose . . . yet everything to gain.

Russ T. is no longer around to miss me. I must make my moves now while I am still able. While my eyes are keen and mind still sharp. The muscles still react with dexterity and reflex. Now is the time. The message left for my Marshals should get the attention I so desperately need . . . .

I imagine the elevator doors opening. With sand falling into the car as Horace exits surrounded by ten men. I imagine he sits down. I imagine the end.

Looking through my weathered binoculars . . . the leather strap nearly worn entirely through . . . I witness the spin drifters catching their daily waves as tall as the side of a house. Even higher. Carefully navigating the twisted rusty skewers of the buildings' root structures which jut from the salty churn. Now that sea levels are steadily on the rise again. The surfing conditions at the old Beverly break have vastly improved. The strong wind is kicking up white-capped walls of water.

The windjammer marauders power surf the wave's steep face. Even performing frontside aerials . . . just before the whitewater swallows them whole . . . they pull back . . . putting on the brakes . . . .

Off . . . . Up . . . . Drifting back behind the line of destruction. Dodging the foaming mouth of doom sent by Neptune. Effortlessly maneuvering out of harm's way. Dropping back onto their bellies and paddling back. To join the line-up just north of the building's exposed foundation.

Shocked back into reality by my kite . . . which pulls violently at my wrist. I set my binoculars on the table . . . I taste the tea which looks an emerald shade. It is perfect. The flavor is just right. No evidence of fungus.

Off in the distance I hear the faint hum of a motor. Rarely does a motor run here in the land of the damned . . . which makes it all the more noticeable.

This is not the motor of an automobile. Too steady for a whining boat motor . . . too incessant. Too heavy to be a motorcycle . . . even the loudest Harley in existence. The dangerous and percussive rhythm gives it away. It's a duster. A helo. A whirlybird. Piloted by some zipper suited sun god.

With my trusty lighter . . . I ignite the fuse of a homemade red smoke flare. Using twenty percent potassium chlorate . . . twenty percent lactose . . . combined with sixty percent paranitraniline red. At roughly 250 degrees celsius . . . the para red melts. As it begins to smoke . . . I toss it over my shoulder.

I raise the binoculars again and discover an Aerospatiale Gazelle on the approach. A French manufactured light weight utility helo first introduced to the french army in the early 1970s. Also previously manufactured with permission by Westland Aircraft in the U.K.

Militaries in countries like Egypt . . . Ecuador . . . Serbia. In addition to many others have come to use the Gazelle in the past. Considered to be the Honda of the helo industry. Powered by a single turbine which tends to offer better fuel conservation. The fantail provides significant reduction in the noise level but not enough to get the jump on me.

Most likely a result of the 2025 United Nations Anti-Armament Agreement. When the American government discontinued weapons trades with India. The French gave us some classic machines as a sign of good faith and loyalty. I guess the suits in Washington are now gifting them to one another.

It's him . . . it must be . . . the blue blood muppy popper is upon me. One of the men who sold the world. He wont be using the elevator after all.

I look over at my little shed. Having spent so many past afternoons inside . . . almost losing my mind entirely. Living inside of a dream . . . inside of that shack. Via PSynaps . . . 8 . . . the dog damned roly poly notifies me of their arrival. The warm sensation informs me of what I already know.

No guns today. What would be the point? He will have more than enough for the both of us . . . I am sure. They are so close.

As I prepare for touchdown, I turn the teacups over. Who wants to drink sand with their tea? Grit betwixt the grinders is more than enough to drive one mad.

The waves lap at the first floor of the **Citadel** these days. Especially during high tide. The lobby is no longer completely dry. However . . . the basement level is proving to be watertight.

The smell of salt is strong in the air. A pelican is diving into the water. Out near the aptly renamed Satan's Muñeca Boulevard . . . chasing after its lunch. My stomach conveniently growls. Wishing I had taken the time for a last supper . . . but it's already past. Spilt milk. **Fuck It. Drive On.** The Gazelle approaches nearby. I hear it just over my left shoulder.

The wind turns into a gale . . . picking my kite up . . . snatching it out from my hand. Held there . . . wrapped tightly around my wrist and cutting off circulation. Jerking violently in the ugly weather . . . ultimately freeing itself from my grasp. Taken then by the wind . . . far out over the waves. Ripped free like some refugee castaway caught in a squall . . . I watch it soar to ultimate altitude.

The helo floats directly above me. Surely . . . they wont do what I think they're going to do. Landing a helicopter on a roof is no easy feat in the first place.

The L.Z. must look like a two-cent oasis from up there . . . and in thirty km/h winds with sixty km/h gales . . . . I wouldnt fuck with it. Better to land in the street and take your chances with hostile locals.

The red plumes of my welcoming party dance happily on the whirling blades of the mighty thumper in the sky. Narrowly missing the lone wind turbine attacked to the roof. The beast drops heavily . . . landing on the skids with force. The rooftop's stucco groaning over steel girders.

Dropping the tail on my flare. The machine rocks forward coming to a standstill. The rotors . . . turning a lazy arc . . . slowing down . . . down . . . down. Once they come to a standstill . . . the crew opens the door. I bask in the sun and rotor wash.

In a matter of seconds . . . the roaring beast is gearing down . . . the blades cease their revolution. Once the dust settles again . . . I turn the cups back over and debate pouring the tea. Still too soon.

I must wait for the guest of honor to show his weathered face before we do that. Tea must be consumed hot. The time is at hand . . . but . . . not . . . quite . . . here.

A group of three exit the chopper. Two enforcers and one general. The zoomy and his VIP remain inside the duster. I wonder which one is the co-pilot? Is it my target or one of the enforcers? The Gazelle requires two pilots for flight.

The general and his enforcers begin conducting a thorough check of the roof. Checking first inside the closet . . . which consumed so many of my days. No ambush waiting inside. So uncreative in their inspection . . . rummaging through the remains left on the closet's filthy floor.

The entire perimeter is then scrutinized by the trio. They continue to secure it by peering intensely into the distance for any hidden snipers or mortar tossing gun bunnies. Or any such activists equipped with Rocket Propelled Grenades. Nothing.

They also search the desk at which I sit. Refusing to stand . . . they leave me in my chair. Then probing the sand beneath our feet for signs of a threat. Nothing but needles. Nothing at all. The little black box catches their interest . . . as it was tucked just beneath me . . . near my feet. I notice the hair on their necks stiffen at the sight of the small container. The one with missing front teeth asks me . . .

"Whud isss thisssssss?"

"My lunch" . . . I reply.

Then I open it . . . taking my time to build tension . . . . I sit and stare him in the eye a half-minute before reaching beneath to retrieve it. Slowly dragging it over the sand . . . implying great mass and density. Raising it onto the old table with a thump. Slowly clicking the latch to reveal its inner-workings. Then taking a moment to look each man directly in the eye. Taking time to steal their souls. I look back down and flick open the cover . . . to reveal . . . my . . . Universal . . . Underwood . . . typewriter.

Having never seen one before . . . it offered them little relief. Still perplexed . . . an investigation of the strange machine within occurs. I do all I can to prevent them from snapping the typebars. As they roughly jam their sausage fingers at it.

Once satisfied . . . they return to the Gazelle. I encase the typewriter once again . . . preparing it for some terrific . . . imminent journey. After another small lapse in time . . . the group emerges once again . . . with my target . . . Horace.

A smallish . . . grey skinned . . . white haired . . . little creep. A man rarely seen but often felt. A man who would kill us all if he had the chance and perhaps . . . he has already.

Clothed in a fine suit of what I determine to be Italian decent. Based on its material. More evidence of its origin lies within the line and cut of it. The suit probably ran him ten thousand euro. Possibly more. No matter . . . it will burn like a wick in the end.

His large porous snout . . . upon which a pair of vintage spectacles perch. They may gaze out at the remains of the world. Titanium wire rims . . . black lenses . . . like the eyes of a great white. Or a possessed doll. Marshals surround him as he crosses to my table.

I smile widely . . . showing teeth . . . but no words yet. Attempting to communicate via telepathic dialogue but he senses nothing. I do not turn to face him directly. Much too soon for that. Only a killer smile on my face. I am having the time of my life.

He reluctantly sits on the old wooden chair across from my own. The legs of which are buried a full three inches in the sand. Making them much too short for me. Though not for this growth-stunted wretch.

Like an asshole that sucks instead of blowing. He joins the party with a certain reluctance. Selfish one way motherfucker. Food converter. Muppy popper. I pour the tea.

Cracking his wide face to force a smile . . . he exposes a large gap between his two front teeth. All of that money and you dont fix those teeth? Once I have poured the libations . . . I raise my cup to his and we drink. The tea will enlighten him before I light him. So well flavored that he gulps it down almost instantly. Sweet. Mint. Psychedelic.

All too anxious to get down to business. Who can blame him with his career at stake? Not to mention his precious plans to annex the hillside. Thereby controlling all primary exports . . . virgins and all types of media. He stands to make a lot of profit in the overthrowing of their fragile system. And he just may get away with it . . . pulling it off with his many resources. His many friends in low places.

He somehow lights a long thin cigar with a short wooden match. By which I am internally impressed although I refuse any outward display of emotion. He drags on his tobacco . . . and I break the filter off mine and light up a Chester with my Zippo. The other lighter remains hidden up my sleeve. He begins to speak. Reaching across the table to touch my face.

"For how long ... will you be able to smoke?"

"Forever I suppose . . . should I retire in hell." I casually reply.

"Not the face I fell in love with ... not the face I came to know ... I've done some checking up ... I know what you have been up to ...."

"Horace . . . you already know me so well."

"Even so. You would be surprised at what we can dig up . . . it is beyond our control at this point . . . we must accept that . . . .

"Saturday night I was downtown. Working for the FBI." I quote.

"You have been a continual fly in the eye for a little over a lifetime now."

"I can live with that," I say.

"I found out about your little sweetheart . . . the one who put you out of the job. You did a naughty thing. Changing her like that. Messy boy . . . we taught you better manners."

"Although I am extreme . . . I am no less a patriot . . ."

It is a lie . . . of course. Well . . . not entirely . . . more of an exaggeration. It's rather difficult to explain. Remember when I mentioned my trouble with the agency? When I was forced to sever ties?

I was not entirely honest . . . I was fortunate enough to discover the agency's ruse in advance. A plan to entrap me in a double-cross frame using a honeypot. One with whom I had a pre-existing physical relationship. Pitting me against her. We had plans of our own. We needed to fake a death. Or two. Both for myself and dear Prudence . . . .

We were experiencing great difficulty with the task of locating a female body. Women being so hard to come by . . . even then. Time being short . . . as it always is . . . we were forced to improvise and use a transsexual.

I was nervous about the switch. Fearing that it would be spotted as an obvious fake . . . I decided to mutilate the bodies. Beyond all recognition. **NMC. Non Mission Capable.** For security purposes . . . .

However . . . he is right . . . I made quite a mess that day. I had to buy enough time to get to Venezuela. My performance was eventually discovered as a hoax. It bought me my walking papers. My death warrant.

They saw what I was capable of . . . that I was on my own program . . . and it frightened them. Enough fear to elicit my erasure. I did it to save her life. All for her. For the child inside of her that no one knew about. Then I went my own way to draw them off of her.

The idea was basic. A fake death . . . a new face . . . and she could go anywhere she wanted in the world . . . . We fabricated a murder scene involving a botched inter-agency parley.

One aforementioned transsexual . . . and another unlucky cocksucker named Arsen Qill Murdter became **permanent believers** that day. So that we could go free. Murdter was an informant we were soliciting in order to learn the whereabouts of Lazlo Gaines.

The tranny was simply in the wrong place at the wrong time. We gained anonymity and freedom by exchanging our lives for theirs. Even if only for a little while. Leaving their mutilated bodies in place of ours. A ruse. I would do it all over again . . . . I pull on my Chester and say . . .

"I lost control when I discovered the double-cross. I never was afraid to get my hands dirty."

"Loved that little cunt did you?"

"Cunt? I did. Love . . . you never learn. Very hard business . . . espionage. You can never tell who is acting."

"Much like show business . . . and politics . . . I have a gift for you."

"You shouldnt have."

"But . . . I did."

"Did you?"

"Affirmative."

"Well . . . let's have it . . . then. Or must I first close my eyes?"

"A reunion is upon you this day. Your long dead sweetheart . . . . Resurrected . . . . Can you believe it?"

"No . . . . I cannot."

"True enough. In room six-zero-eight since oh dark this a.m. Anson and Sils have been keeping her warm for you."

"Fantastic . . . bring her out then . . . I am . . . absolutely dying to see this. Where was she found?"

"Key West . . . of course. At the International Airport . . . on her way to Dubai."

"Oh . . . how many fingers does she have?"

"Fingers? You never change. All in good time . . . little Frankenstein . . . first you must tell me what it is you know. Where you've been . . . and what you have been up to."

"I know that you are a mere scoundrel . . . a rapist . . . a deviant . . . and you enjoy having me in the lean position ."

"You dont even know the half of it . . . half-breed . . . . I will have you screaming by sundown . . . you already know what you are dealing with."

"Run a carbon black test on my jaw . . . and you will find . . . it's all been said before . . . ."

"Can you remember who you are? Who your grandfather was? What you came from? Think hard on it."

"Maybe I do . . . . Maybe you tell me."

"I want to tell you a story from my own childhood . . ."

"What? You slithered from the womb bearing a full set of teeth and a pointy tail?"

"I once won a spelling bee."

"You dont say . . . ? Spell magnanimous."

"I would rather spell assassin. You know your grandaddy shot a president in Dallas. We acquired his son . . . later . . . you arrived . . . with your Extra-Sensory Perception . . . well . . . the choice was clear."

"Lies. My grandfather would have been dead long before my birth. The one you mentioned was killed on live television . . . I've seen it. Ridiculous."

"I would never refer to the household name . . . the true assassin . . . . was never caught . . . . . . No soul knows his name . . . ."

"Known only by old Scratch himself . . . . Known by you . . . ."

"He is the reason you are in this mess. He is responsible. He made it this way for you."

"We are all responsible for this . . . you especially. So remove the sand from your ovaries."

"We never would have known of your existence . . . were it not for him. You could have lead a normal life."

"As a fucking t.v. baby? Hypnotized like some chicken?! I prefer to use my glossa to spit shine shit shrouded shoes."

"What I want to discuss . . . is the compound . . . on the hillside . . . . I want to turn you back on."

"Why else would you risk a sloe afternoon in purgatory?"

"I could reinstate you . . . outside of the . . . Citadel . . . at least. Like before . . . or maybe . . . this time . . . you might prefer fame."

"I like it here . . . alone with my anonymity. Nothing feels better than kicking the shins of giants. Death in this state . . . would be . . . sublime . . ."

"Enough talk of death. Let us speak of time and the tampering of it. How you do it? It will change human existence as we know it. Tell me this . . . and I will reinstate your clearance."

" . . . I have a license to kill here and now . . . reinstatement . . . is not an option . . . I am not for sale . . I rather prefer the life of a 1369. It has its perks."

"Remember . . . we can always force our way inside . . . if need be. It's been done before . . . it is much easier if you comply. Struggling can be so painful."

"I couldnt simply let you inside. It's mine . . . and as you know . . . I enjoy doing things the hard way . . . as most unlucky cocksuckers do."

"So they do . . . let's start the music and roll the credits . . . . Let's move to the beat like we know that it's over. BOHICA."

"Bend Over . . . Here It Comes Again." I mutter. "I've been in the lean position ever since we met . . ."

I continue . . . Singing a tune I recall . . . from an early pop sensation's catalogue,

"It's not like me . . . to pretend . . . but I'll get you. I'll get you in the end. Yes I will . . . I'll get you in the end . . . Oh yeah . . .Oh yeah."

With that . . . the general . . . the third man . . . strikes my grape with the butt of his revolver. I greet death for a moment. Appearing before me in all its glory as I drift off . . . the prune offers me this . . . .

"You're a regular piano-wire man . . . in love with an uptown girl. Always were a sucker for them. Do you think it was an accident that you found that brunette in 909? Picking up the strong dope just like we knew you would. You helped us get inside."

"I pray you'll beat me for ten-thousand years. Beat me. Beat me . . . oh ho oh oh oh!"

Another blow follows. A left hook to my face. Dislodging a molar though not the transmitter, which I promptly spit into the sand. I left my channel open so that 8 can hear. I have told him to stay away . . . in case this doesnt work out.   No casualties this way . . . no blow back bullshit.

See . . . the problem with the transsexual that we used in place of Prudence . . . I later discovered . . . was that s/he was somehow related to this prune. What are the odds? I dont know if he was fucking it . . . or what? S/he was a part of his bloodline. Somehow. Some fucking way.

When I say transsexual . . . you may picture a thirty something . . . potentially homosexual male . . . from the suburban community of Trinidad in Colorado. One who finally realized the need to live out his days with a cunt instead of a cock. That . . . at least . . . I can attempt to understand. But this thing here . . . was a totally different situation. All together different . . . .   You are attempting to grasp this concept . . . but you are not even close.

This particular transsexual began life as a little boy . . . an unsuspecting child. Forced into the procedure at around age nine. Before puberty. That way the skin has more than enough time and elasticity to adapt to any alteration.   With a skilled surgeon at the helm . . . no true proof of sexual reassignment exists. Seamless. Like the song says,

"Daddy's little girl aint a girl no more."

Upon discovering the death this particular tranny . . . the prune developed and extreme interest in the case. I assume he found out about the switch rather quickly because they were on my trail in Venezuela within two weeks.

I took preventative measures there as well . . . I purchased my face while I was abroad. A separate . . . secure option. A guaranteed face. A four-way switch in all.

The donor for my face was deceased and anonymous to everyone but myself and the man I paid to find it. My face was removed and replaced. Then the old "wanted" face was destroyed. Not even the surgeon performing the task was informed as to the original identity of any patients involved. Leaving the agency to chase a ghost.

Exactly how do you guarantee a face? You may wonder. Allow me tell you. First you capture the wife of the man who will procure the face for you. Capture his children. His lover or mistress. Capture their dead photographs. Then show this skin dealer the pictures. Leave him with his world in ruins. Give him twenty-four hours to digest. Allow him to mourn . . . .

Then let him in on the joke. Return him to his family. Assure him those photographs could easily become a reality. Assure him of your dedication to the cause. Your cause. Because. Because you'll fucking do it and he knows that now . . . doesnt he?

"We -will -not -do -what -they -want or -do -what - they -say . . . oh no."

I manage to squeak out through broken bits of teeth. A song from an ancient political band. My cheekbone sagging low. I quote another legendary activist.

"Total destruction is the only solution."

Then I repeat my previous question.

"Hey . . . Horace . . . the girl in six-oh-eight . . . how many fingers does she have?"

Fucked Up . . . Got Ambushed . . . Zipped In. They only think Prudence is down there . . . . If they have anyone down there at all. Could be a bluff. Always so sure of what they couldnt possibly know.

What they do not know is that the girl in the six-oh-eight . . . if there even is a girl . . . is only a plant wearing Prudence's face. If this is my decoy . . . then she is missing the top digit of her left pinky finger. I should know . . . I bit it off myself for identification purposes during the facial exchange procedure. Regardless . . . this may be the only opportunity I ever have to take Lesher out.

Surely she's just the damn throwaway. Just another . . . more unlucky . . . and less likely to be missed type. The female donor -let's call her Sylvia-had to be someone who was attempting to outrun fate. Usually a drug related fate . . . exchanging it . . . for one with a less immediate ending. Sylvia needed a new identity . . . whatever the reason. So she got me. Me and my reason.

Little did Sylvia know . . . her new face (Prudence's old one) was wanted by the agency. As always . . . life is about who you know and how much you are willing to pay. I anonymously paid off Sylvia's debts so that no one would come looking. Then I paid her an arm and a leg for her face.

First . . . secure faces must be located then harvested from living or recently deceased donors. Naturally . . . all organ donors must match the recipient's blood type among other things. Then the bodies of the transsexual and Mr. Murdter were found in place of Prudence's and my own.

The first face switch is then performed on Prudence by a local licensed underground surgeon. One that owed me a favor. Then we split up. I went to Venezuela for my procedure . . . and she went . . . to some location that I am sure I cannot recall.

Prudence is far better protected than the unlucky slag currently tied up in six-oh-eight. She is far . . . far away from here . . . and always will be if I have anything to say about it. Finally . . . Lesher answers my final question.

"She has nine complete digits ... a piece missing off her pinky"

All systems go for countdown. Ready to launch. Before I unleash my surprise . . . I want to hold my maker close . . . one last time. I draw him in . . . speaking in a low tone. I put a busted arm around him . . . beckoning his ear.

As I held him close . . . I put my ear to his . . . hearing a familiar sound. A sound I recognize from my childhood. When I held a sea shell to my ear . . . hearing nothing but the ocean from anywhere in the world. Everything seems to be so quickly coming to an end . . . and I pull out another Chester . . . putting it to my lips. I painfully move my broken jaw . . . to say . . . gutturally . . .

"You've got it all figured out . . . every last detail . . . .
But you forgot one thing . . . "

Attempting to lick my dry and cracking
lips . . . pulling from my sleeve the lucky revolver
cigarette lighter . . . one that has seen me through
many steely moments.

A funny birthday present from a past life . . .
but dont be fooled. This is no pistol . . . . Though the
security team tenses accordingly. No. This lighter is
noteworthy because it is electric. It must be. It is the
only way. A detonator also works via electrical
current. I say . . . .

"Top of my class in ordinance demolition. You are
here to finish this. Consider it finished! **FUGAZI** . . .
baby! **Die With Your Mouth Open!**"

Pulling the trigger on my little snub-nosed
incendiary device. Click . . . .

Nada.

Fuck.

Now who's bluffing? I trade an uneasy smile.
Then the prune quotes a Flux of Pink Indians song.

"Come on Thomas eat it up . . . sometimes I dont think you were worth the fuck!"

His lepers are quickly moving in for the kill.
The detonator may have jammed. Only
temporarily . . . I hope. It happens from time to time.
It has become increasingly difficult to find reliable

285

components any more. Most cartridges purchased on the market end up being duds. Which is why I mold and assemble all of my own ammunition. Ordinance however . . . is not so easily homemade in our workshop.

Ordinance tends to require a little outside help. Sometimes involving outside resources . . . this results in a general lack of quality. I shake it my lucky torch . . . attempting to align the connections.

I need only a split-second connection with the electric blasting caps and I am home free. I try again to complete the circuit . . . depressing the trigger . . . and as the flame ignites . . . lighting the Chester currently lodged between my dick suckers . . . .

. . . a bullet from a Marshal shatters my hand and the lighter inside . . . driving tiny slivers of silver into my palm . . . I feel my metacarpals go numb. Dead. Then a sharp and hot pain. In a stroke of luck and irony . . . it completes the circuit and signals the detonator . . . as I inhale the first drag of my last fag . . .

. . . the **semtex** is incinerating from beneath the sand now collected over a decade and a half. Atop this debacle of commerce. The building shudders violently. Though . . . I had not planned for the helo . . . .

The **Citadel** can withstand the blow . . . and has long been reinforced to tolerate powerful earthquakes. A little off the top wont hurt too much. The entire basement levels are lined with diamond plated steel . . . so I pulled sections of it from the walls and brought them to the penthouse level.

I then booked the penthouse out to a very prominent artist who desired utmost secrecy. A shrouded Graycie arrived at midnight a few days earlier to check in as said artist.

I escorted her upstairs but we went to the ninth floor instead. There I left her with Rambeaux. I proceeded to the twelfth floor to turn on the jukebox and place a Do Not Disturb placard on each entrance. Leaving rooms vacant ever since.

The plating will do two things, protect the lower floors and direct the blast upward. Into the sun. The Detasheet I placed on top of the steel sheeting will have only one direction to go . . . up and away.

Semtex for reliability. Comprised of a sultry union between PETN and RDX primarily. Bonders and wax then complete the equation. Toss in a reliable detonator and you are home free.

Pentaerythritol tetranitrate or TEN . . . also found in TNT . . . a few WMDs . . . and vasodilators . . . is mixed with Research Department eXplosives . . . a.k.a. cyclotrimethylenetrinitramine. Often shortened to cyclonite . . . hexogen . . . or T4 . . . for obvious reasons.

PETN serves as the base. Add this to a near equal amount of RDX . . . specifically chosen for maximum brisance . . . because it has a VoD of 8750 m/s. That's Velocity of Detonation calculated as meters per second.

All components are water insoluble. This being the reason they were selected for this particular mission. The **Citadel** may be impervious to many things but moisture is not one of them. If you have cleaned yourself once handling it . . . which I have . . . the detection of **semtex** is extremely limited.

Beneath the sandy rooftop lies the twelfth floor. In those rooms I have laid my trap. A daisy chain of **detasheet** and three kilograms of **semtex**. Undetectable from up here. Which is why . . . even after a thorough search of the roof . . . these army ants could not find me out.

I have also taken the liberty of reinforcing my chair with a piece of v shaped steel plating. Welded to the bottom tips of my chair's legs. I used a rusty chunk of diamond plate pulled from the walls of the abandoned basement levels. The same steel plating I used to line the entire twelfth floor.

The legs are attached to the diamond plate. Then buried in the sand. This will absorb some of the blast . . . deflecting it out and away from me . . . . Even if only slightly. Every little bit helps. The little handles I welded onto the top edge of my seat seem a bit insignificant. I must confess . . . a seatbelt would have been more gratifying. Hindsight is always 20/20.

I packed the rooms with ammonium nitrate treated with urea. To minimize nitrogen loss. I had not planned for the helo but it will only add fuel to the fire. Shrapnel too . . . meaning that this will be more painful than initially anticipated.

As the blast lifts me from the sandy rooftop . . . the fuel tank of the chopper incinerates . . . I feel pieces of shrapnel tearing through my kevlar suit pants. Then through my burn suit underneath my pants. Pieces of the turbine fire past . . . and the wind takes me. This song fills my mind,

"This is the coastal town that they forgot to close down . . . armageddon . . . come armageddon . . . come armageddon . . . come."

My legs are on fire. I smell my skin smoking . . . and I think I am screaming. Trying to . . at least. My hands burn as they cling to the chair . . . . Death . . . my oldest friend . . . and always beside me . . . . I think I am screaming this . . .

". . . I'm a building jumper . . . roof to roof . . . you'll see me flying in the air."

Fingers . . . knuckles . . . shot and charred to the bone. Soon I cannot feel them at the ends of my forearms. Nerve damage. Probably worse. Much worse. Somehow I hold tight. The sun seems to be setting early today.

Having taken all of the abuse I can stand . . . I go black again. Blackness consumes me. The dark welcoming me again . . . and hours seem to pass . . . .

. . . .
. . . .
. . . .
.

*It's about Doing something and
Getting off your ass
Saying something
Seeing what a shitty place this Is and
what a Jam place it Could Be . . . .
*ANONYMOUS**

Is this it? Have I arrived at my final resting place? Deep within the terra firma. Some zombie embryo . . . in hibernation . . . deep beneath the sandy loam. Above me I hear a child playing . . . making some fantasy come true. A little princess and her sandcastle. Digging in the wet sand as the ocean churns behind her . . . gaining momentum . . . then egressing.

Children are like the sea . . . raw . . . untamed. Capable of anything. Unearthing my hand as waves lap nearby. Showing no fear. I imagine there is little left of my metacarpals. She continues to dig. Unearthing my wrist . . . down the arm to the shoulder. Slow and steady . . . she digs. Then an eye. A nose. What is left of my face. Brine lapping at the edge . . . of the deep hole . . . I watch the saltwater as it climbs down the sandy walls of my peripheral.

It is then that I hear . . . ever so faintly at first . . . then the driving percussion of a song I have long known . . . long loved . . . and been loved by . . . for most of my existence. Most especially . . . in my formative years . . . it was this anthem that jarred my soul completely . . . .

"So unplug the jukebox . . . . And do us all a fa-vo-ur.

Yeah. Yeah . . . .

That music's lost it's taste . . . . So t-ry another fla-vour . . . .

Ant-muse-say-ic!!

Ant-mu-saic!"

The eternal call to all emanating from within my head. Not in the usual way wherein I would play my own version created from what I remember and also enjoy most about a song. This was the real thing. Not some mental imitation. This cannot be a memory. I would know the difference . . . believe me. I have been dealing in memories for decades now. Nor does it sound like a cover of the song. No bastard renditions welcome. Sounds like the industrious originator to me. The lyric warns.

"Dont tread on an ant . . . he's done nothing to you . . . . You cut off his head . . . . Legs come looking for you"

An electric shriek of guitar rages in my ears. Followed by the Antmusic chorus . . . driving me on . . . calling me over the horizon . . . toward the insect nation . . . in the hillside compound.

The sonic impulse seems to come from within. Not from without. My ears picking up internal vibrations. The signal seems to be channeled through my PSynaps. It may have to do with my proximity to the hillside compound. It must be. Sounds like a live recording in fact. Very vintage. Very old. Still beautifully clear. Radio for the mind. Sonic rhythms for the soul. **P**Synaps . . . it appears . . . is losing the . . . **fear of music** . . . .

I can hear the waves crashing heavily in the background now. I am in darkness still. I feel the warm sun on my charred skin . . . .

The child takes up my extremity . . . tugging on my near lifeless body. I feel a dead layer skin slough loose and slide from the back of my hand. Causing her to lose equilibrium and fall back on the wet sand. I feel her weight compact the earth around me.

She stands up . . . regaining her composure. Discarding my extremity's dead husk . . . come loose in her soft hands. Taking hold once again. This time at the wrist . . . tugging at my mortal coil.

She begins to unearth more of my remains . . . my face blackened with soot . . . my clothes wholly charred. Tattered. Ashen.

The flies begin to hover . . . searching my open wounds for a warm place to breed. Little do they know . . . the **Scarabaeidae** have already done the deed.

She lifts me to my feet giving the sensation of levitation. One that I can only compare to a wave . . . when it picks you up as you drop into it. Weightlessness.

Then . . . I am half free of my premature burial. She removes a crumpled wad of brown paper from her dress pocket . . . handing it to me. I cautiously open the mystery lump . . . half expecting a human heart. A woman's . . . judging by the size. Or a pair of eyes . . .

. . . I was fortunate enough to be wrong. Dead wrong. The ragged paper only reveals a list of performers. The edges flickering abruptly in the breeze. The flyer foretells of a show. Tonight. Up on Cielo Drive in Benedict Canyon. A three act performance.

Now . . . the **Make a Death Wish Foundation** opening for **Christkill Motherfuckers** were a terrifyingly good scream. Let me tell you. Absolutely amazing . . . like **NIN** w/ **DFA**. If you follow that up with the **Drill Team Abortion Clones** opening up for **Foul Mouth vs. Glassy Eyes** . . . . Then you may have some semblance of what was in store on this very day.

Nothing could have prepared me for what it said . . . even for someone who truly has been around . . . . Damn . . . this . . . this is an entirely new kind of show.

It seems that . . . tonight . . . Darby Crash is opening for G.G. Allin . . . who will then be succeeded by . . . Kurdt C. Preferably pronounced "curtsy" (kurt-see). Lenin will be headlining . . . or that might be Lennon . . . I cant be sure . . . my eyes are failing a little. And Jagger will be making a special guest appearance for the encore but most likely . . . it will end up being David Johansen. The old bait and switch.

My vision is beginning to go altogether at this point . . . well . . . . Whatever . . . . **Nevermind** . . . I must be on my way anyhow . . . I gather my heavy feet from the moist sand and make my way for the hills.

As I take my first step . . . my foot falls on something solid within the sand. I toe at it . . . to reveal the black case. A small handle on its side. I remove it from the sand and press on . . . toward the hills.

Plastic surgery has taken on many vast improvements since The Ant's famous anti-slogan . . . . In the hills . . . cellular regeneration has progressed in great undogly strides. In Tinseltown both the supply and demand are at their utmost.

Wherein . . . the legal tender required for research and development meet the neediest of cynics. People who search in manic desperation for the fountain of youth. While destroying themselves from within . . . they rapidly renew from the outside . . . hoping that somewhere . . . at some point . . . the good will manage to outweigh the bad.

I have personally undergone two complete facial procedures that were performed by hillside surgeons. The quality is unparalleled. Which is what my line of work calls for . . . and in my current shape . . . I must rely upon a few dusty allies to pass the front gate. Perhaps . . . I may even call upon a few old nemeses.

I wish more than anything else that this was all a fantasy. Some horrible delusion . . . . Dream or afterthought. I have wished many times that I could awake with a start.

Only to realize that I was safe in my childhood bed. Coddled by ambition . . . satiated by exclusivity . . . and repulsed by general moral priorities . . . but I cannot.

What I can do . . . is assure you that this hell is mine. Quite literal and real to me. Ultimate reality. This is the story that begins with the end. There is only one way to change it . . . you must alter the way it begins. Or . . . one chooses the life of a puppet on a string.

One day . . . this reality will become your own. I have given to you all that I am able. Given you every advantage you could possibly require. If you think you are ready for this . . . hell . . . to which I have become so . . .

. . . accustomed . . . .

. . . . Allow me to tell you . . .

. . . it is not likely . . . .

. . . . It will happen when you are most alone . . . .

. . . . Depressed.

Abandoned.

Hungry.

Parched.

Beaten.

Sleep deprived . . .

                              . . . or unconscious . . . .

. . . . Weak and afraid . . . .

. . . . Broken and damaged.

Forgotten . . . .

. . . . Thrashed.

When your guard is down and your self-esteem even lower.

It will be on your birthday or Thanksgiving.

Just after your big promotion.

On super bowl Sunday . . .

            . . . around midnight . . .

. . . after your team has won the game.

During happy hour.

During sex.

While you are asleep.

You will never see it coming . . . that day . . . when the entire world plunges into chaos.

You will not be afforded the luxury of putting on your shoes or of having the chance to scream.

Here is that chance . . . .

Learn to swim . . . trim . . . repair . . . farm . . . and hunt. Become an apex predator. Familiarize yourself with popular mechanics and consume your mind with lateral thinking. Learn to read . . . read often . . . and know the classics. They are full of morality.

Otherwise . . . .

By my estimation . . . you are headed in my direction already. But you have not arrived here yet . . . and it is not too late . . . . But I am not entirely sure.

You may choose to wish it away. Or pray for an answer. You would only be wasting what little time you have left. Ask yourself . . . am I a 1369?

As for me . . .

. . . I am

. . . more or less . . .

. . . . a space traveller . . . lost . . .

. . . too worn to withstand the stress of a return mission . . . a burden now too great to bear. I stay here on the fringe because it has become familiar . . . my home . . . my plain . . . .

. . . . My destiny.

I have gone too far . . . witnessed too much . . . now there . . . is . . . no . . . return.

Present status being Non-Mission Capable . . . .

This is your chance.

I write this journal . . . on paper made from discarded stacks of headshots and resumes collected from the fill . . . . Hand-struck by way of typing machine. One which survived the first and terrible Great Depression . . . then bearing witness to the more horrific second.

Born in the wake of disaster. A typewriter from which the comma key was broken one month back . . . forcing me to ellipsis ever since.

Here one month can become a year. The days only recorded by sunsets and rises. Never knowing if the next will ever come.

What I find most bizarre . . . is the fact that this all began as a thought put down on paper. Is was then uploaded and converted into an organized stream of data . . . before it was shot into cyberspace.

To you.

This message . . . sent from the future or past . . .

. . . like mailing a letter to yourself . . .

. . . prior to the embarkation of a world tour.

Uncertain of when . . .

. . . or where . . .

. . . exactly . . .

. . . it will find me again . . . yet assured that one day it will.

A message in a bottle . . . in time.

Not that it matters.

It only matters that it has found you. This . . . report . . . of . . . my conclusions . . . my findings here . . . from the edge . . . of the brink . . . of the blackest abyss . . .

. . . deeper than the great divide . . . .

A ghastly void . . . one which has quickly grown grander than galaxy.

Left for whomever may cross its path while . . .

. . . navigating . . .

. . . through . . .
                    . . . this . . .
                              . . . my . . .
                         . . . your . . .
                                    . . . our . . .. . .

. . . . trail of . . . dead.

Special Thanks to these artists . . .

Faye, Jon, Michael, and all of my family and friends.
"Blank Frank" (Eno/Fripp) Brian Eno, Here Come the
Warm Jets
"One After 909" (Lennon/McCartney) Beatles, Let It Be
"Dancing With Mr. D" (Jagger/Richards) Rolling Stones,
Goat's Head Soup
"Dance This Mess Around" (Pierson/Schneider/Strickland/
Wilson) B-52's, B-52's
"You're Late" Bone Awl, Night's Middle
"Marquee Moon" Television, Marquee Moon
"Money for Nothing" (Knopfler) Dire Straights, Brothers
in Arms
"I Against I" (H.R.) Bad Brains, I Against I
"Broken Glass" Murder City Devils, The Murder City
Devils
"Ladytron" Roxy Music, Roxy Music
"Garbageman" (Interior/Rorschach) The Cramps, Songs
the Lord Taught Us
Secret Machines, Now Here Is Nowhere
"Baby's On Fire" and "Dead Finks Don't Talk" (Eno)
Brian Eno, Here Come the Warm Jets
"Kiss Me Deadly" Lita Ford, Lita
"Three Days" (Farrell) Jane's Addiction, Ritual De Lo
Habitual
"Do the Beng Beng" Derek Morgan, Moon Hop
"Fatty Fatty" (Eccles) Clancy Eccles & Friends, Fatty
Fatty
"All Women Are Bad" The Cramps, Stay Sick
"Hairdresser On Fire" Morissey, Viva Hate

"Contrapunctus Four" Bach
Two of Us" (Lennon/McCartney) The Beatles, Let It Be
"Good God's Urge" Porno for Pyros, Good God's Urge
"Dirt" The Stooges, Funhouse
"Message From Another World" Harry Perry
"Who Loves the Sun" Velvet Underground, Loaded
"Long Cool Woman in a Black Dress" The Hollies,
Distant Light
"Hairshirt" R.E.M., Green
"Fascination Street" The Cure, Disintegration
"I'll Get You" The Beatles, She Loves You
"Beat My Guest" Adam Ant, B-Side Babies
"Negative Creep" Nirvana, Bleach
"We Will Not" Bad Brains, Rock For Light
"Real Situation" Bob Marley, Uprising
"Background of Malfunction" A Flux of Pink Indians,
Not So Brave
"Everyday Is Like Sunday" Morrissey, Viva Hate
"Cactus" The Pixies, Surfer Rosa
"Antmusic" Adam and the Ants, Kings of the Wild
Frontier
"Whip In My Valise" (Goddard) Adam and The Ants,
Dirk Wears White Sox
"Beat My Guest" Adam and the Ants, B-Side Babiez
"Happiness is a Warm Gun" (Lennon) Beatles, The White
Album
"American Pie" Don McLean . . . .
Chet Baker . . . .
Nathaniel Hawthorne . . . .

All characters depicted herein are fictional.